JIM HARRISON

Returning to Earth

W9-AWO-346

Grove Press
New York

to Peter Lewis

Copyright © 2007 by Jim Harrison

All rights reserved. No part of this book may be reproduced in any form or by any electronic or mechanical means, or the facilitation thereof, including information storage and retrieval systems, without permission in writing from the publisher, except by a reviewer, who may quote brief passages in a review. Any members of educational institutions wishing to photocopy part or all of the work for classroom use, or publishers who would like to obtain permission to include the work in an anthology, should send their inquiries to Grove/Atlantic, Inc., 841 Broadway, New York, NY 10003.

Printed in the United States of America

Library of Congress Cataloging-in-Publication Data
Harrison, Jim, 1937–
Returning to Earth / Jim Harrison.
p. cm.
ISBN-10: 0-8021-4331-8
ISBN-13: 978-0-8021-4331-0
1. Amyotrophic lateral sclerosis—Patients—Fiction. 2. Death—Fiction.
3. Indians—Mixed descent—Fiction. 4. Upper Peninsula (Mich.)—Fiction.
5. Family—Fiction. 6. Memory—Fiction. I. Title.
PS3558.A67R4 2007
813'.54—dc22   2006050802

Grove Press
an imprint of Grove/Atlantic, Inc.
841 Broadway
New York, NY 10003

Distributed by Publishers Group West

www.groveatlantic.com

07 08 09 10 11 12   10 9 8 7 6 5 4 3 2

Praise for *Returning to Earth:*

"A force of nature in American letters . . . Harrison's trademark prose, lyric and fluid, seamlessly melds perceptions, memories, and dreams to capture his characters' inner lives. The narratives in turn pull readers into the underlying depths and currents of this tale with the quiet force of a river. *Returning to Earth* is a watershed work for Harrison. . . . [A] view of death that is as earthbound and humble as it is spiritual and profound." —*The Seattle Times*

"Harrison has always written with muscular force and startling compassion. . . . We watch as Donald's family members enter the essence of grief and as they take the first small steps towards acceptance of loss. When the book ends, many readers will, I suspect, hold it quietly and wonder how to let these people go." —*The Oregonian*

"Each voice has its Joycean digressions and obsessions. . . . Although these characters share a common heritage and interests, they remain so distinct, so memorable, that you would recognize their voices in a crowded bar, even if you had your back to them. As for the places they love and inhabit, the chokecherry and dogwood and porcupine-quill baskets and feathers and stones—well, let's just say that all five senses were used to re-create them." —*Los Angeles Times*

"Harrison's newest novel, *Returning to Earth*, contains some of the most poignant moments he has ever imagined. . . . [He] has crafted something remarkable, a set of interlocking stories set in a complex, evolving geography. Any reader who emerges dry-eyed from this powerful but beautifully underwritten scene isn't paying attention. . . . an important work by a major writer." —*The Plain Dealer* (Cleveland)

"Jim Harrison is a writer with bear in him. Fearless, a top predator, omnivorous, he consumes all manner of literature and history and philosophy. . . . one of the great writers of our age . . . I never miss a book by Harrison, and am glad I did not miss this one." —*Star Tribune* (Minneapolis-St. Paul)

"Time, memory, and the land all play key roles in Harrison's remarkable new novel. . . . A deeply felt meditation on life and death, nature and God, this is one of Harrison's finest works." —*Library Journal* (starred review)

"A quilt of family intimacy narrated by disparate voices . . . Harrison deftly shows the intimate details of a family facing the death of a loved one. . . . *Returning to Earth* is a beautifully written account of one man's passing and the effect on his multifaceted and multicultural family." —*Rocky Mountain News*

"Vintage Harrison . . . The themes are as stark and inevitable as life itself: love, loss, death, guilt, redemption. . . . More like Faulkner than Hemingway in the telling . . . It is told in a prose so pure and scraped of excess that a paragraph can seem like a novel, a sentence a poem. . . . Breathtaking." —*The Grand Rapids Press*

"[Harrison's] books glisten with love of the world, and are as grounded as Thoreau's in the particulars of American place—its rivers and thickets, its highways and taverns. Bawdily and with unrelenting gusto, Harrison's forty years of writing explores what constitutes a good life, both aesthetically and morally, on this planet. . . . A luminous, sad calm pervades this novel." —*The New York Times Book Review*

"[Jim Harrison] has become a major figure in American literature, and nowhere are the reasons for that more clear than in his newest novel, *Returning to Earth*. . . . A prodigious achievement. It is both familiar and strange, rooted and rootless, endlessly dark and occasionally hilarious. It is above all human: raucous, literary, bawdy, goofy, and wise. It is heartbreakingly sad. And it registers the redemption of love, the power of the word to speak the truth, the peace that comes to those who live even when it is time to die."   — *The San Diego Union Tribune*

"Harrison's meticulous attention to the sensualities of life are still present in the beautifully lucid writing. . . . *Returning to Earth* is a poignant and powerful reflection of how all stories become one in the end, and it is a story told with bare-bone honesty and simple eloquence."   —*Livingston Weekly*

"Poses the big, searching questions about life and death that we've come to expect from this robust, vibrant author . . . He posits an intriguingly receptive attitude toward mortality in a society that largely finds death aberrant and unfathomable. . . . Harrison is one of few American writers equally at home writing about backwoods, mixed-race construction workers, and wealthy university intellectuals . . . [the] saga bears strong traces of Southern classics by William Faulkner and Walker Percy."
                    —*The Boston Globe*

"[Harrison is] one of America's most life-affirming writers . . . with a vision of life as a stormy and hardscrabble affair. . . . Recalls Williams Faulkner and Louise Erdrich—two writers who stand behind Harrison's writing, not to say his vision of reality. . . . What drives these knotted stories forward is Jim Harrison's acute sense of abundance: the abundance of talk—these folks are such talkers—of food, of spirit, of drink, and of life itself."   —*The Buffalo News*

"Harrison is one of the most remarkable writers on the planet. He is one of the few who can write a book about death and dying that is at once dignified, uplifting, and hilarious. . . . Redemption and courage flow from Harrison's heart to ours. We're lucky to have him. He's a genuine treasure."   —*The Wichita Eagle*

"For more than four decades his sinewy prose and poetry have been exhorting us— without timidity—to embrace life in all its sensuality. Now, with his splendid new novel, [Harrison] delivers a treatise on love, loss, and longing."
                    —*Santa Fe New Mexican*

"[Jim Harrison's] fiction is rooted in primitive feelings of earthy connectedness and the mystical bonds shared by human beings and nature, or that could be shared were not our innocence corrupted by greed and unholy aspiration."
                    —*The Commercial Appeal*

"At the center of the novel, the irreducible conundrum: what matters after life is stripped away? That is the question. It is not an easy question and it is the question we most often look away from, in a culture swept up in the distractions of the everyday. Be kind, Harrison might say by way of a sideways answer. Be true and be kind."   —*Ft. Lauderdale Sun-Sentinel*

Also by Jim Harrison

FICTION

Wolf
A Good Day to Die
Farmer
Legends of the Fall
Warlock
Sundog
Dalva
The Woman Lit by Fireflies
Julip
The Road Home
The Beast God Forgot to Invent
True North
The Summer He Didn't Die

CHILDREN'S LITERATURE

The Boy Who Ran to the Woods

POETRY

Plain Song
Locations
Outlyer and Ghazals
Letters to Yesenin and Returning to Earth
Selected & New Poems
The Theory and Practice of Rivers & Other Poems
After Ikkyū & Other Poems
The Shape of the Journey: New and Collected Poems
Braided Creek (with Ted Kooser)
Saving Daylight

ESSAYS

Just Before Dark
The Raw and the Cooked

MEMOIR

Off to the Side

Part I

Donald

1995

I'm laying here talking to Cynthia because that's about all I can do with my infirmity. We're living in Cynthia's old house in Marquette in order to be close to the doctors. Her brother David usually lives here but he's off taking a look at different parts of the world but mostly Mexico. Cynthia and I ran away in our teens and got married and now she's back where she started. My dad, Clarence, did the yard work for her family for about thirty years. My bed is in her father's den because it's too hard for me to get upstairs. One wall of the den is full of books with a moving ladder to get to the top shelves. Cynthia says her brother lives inside these books and never really got out. I'm forty-five and it seems I'm to leave the earth early but these things happen to people.

    I don't have the right language to keep up with my thinking or my memory or all of my emotions over being sick so I'm speaking this to Cynthia [I'm interfering as little

as possible. Cynthia] because she wants our two children to
know something about the history of their father's family.

Starting a long time ago there have been three Clarences
but when they got to me my father thought there hadn't been
all that much luck in the name so they called me Donald in
honor of a young friend of his who died in a mining accident over near Ishpeming. The first Clarence, named after
a Jesuit priest who was a missionary to Indians out in Minnesota, waited until he was fifty to father children because
he wasn't too sure about the world. He had tried to come
east in 1871 because his mother had told him about the great
forests of the Upper Peninsula. Some of her family had
moved west to Minnesota from the U.P. because the white
men were moving in for the copper up in the Keweenaw
Peninsula. Her people were Chippewa (Anishinabe) but she
slept with an immigrant who had come over to the Pipestone
area of southwest Minnesota. This man was from the country of Iceland and a bunch of them had come over to farm
that real good soil down that way. It was hard on Indians
then because the Sioux had killed a bunch of farmers near
New Ulm and the settlers were leery of any kind of Indian.
So the first Clarence's mother died when he was about
twelve and he had never met his father in person. He was
real big for his age and he ran off and worked for a farmer
near Morris for a year but they made him sleep in the root
cellar beneath their pump shed. He was a good worker and
they didn't want him to get away. They kept him locked
down there a whole winter week for stealing a pie. Who is
to say how angry a young man would get trapped in a root
cellar for a week? By and by he got loose and walked down

to Taunton near Minneota and found his father, whose name he had memorized, a farmer named Lagerquist. It was a Saturday morning when farmers come to town but the man was with a wife and two kids so that young Clarence wasn't sure what to do. The story goes that the man came up to him and said, "What do you want, son?" Clarence was real glad the man recognized him. So Clarence said, "I'd like a horse to ride to Michigan if you can spare one?" The man got him a horse but it was a draft horse so it was slow going. That's how the first Clarence started out for Michigan. It's hard to think of a thirteen-year-old doing such a thing nowadays.

Here I am on the sofa at age forty-five and I have Lou Gehrig's disease. [Donald has had amyotrophic lateral sclerosis for nearly a year now. His case is especially aggressive and it appears he will fall short of the three years of the disease that fifty percent of patients last. Cynthia.] I never knew much about Lou Gehrig though my dad, Clarence, used to talk about him. Gehrig played baseball, which I never had any time for because the coaches at Marquette decided they needed me for track where I could be counted on to win the 100, 220, and the shot put, though my true love was for football where I was the quarterback, and a linebacker on defense.

The children are both in California where Herald is taking advanced degrees at Caltech and Clare is an apprentice for wardrobe in the movie business. We talk on the phone to them for about an hour every Sunday.

You wonder how a girl from the Upper Peninsula could end up working on movies but that's the way the world goes these days. Clare got this interest from her stepcousin

Kenneth, who doesn't like his name and just goes by the letter "K." He's Polly's son and is a crazy bastard but I like him. Years ago K would ride his bicycle all the way two hundred miles from Marquette to Sault Ste. Marie for a visit. Herald is more like his uncle David. Mathematics is enough for Herald though he's also interested in botany. He's a big strong young man but finds people confusing. Herald and Clare have an apartment together in Los Angeles and look after each other like a brother and sister should. Why I say Herald takes after David is because when I read David's rundown of what his family did in the Upper Peninsula for a hundred years I was puzzled. It was published in the Sault Ste. Marie newspaper among others and I was proud that a relative knew so much but there weren't any real people in it. I like the stories with people myself. I mean he told the story of the bad details of the logging and mining his ancestors were involved in but not the actual story of the people who owned the logging companies and mines and the working people. I'm not being critical; I just prefer stories.

Of course I've got a foot in both worlds. My dad figured I'm over half Chippewa. In fact I'm due benefits from the tribe for my sickness but Cynthia has some money salted away and we figure tribal money should go to the folks who really need it.

Let's go back to the first Clarence. I remember when I first heard the story from my dad when I was a kid and I worried about the hardship. Here was this boy only thirteen being kept in a root cellar who after he escapes sees his real father only half an hour and then he's gone to the northeast riding a big draft horse toward a future. The story goes that he only had seven dollars and a letter that said the horse was his because he looked pretty Indian and people were liable to take the horse from him claiming it was stolen. I said all these worries to my dad and he said, "Life is real hard for some folks," but then he added that riding off on that horse was likely a good feeling for his grandfather compared to losing his mother and being trapped in a root cellar. So maybe it wasn't too bad to be him on a draft horse riding east. For instance I'm real sick right now but I've been able to live with it except for a few times when it got out of hand. Back in high school when I ran track or played football you were likely to get a cramp. With this disease at times you are a cramp, your whole body seizes up so that even your mind seems inside a cramp. You're all cramp, pure and simple. That's why K goes with me when I feel good enough to take a walk. I'm too big for anyone to carry but K can go for help.

When I was a kid of eight or nine years and first listened carefully to the story of the first Clarence I was upset when Dad said that he rode his horse through fields so wide out on the prairie that you couldn't see across them. This fact upset me for a few weeks because I couldn't imagine such a landscape. In most places in the Upper Peninsula you can't see very far because of the thickness of the forest and that's why it's a relief to be in the hills along the coast of Lake Superior, where you can see a long ways. When I finally questioned my dad about these fields with no end to them he said they were something like Lake Superior, which you can't see across to the other side in Canada. This all became clear to me when Cynthia and I took the kids on a camping trip out west years ago. Cynthia explained that in 1871 when Clarence began his trip there weren't many trees in western Minnesota and the eastern Dakotas except for cottonwoods along the creeks and rivers. At that time the trees the settlers had planted hadn't grown up much to speak of.

The upshot was that it took the original Clarence thirty-five years to reach the Marquette area, in 1906. His first try heading east frightened him because by late September in 1871 and early October every morning the sun rose red and the world was full of smoke. It had been a real dry season in the northern Midwest and there were fires everywhere, mostly the tops of trees and limbs left behind by logging. This was the year of the great Peshtigo fire in northeast Wisconsin that killed over a thousand people. Clarence heard from travelers that rivers boiled, and birds high in the air caught fire, and the wind everywhere was a hundred miles an hour, more than the worst November gales on Lake Superior.

So he turned around near Bad River and never saw the great uncut forests his mother had told him about. He had some bad luck and then some good luck. He was camped on the Red River north of Grand Forks and two outlaws tried to steal his horse. He threw them in the river and one drowned. He moved his camp north and one day a rich farmer up that way saw him riding the horse, which was a sorrel mare by the name of Sally. The farmer wanted to buy the horse and Clarence explained that the horse was all he had of his father and needed to keep it. The farmer hired Clarence to take care of his twelve teams of draft horses and work on his farm. Clarence got to live in a small log cabin, which was good after many months of camping and besides it was November and getting pretty cold that far north. The farm was so big that there was a cook to make food for the many hired hands so he got to eat regular. Snared rabbits, muskrat, and beaver can be pretty tasty but anyone hankers for some beef, cabbage, and potatoes.

The horses were how Clarence got to see his father again. The farmer was impressed by Sally and wrote off to Clarence's father to see if he might have any other horses of Sally's breeding. By and by his father showed up by railroad in Grand Forks with two fine teams, which the farmer bought. Clarence was right there in Grand Forks with the farmer and they had a steak dinner together so it was a real good experience to be acknowledged by your dad. Cynthia tells me that the Icelandic on their remote island don't grow up with much in the way of prejudice. I've always had an urge to go to this island but I've had this problem of not wanting to get on a plane. I've never been on one and now it's not likely I will. I've always loved winter and ice and snow. I've been on a helicopter twice a year ago when K took me up to western Canada to see a glacier. After I got diagnosed with this disease Cynthia said to me that if I had any special wishes for travel I better jump on them. I had always wanted to see a glacier and K figured out the whole trip with his computer. K told me that a helicopter was more like a huge metal hummingbird than a plane. I'll tell about this trip at some point because it got me over wanting to murder a man.

It's hard to understand your fears. For instance I don't fear death. As far as I know every living creature dies but as a boy after they took my mother off to the asylum in

Newberry I had to stay with my dad's cousin back in the woods over near Au Train. I cried about a month over my mother. [She was diagnosed with schizophrenia I learned from the records. Cynthia.] I also cried because I was scared of my dad's cousin. I couldn't stop crying so they sent me home from the third grade. The principal tried to tease me out of it by saying here I was a foot taller than any other boy in the class and crying like a baby. The principal was a nice man from down in Ann Arbor and took me for a walk way out to Presque Isle but that didn't stop me from crying. Anyway I lived for about two months with my dad's cousin that early summer when I wanted to be back in Marquette playing football with other kids. Such is the nature of athletes that I was already being watched when I was ten. It was the accident of me being big and fast, which is what coaches look for.

My dad's cousin was named Flower, her white name anyway, but she was a pure-blood and traditional. For all practical purposes my dad and I weren't the least bit Indian but were just among the ordinary tens of thousands of mixed bloods in the Upper Peninsula. Of course we had a bunch of relatives, especially on my mother's side, who were more like real Indians but we thought of ourselves as city people with Marquette being the biggest city in the Upper Peninsula with a population of 20,000 in the mid-1950s. All our relatives were such a mixture of Finn, some Cornish, a few Italian, and Chippewa. A lot of these nationalities turned up to get work as miners and loggers. Take my Great-Uncle Bertie for instance. He worked on the ore boats out of Duluth and could be gone for years at a time. Both Bertie and his wife were half Chippewa and had three of their own children but three more came along fathered by a Finn miner when Bertie was gone so much. Once when he was in the merchant marines sailing out of Los Angeles and he was gone for seven years, he wrote a card that said, "I am in the country of Chile. Say hello to the kids." The upshot of this is that of my dad's six cousins in Bertie's family three look like Chippewa and three look more like Finns.

So I didn't know anything to speak of about Indian life when I went to live with Flower for those two months, but then what can a ten-year-old know? Quite a lot, says Cynthia, though they don't have the language to express what they know. That's like me. Anyway, Flower shook my brain like one of her many rattles hanging from the rafters of her tar-paper shack. To make a living she cleaned cabins and did laundry for cottagers, sold her wild berry pies, collected herbs with some like wild ginseng bringing good money. In winter she trapped and was pretty good at it my dad said. She wouldn't take any money from the state, county, or federal government because she wouldn't sign papers. Her grandpa had lost a lot of land by signing timber leases for white lumbermen. Her grandpa couldn't read and they slipped landsale papers past him and then had him kicked off his land down toward Trenary. These things happened in those days with evil men for whom everything is money.

So I tagged along with Flower in the woods while she was finding herbs, or picking berries for pies, or cleaning cottages when I would sit out in the car though twice I got invited to go swimming with the kids of the cottage owners. I mostly swam with Flower in the Au Train River or in

Lake Superior when it was warm enough. Flower had an old rickety '47 Plymouth that wouldn't go very fast and this is how I started getting scared. We drove over to Grand Marais to see a friend of hers and to catch some pike in early June. We were out in the rowboat on Au Sable Lake and this old woman friend of Flower's pointed toward the huge sand dunes to the north along Lake Superior and said that long ago there was a bad tribe that lived up in the dunes. They could become beasts and fly down in the night and cannibalize the peace-loving Indians that lived near the Grand Marais harbor though there was no town back in those days. Up to the point of this story I was happy because I had caught two nice pike, which pleased Flower because pike were her favorite dish. Well, after the story I could imagine these bad Indians becoming bears with huge wings and flying down to the harbor in the moonlight and eating Indian children like myself. I almost peed my pants right there in the boat.

During our two months together Flower told me dozens of old stories, most of which scared me especially the ones about the Windigo, but then the story of Iona, the Night Flying Woman, calmed me down. Cynthia said that I was already frightened because my mother had to be hospitalized forever. That's what my dad told me anyway. I think at ten I already sensed this because we were always looking for her whether in our old house on the edge of town where the city was going to tear down the house to build a road. It had been a farmhouse before the city moved outward and was cold as a barn in winter. We pretty much lived in the kitchen during the coldest parts of winter. That's when my dad worried the most because Mother would wander off into the coldest part of the house, or worse yet into the frozen swamp behind the house. Her cousin from Negaunee would babysit her but she liked our phone too much because she didn't have a phone in Negaunee. The last straw was during a cold snap in March and mother lost the tips of two toes when she walked out barefoot in the swamp. Our best help during this hard time was a Mexican I called Uncle Jesse who also worked for my dad's boss, Mr. Burkett, who was Cynthia's father. Mr. Burkett often didn't have both oars in the water as they say, which means he wasn't a stable man. Some of the drugs my mother had to take tended to eat up the paycheck but Jesse was there to help. Sometimes he would come over with one of his many girlfriends and a six-pack and my dad would fry up some fish or venison, which Jesse loved to eat. Jesse would tease me because at ten I was already as big as he was and every time he would come over he would give me four quarters because on the side he owned a Laundromat.

So the city took our house and by the time Dad found one and got it ready I had been two months at cousin Flower's. Strange to say, at first I missed Flower's place when I got back to Marquette but then it faded away except at night when her stories would come back to my imagination in full Technicolor, especially the flying beasts which I took to mean bears with huge wings. When that happened I might come down from my room and sleep on the front porch where there were always street noises nearby our bungalow, which was fairly close to the college. A car passing would send the flying bears away and then I could think

of the good things about living with Flower like looking for
a buck for the deer season months away. Flower guided
this rich man from Grand Rapids who came up alone every
November. Dad said this man liked bringing home a huge
buck every year though it was Flower who had the deer
completely scouted. Dad told me later that he thought the
two of them were "sweet" on each other. Once when a drunk
hit her when she was walking a two-track this hunter paid
her doctor and hospital expenses in Munising.

I feel like I'm running on at the mouth but Cynthia says
no. I should get back to the beginning of the story but I'm
still in an odd mood from waking up at first light on this warm
morning and smelling the lilacs in bloom. It seemed like
when I woke up I couldn't understand anything and my
heart ached. I looked down and took the sheet off and my
muscles are nearly gone. Cynthia says not but I know otherwise. Even a pencil or a glass of water weighs something
now. For twenty-five years I made a fair living laying blocks,
pouring and finishing cement, and sometimes roughing in
houses. Now I have too much spit and I don't want to eat.
On Sugar Island I used to carry the rowboat down to the river
for the kids and it weighed three hundred pounds. I would
hold an arm out and my little daughter would swing on it like
a monkey. I could hold a ninety-pound corner block out
straight and now I can scarcely hold my arm out. These things
happen to people but some days it can be hard to handle. So
this morning my reality broke down and I wasn't sure of anything. Just before I got sick I finally made a three-day fast,
which I'd failed at four times before I succeeded. What you
do is go up into Ontario to a certain mountainside and spend

three days without food, shelter, or water. I'm not going to talk about my religion because it's too private. Maybe a little. There's another hillside from which you can see Lake Superior where I'm going to be buried. You can't think of a thing that lives that's not going to die. I had hoped in these three days to find out how I was going to get rid of my fears and how to grow older with grace. I found out in a hurry! Here I am on my way. [Donald is now laughing. It takes courage to laugh until you cry at death. Cynthia.] Anyway, while I was up there after about a day and a half reality fell apart, which I'll explain to you later without any religious conclusions.

My last long walk alone was only a few months after I got sick last year. My doctors told me I had been sick for a while but I didn't want to let on. Cynthia noticed because it's an old joke in our marriage that when I really want to make love I charge upstairs in the evening while she reads in bed. Cynthia has always just read and not watched television where I like to watch sports. Only suddenly one day I couldn't charge upstairs. That was that. She waited a long time to question me but it scared me too much to talk about it until we finally went to the doctors.

Well, on my last long walk K drove me over to Grand Marais so we could fish for early pike just like I had done thirty-five years before with Flower. The fishing was so good that K drove into town to get some ice so we could keep the fish in good shape. I told K I was going to take a stroll up into the dunes and he wondered if this was a good idea because Cynthia had told him not to let me out of his sight. I said I was feeling fine, which wasn't quite true. It was hot and sunny and I knew if I got up into the dunes I could get away

from the deerflies. I'm not so fast at swatting them away anymore. What I was hoping to find was this beautiful, cool grove
of birches that my brother-in-law David had shown me years
ago. My kids used to refer to their uncle David as "the loon."
He heard about his secret nickname and just laughed. David
has spent so many years around here at this cabin that he
knows some fine places that seem to carry a weight of their
own. Flower knew such places. Actually there's a tinge of
resemblance between them. If you spend that many years in
the woods it's bound to be a share of your body and soul.

So I half crawled up the dunes because I already wasn't
very strong but I made it up and over a ridge and descended
into a bowl of sand about a mile wide. Out in the middle of
the bowl was the grove of birches and poplars. It occurred to
me that this place was the same as it was back in the time of
the first Clarence. Maybe I'm him, I thought, which is an odd
thought. I had a handkerchief and wiped the sweat out of my
eyes feeling lucky because there weren't any deerflies up in
the dunes. Way off to the northwest I could see a single bear
grazing on beach pea and wild strawberries on a grassy hillside. I wasn't worried though he was close to the birch grove
because there were no cubs. It's the female who is ornery
when she has cubs. Well, it took me about a half hour to reach
the grove because my muscles were seizing up and sometimes
I crawled because it was easier, also faster. I made my way
into the grove and crawled up on this huge low-slung birch
limb where David showed me how you could lay back on it
and the slightest breeze off Lake Superior would rock you
gently. That's what I wanted. It was a miracle of sorts but
there was no breeze until I laid out on the limb and my body

calmed down. Within minutes there was no inside or outside to the world if you get what I mean. My sick body disappeared plain and simple, at least for a while, and then it slept. There was a spirit in the place that gave my body some peace. Maybe it was only because the wind came up and the huge branch rocked me as my mother once had in the rocking chair. My eyes were closed but I started to see things just as I had up in Canada in my three days on the hill. My mind brought up the vision of the bears with big wings the old woman told me about when I was in the boat with Flower. One had a face that looked a little like my own. I wondered how you could see things with your eyes closed? [Donald wants an immediate answer to this but I'll have to ask the neurologist. Cynthia.] Of course when I die sooner rather than later and my eyes don't work I wonder how long my mind will keep seeing things and what I'll see? This seems to me a natural question. If we have a spirit how and what does it see? All around the bears were ravens, which always follow bears to share the food. They follow the wolves up here too. I was there a fair amount of time and when I finally opened my eyes there was K sitting against the tree smoking a cigarette.

"How did you find me?" I said.

"There was a little rain last night and you leave a real big track, especially when you're crawling."

K helped me up and it wasn't too hard to get back to the lake though I knew I'd never again be able-bodied.

Enough of me. Back to the first Clarence. He worked for that farmer about five years the story goes but then the

farmer died of heart problems and his wife and son, who
were spoiled, put the farm up for sale. They wanted to
move to Minneapolis and live a higher sort of life. Their
lawyer wouldn't pay Clarence the five months of wages still
due to him but these things happen so Clarence headed toward Duluth, where he heard there was plenty of work to
be had. Here he was back on Sally and still only seventeen. Now he was at the age when he needed the company
of women and they weren't hard to find in those days because this was 1876 and there were so many Civil War
widows in the towns and countryside. These women also
needed affection. Up near Crookston he stayed with a widow
and her three children on a farm for a year but then she
got a chance to marry a pure white man who owned a hardware store so that was that. In his sorrow he got drunk and
when he woke up at this campsite an Indian was trying to
make off with Sally, so he hit the man a bit too hard and
then had to take care of him for a week until he was up
and around. Though it was early May one night it snowed
a foot and then the next day a rain began that lasted seven
days so that Clarence and the injured man were stuck between flooded creeks. Lucky for them Clarence snared a
young deer so they had plenty to eat and wood to main-
tain a big fire. I mean it was still a hard life but if you're
warm and got enough to eat and a tarp over a lean-to to
keep dry, you're about covered for your needs. The horse
thief turned out to be a pretty good person and when they
parted ways after the man's ribs felt better from the punch
they agreed they'd probably meet up again, which they did
in Marquette thirty years later.

Clarence had a stroke of luck when he reached Bemidji and met a logger who admired the size of both Sally and Clarence and gave him a job skidding out big logs, which were used to build ore docks over in Superior and Duluth. He had bad luck in love, though. He was struck down with love for this Indian girl but her father said no because he wasn't pure-blood. First he lost the widow because he wasn't pure white and then he lost this girl because he wasn't pure Anishinabe and her father was a Mede-wi-win. Clarence couldn't believe it and stuck around Bemidji for two years but then the girl married someone else so Clarence moved on east to Duluth. He hadn't yet seen the "big waters" that are Lake Superior. Well, he was thrilled with Lake Superior and camped out over east near Odanah for a month just looking at the endless sea. For some reason Sally loved big waves and swimming and he'd ride way out in the lake on her broad back even if the waves were high. Of course this was June and swimming would take her away from the blackflies, which drive both man and beast crazy. My dad said when he was young and cutting pulp down near Seney he just went crazy one day and dropped his chain saw and started running and jumped into this lake scaring the deer, who were already there submerged with just their noses peeking out.

Before Clarence went to work in Superior he rode even farther east to see some remnants of the big forests and didn't know until later that he didn't go far enough. He avoided settlements and loggers because people were always trying to get his horse, so he didn't have much information. He found a river gorge that was over near Nisula or Pelkie I

think and on a flat there was a group of the largest white
pines in creation. It was Eden he told his son, who told his
son, who was my dad killed years ago when a boat slipped
off a hoist. Anyway he got starved out of Eden because you
can't just eat wild meat you also need flour for bread or
potatoes. As I've said Clarence was real big but he measured
one white pine as the spread of his arms four times around
the tree. I wish I could have seen a tree like that. My brother-
in-law David has found some great big stumps southeast of
Grand Marais, which is not the same thing. He and I sat
beneath one during an August thunderstorm once and you
could almost imagine the tree that lived on that spot. Even
one of the roots was bigger than about any tree you see
nowadays. I went back there several times including once
alone when I spent a moonlit night under there and a small
bear looked in between the roots and I said, "Hello, mugwa,"
which means bear in Anishinabe, but there's a lot more to it
than just saying "bear." Suddenly laying here talking to
Cynthia I'm falling apart in many directions.

    [Donald is having a real hard time. The neurologist has an
elaborate word for it, *dysarthria,* but it means Donald loses his
ability to talk. Sometimes he thinks he's talking but it's not comprehensible. Once I get him started he so badly wants to finish
telling the story of his family for his children. These people are
good storytellers but they never write anything down. When I
was a little girl his father, Clarence, would tell me stories while
he worked in the yard constructing elaborate flower beds for my
ditzy mother, the gardens being the only viable part of her life
(her problems being pills, alcohol, dealing with my father, who
moment by moment could drive an auditorium full of women to

batty tears). Clarence and Donald tell their stories in measured tones, ever so slowly, as if they are re-creating the story's content visually in their minds then sending it out in words. They would not dream of writing the stories down, Clarence quit school in the fifth grade and began working full-time at age eleven. Donald is the most purely physical person I've ever met in my life. After an exhausting summer day working construction he would take Herald and Clare fishing until darkness fell. He would sleep five hours and then be up at six a.m. to cook breakfast because I'm slow in the morning and because he liked to cook breakfast, a habit that started when his mother was taken away and Clarence often worked nights running his trapline or reconditioning boats in addition to working for my family. Right now I'm trying to make sense of my exhaustion. Our kids, Clare and Herald, wanted to move home from Los Angeles to help out but Donald wouldn't allow it. David volunteered to return from Mexico early but I told him frankly that he would generally be more of a problem than a genuine aide. My main hope is when Polly's son K comes back from Ann Arbor in three days. He's going to live in the garage apartment out back and Donald likes and trusts him. Other than K it's just me. He turns to stone with the neurologist and nurses. The simple fact is that Donald is deeply embarrassed by his illness and I don't think that he's going to get beyond this state. When I sleep on a single bed beside his own in the den it's like when Clare was sick as a baby and I could hear her every breath even when I thought I was asleep. We've been lovers since I was fourteen and he fifteen, almost sixteen. Our children were raised almost by the time we were forty. We were so proud of them and then they were gone. I have enough money from my parents, mostly from my mother's estate, but it was unthinkable for Donald not to go on working. Despite this money when we went on trips, usually to the West with the kids, we didn't stay in lodges or motels but camped. Donald wasn't a tightwad, he just liked to camp. And not at regular campsites but off in the woods or beside rivers. Once in Wyoming we were camped beside the Green River and this old gentleman rancher came by on a horse and told us we were trespassing but then he and Donald started talking and we ended up staying four days while Donald and Herald, who could do a man's work at fourteen, jacked up a bunkhouse and laid a course of cement blocks under it to stabilize the foundation. Like his father, Donald liked to be useful. I used to wonder if I first loved him because he was the opposite of my father, who was so aggressively useless and would lamely put on a pair of calfskin gloves while rigging his sailboat, which almost never left the harbor. Once Laurie and I caught my dad with a ninth-grade classmate of ours on his boat but I didn't tell my mother because I didn't want to hurt her feelings. I know K has an affection for me though at forty-four I'm nearly twice his age. I do realize that I'm not exactly homely. I like the neurologist, who is divorced, but he has an odor of offices and medicine, which I find repellent. Donald teases me that I better start looking for a boyfriend and that was nearly a year ago. When Polly came over for dinner two weeks ago she said she was worried because I was getting skinny and haggard from being with Donald around the clock but I said I love him and that's what you do. Polly was very smart not to remarry my brother David, who is very nice but has been basically goofy since he was a little boy. He couldn't accept the fact that Dad was a lost cause. I went through a long stretch when I thought the male and female were more similar than they turned out to be. Strangely, though there is a big age difference, Donald and K are more like boyhood friends. When they packed the SUV for their trip to see the glacier early last fall, they acted as if they were simply off on a fishing trip though Donald stumbled twice in the yard. K is slender but very strong and could help Donald to his feet. K used to ride his bike all the way from Marquette to Sault Ste. Marie and later Bay Mills to see Clare, whom he had a crush on, and also, frankly, myself. Polly is always worried about K partly because she has given up on her daughter Rachel, who has always had drug problems and lives in New York City. Before Donald got sick I went to New York City with Polly to do a possible "intervention" with her daughter. David wanted to go along and help out but Polly said that he'd probably just give a lecture on the history of drug use in America. We had a fine time in New York City because it turned out Polly's daughter wasn't in bad shape. She worked as a receptionist and a general helper for a small off-brand record company in the Lower East Side. Her hair was orange, she had tattoos, and rings in her nose and belly button. We went to a strange concert with her and all her friends, who seemed to comprise a tribe of sorts. She lived with a rather tiny young man who was a singer with a large discordant voice. All in all we were relieved. I'm going to stop interrupting or maybe I'll just edit out my comments. I think that a good deal of my exhaustion comes from trying to make sense out of all of this. I envy Donald's mostly unspoken religion though it is maddeningly stoic. This religion has evolved from both his life and childhood stories plus the traditional three-day fast. Cynthia.]

The next piece of luck Clarence had over near Duluth was again caused by his horse Sally. They were building ore docks near Superior and Clarence got a job as a teamster hauling timbers, but then finally became a foreman of a big crew building the ore docks before he was twenty years old. I've spent quite a bit of time worrying about this man even though he's long dead. Here's the idea. The hours were so long your work was your life. Clarence's workweek was six days a week, twelve hours a day. The only vacation you might get was if you got injured and then you didn't get paid a dime. The powers that be could get away with this because there was plenty of available labor, a lot of them immigrants — Finns, Swedes, Germans, Norwegians, Bohemians, and such-like. There was an endless supply of iron ore from up on the Mesabi Range near Hibbing and Grand Rapids in Minnesota. That was open-pit mining while over in the Upper Peninsula it was deep-shaft for both iron and copper. My dad said that at least Clarence got to work aboveground. By and large your basic Indians don't want to be deep-shaft miners. They're leery because of the idea that to go deep underground would be coming close to the living world of spirits. For all I know this may be true.

Anyway, I've been troubled by this idea of work. On occasion I've worked a fourteen-hour day laying blocks or finishing cement and I can tell you that you just become cement. That's your life. The same with miners or loggers for that matter who got a day off a week at logging camps for thirty bucks a month. It must have been twenty years ago that David told me that between 1890 and 1910 in three mines over near Republic, west of Ishpeming, two thousand miners died in accidents. You can't believe everything David says so I had Cynthia look it up in the Soo library and it turned out to be true. It was like the owners sent men to war underground. The company gave the miners a house and a milk cow and if the miner died the family got to live in the house for a month and then they had to move on. This is the history of our life up here. Cynthia helped me calm down a bit by having me read two books to show me it also happened in other countries. One took place in the mining areas of England and was authored by A. J. Cronin and the other was based in France and called *Les Misérables,* which of course means the miserable ones and that's putting it lightly. I can't tell you what good it did me to learn all of this but I think you're better off understanding things like this than simply being pissed off. When you work a man twelve hours a day he becomes exhausted and careless and that's when the fatal accidents happen. Men and women fall in love, mate, and have children and they have to be fed.

I know something about what Clarence was up against building those giant ore docks. I'm modest about my knowledge but I was pretty good at geometry and algebra in high school. They were the only subjects I got A's in. I nearly flunked Civics and History because their subjects never dealt with the raw deal the Indians got, which made me quite angry. I knew the story of how Flower's grandfather lost a whole section of land, which is 640 acres. Anyway, my son Herald did some research on his computer and at libraries and came up with all of the details on how these giant ore docks were built. They had to be about a hundred and fifty feet high so that the ore could gravity-feed down chutes from the train cars to the huge freighters, which would then take the ore to Cleveland and Chicago to be made into iron and steel.

It was on a March morning after an ice storm that Clarence lost Sally. He was hauling a load of planks out to the end of the ore dock. A man had been supposed to throw out rock salt on the side planking next to the rails but had run out of salt. The wagon started to slide and Clarence jumped clear only to see the full load skid off the side dragging the fully harnessed Sally with it. Clarence went down hand over hand on a big rope but Sally had hit the solid ice, which often doesn't melt until late April or early May. The fall was about a hundred and fifty feet and Sally was just short of twenty years. Clarence borrowed a team and a log sled and supplies and took Sally about ten miles east along the shore and then up into the woods to a place they had once camped together. The ground was frozen deep because there had been a cold spell where it was below zero most of February, like in Ishpeming a few years ago when the city pipes froze eight feet down. The story goes it took Clarence three days and nights to bury Sally deep enough to be safe from the wolves and also the bears that would soon be coming out of hibernation. Clarence built a huge driftwood fire and worked right through the three days and nights until his beloved horse had her proper burial.

Clarence quit his good job, bought a barrel of whiskey, and drank for a month or so. He lost his heart for a while. I was thinking just now that I understand his feelings because I have lost my body, which has been mine for forty-five years. [Donald stops talking and looks at me because I'm crying. When he resumes talking I can't understand what he says except that I know he's talking about a pet crow he had as a child. Donald is making squawking noises. Later on about midnight the new Rilutek drug seems to have a good effect because Donald wishes to talk. I've dimmed the lights, so I can barely see to take dictation but we are both staring at the moonlight on the lilacs out the screened window. Their odor is nearly overpowering and it's as if we've both given in to this living memory of earth. Moment by moment it's lilacs. C.]

Clarence had a sense of humor. He told his son, who was my grandfather, that he would have buried himself with Sally but couldn't figure out how. There are things a man can't accomplish. When he finished the whiskey he didn't have any more to drink for years until he went to the World's Fair in Chicago or St. Louis in 1903. Meanwhile he used the empty barrel as a food cache because flies didn't like the whiskey smell. He ran it up to a tree limb with a rope and pulley because now he lived way back in the woods and had a problem with bears getting his food. He raised a tiny bear cub after a hunter had shot the mother. She slept with him until she was three except in winter—then Clarence talked to her down the blowhole in the snowbank covering the deadfall where she hibernated. Her hot slow breath melted this breathing hole but so deep was her sleep she didn't hear him. This old Indian jokester in the area asked Clarence if he made love to this bear and Clarence said that like many women she plain didn't want to. She made love to a male bear but stayed in the area and would visit Clarence and sit by the fire with her two cubs. He lived only a mile from Lake Superior and they would share a pail of lake trout he'd catch. Naturally he called this bear Sally. Any dog or horse that lived with him the rest of this life he called Sally. When he married this mixed-blood French-Canadian woman named Lucretia when he was fifty

he also called her Sally. Clarence believed spirits were alive
and moved in and out of creatures. Even birds could carry
human spirits and vice versa. I have no proof of this but it
might be true. It's not for us to say no to it.

One winter night Clarence had a dream of horses. In
the dream there was a green pasture with many draft horses
that were related to Sally. There was a marsh nearby full of
red-winged blackbirds, which have a song Clarence liked,
so in April he headed toward the southeast and worked at a
sawmill in Ladysmith, Wisconsin, for a year to gather a little
money. By the time Clarence left the woods he was about
tired of just eating fish and venison, and the rutabagas, cab-
bages, carrots, and potatoes he grew in his garden. He had
a craving for tomatoes, which are almost impossible to grow
that far north. Once when Cynthia's tomatoes froze in mid-
June on Sugar Island near the Soo she was steamed up all
summer and then in August drove a couple of hundred miles
to buy five bushels of the right kind of tomatoes both to
can and to make sauces for the freezer. If you want tomatoes nothing else will do. Unlike many in the Great North
Clarence wouldn't eat bear meat.

Clarence got tired of Ladysmith and moved on farther
south to find the sources of his horse dream. He was a month
or so around Marshfield and won fifty bucks at the county
fair in the anvil-lifting contest, which was a lot of money in
those days. Clarence knew his limits because he had met the
big Chippewa up north who had portaged nineteen miles
carrying over four hundred pounds but this fellow weighed
over three hundred fifty. Some of these Indians got real big
because they had hundreds of years of all the fish that they

wanted to eat from the Great Lakes just as Cynthia tells me the Crow Indians got so tall because of centuries of buffalo eating. She says that's why Desert or Pueblo Indians are smaller. The food is harder to find down that way.

The stroke of luck at the county fair at Marshfield was that Clarence met the foreman of a big farm over inland from Milwaukee. This farm was owned by a German that also owned a big Milwaukee beer company. This farm bred and raised hundreds of draft horses to pull beer wagons and suchlike but also for sport like pulling contests. When Clarence arrived at dawn after walking ten miles in the moonlight he saw the marsh full of red-winged blackbirds and the field full of horses just like his dreams.

Just now I thought of the walks I used to take with Clare near Bay Mills in the moonlight. Herald was always a little scared of the dark though he denied it. Clare and me would walk up the hill to the cemetery and she liked to pretend she was afraid of the spirits but I knew she wasn't. When she was just a child she was a tough little cookie. Once over near Rudyard when the whole family was picking huckleberries on a hot day we went swimming in a creek and when we got back to our pails there was a small bear eating our berries. Well, little Clare ran at the bear screaming her head off while Herald and our dogs got behind Cynthia and me. Most dogs know better than to bother a bear. Once in the woods I helped a bear hunter staple about two hundred stitches in a hound that mixed it up with a sixty-pound bear. Well, Clare loved to walk in the moonlight. In high school she was six feet tall and was a real good power forward on the girl's basketball team.

Clarence thrived on the horse farm and moved up the ladder among the help so that in a couple of years he had his own shack rather than staying in the bunkhouse. He went down to the World's Fair in 1903 and drove a twelve-team hitch, that's twenty-four horses, pulling a big McCormick reaper in a parade. I still got the medal he received at the World's Fair. It's not gold but it's a nice medal, sort of like the one I got for winning the shot put at the state track meet down in Lansing.

Clarence didn't like Chicago too much. He thought it might catch fire again like it did in 1871 when he first traveled east on Sally and the world was full of smoke. He was also upset that his boss sold the twelve-team hitch to another beer company owner from St. Louis. He had worked with these special horses for two years and now they were sold. He had come down to Chicago from Milwaukee in a railroad car with the horses and returned in the private railroad car of his boss and started taking a few drinks. He went on a bit of a bender and got in trouble when he took this French-Canadian girl out of a whorehouse where she had got roughed up. Out on the street the whorehouse bouncers had followed Clarence and attacked him, which was their mistake. They wanted to get their girl back. Clarence made short work of the three of them though they had blackjacks. The police tried to arrest Clarence but one of the spectators of the fight worked for the big-deal brewing owner and interfered. Clarence took the girl home and they stayed together until she died on their little farm near Ishpeming thirty years later. She didn't mind being renamed Sally.

[Donald seems asleep with his eyes open. I am thinking that I must let Herald and Clare come for a visit despite Donald's embarrassment. His decline is precipitous. The neurologist is from Cleveland and doesn't really understand why Donald hid the early stages of his illness for God knows how long. I said some old-style men in the Upper Peninsula are like that. Life is hard and you don't complain. If you smash a hand while logging you joke about it. So many of them are broken-down and crippled early, like the cowboys in their forties and fifties I saw in Wyoming. My other reason for getting Herald and Clare home is my worry about having overheard Donald on the phone with K in Ann Arbor. I thought I heard Donald say that he doesn't want to live beyond his ability to walk down the street to the water near the old Coast Guard station and museum. I was immediately damp with cold sweat. K brings Irish smoked salmon up from Ann Arbor. Donald has always smoked lake trout and whitefish and can't understand how the Irish turn out a better product. The salmon is easier for him to eat than most things with his disease. Later: I slept two hours and now it is dawn with loud bird noises and a cool breeze off Lake Superior. Donald is awake and I can tell he wants to make love but we tried it a week ago unsuccessfully. I could see his rage at life, similar to early last fall before the trip to the glacier when he still wanted to murder that man over near Baraga.]

I like to look at this photo of Clarence and Sally when they got married out on Presque Isle in 1906. Her mother and some relatives who were mixed-blood Cree and French came down from Manitoba and stayed a couple of months. One of the relatives was a shaman type. He was a real little

fellow and liked to play jokes on people and had the talent of
being able to disappear at will. Sometimes he scared people
but mostly he was an ordinary fellow. He was said to commune with certain animals that God had never invented. He
camped in a little tent in a thicket out behind Clarence's
house. Early one morning Sally saw out the kitchen window that the man's tent and whole thicket were shaking and
suddenly the man was up in the top of a fir tree. Sally was
frightened because she was already pregnant before marriage and she sure didn't want this man's spirit to enter her
baby. Outsiders don't understand that no one wants to be a
medicine man. It's a calling, and the so-called spirits draw
the man out into direct communion with what we can't see
but suspect is there. I don't even want to say this man's name
though I'm not sure of much of this and my dad didn't want
to know anything about it. With the Anishinabeg you have
the *jessahked* and the *wabeno,* who are men of dawn. That's
about all I'm saying as it's coming close to my own religion,
which is nobody's beeswax as we said when we were kids.
The Cree however left early because he thought he was
being pursued by local spirits known as *manitous.* He needed
to get back home up near Hollow Water in Manitoba, where
the local spirits knew him.

Clarence raised some draft horses but his meat-and-
potatoes trade was that of a commercial fisherman. They had
a pretty good life though Sally was upset that she could only
have the one child. In addition to commercial fishing for lake
trout and whitefish and raising draft horses, Clarence also
built a smokehouse to smoke fish. Of course back then re-
frigeration was limited to ice boxes so that food that lasted,

like smoked fish and meat, was much in demand. My own dad learned back in the Korean War from some guys from down south how you go about smoking meats like hams, brisket, and pork shoulder, which is my own favorite though Cynthia says it's too fatty.

The main content of my life has been getting married and raising children, but then when the children left a few years ago I felt high and dry. I missed fishing with Clare. If Herald was along he'd stay back at the campsite reading a science book or wander around identifying plants and flowers from one of his guidebooks. Herald was a bit spooked by the woods but we always took along our old malamute Jeff, which relaxed Herald. Jeff hunted ground squirrels all of his long life but never so far as we knew caught a single one. Cynthia liked us to go on these fishing trips because it gave her a chance to be alone. We'd go as far as the Nipigon area of Canada because Clare liked to fish for large brook trout. Her uncle David gave her some nice fly rods that I'm sure cost an arm and a leg. Clare always teased me because I'm a bait fisherman, either minnows or worms. She's hoping to get in the movie-wardrobe business in Toronto rather than Hollywood because Toronto is closer to brook trout. She once caught a five-pounder when we were camped between Wawa and Chapleau. Herald was nervous because we heard wolves at night. Even Jeff the dog got into the tent with Herald when the wolves started howling. Herald was always in his own tent because he'd be up half the night reading by a lantern. He was a good camp cook though Clare rode him hard for following all recipes as if they were science.

So when the kids left for the university I got a bit lonely
though I had Cynthia and some pretty good friends. Cynthia
and K found me some books to read in the evening and I
can't say they brought happiness. I'm a slow reader because
I have dyslexia and maybe I dwelled too long on each page.
A couple of years ago K sent me *Rites of Conquest,* which is
about the history and culture of Michigan's Native Americans. I wish my dad had been alive to talk this book over. K
took me down to Mackinaw City, where the author, Charles
Cleland, was on an archaeology dig but I was too shy to ask
many questions. Though he was a professor the man was
as regular as a keg of nails. Despite meeting the author I
was lower than a duck's butt for a couple of months. Cynthia
and K cautioned me by telling woeful stories about the history of Jews, blacks, and Arabs. On Third Street near the
IGA I saw a very white man and his white wife getting into
their real expensive car which was also white and I wondered how much he knew of what his people had done to
us back in history. I had insisted on walking way down to
the IGA in the morning because I was going fishing with K
and we needed something to take along on the Deadstream
for lunch. Well I got dizzy from my disease though this was
early on last year and I sat down on the curb. Within minutes a cop car wheeled up and I decided to just look at my
feet. A cop yelled out his car window, "Are you drunk, boy?"
But then he said, "Jesus Christ, Donny, is that you? Are
you okay?" It turned out to be Ray Nurmi, who played
defensive end in high school. Ray gave me a ride home in
the squad car and I didn't ask him if he called Indians "boy."
I asked him if he knew where Floyd was living and Ray said

he'd heard Floyd was living up near Baraga and did I still have it in for him? I didn't say anything. Floyd's the man I wanted to murder for years.

[Donald falls asleep from all the ibuprofen I gave him a half hour ago. This ordinary drug helps relieve symptoms tempo-rarily, especially the severe cramping. Donald has never wanted to admit to me certain of his characteristics that he is thinking of as weaknesses. This Floyd thing has largely passed now though I see it can still arise as a minor blemish. Donald can be so se-cretive about such things except with K. I know that K and Donald drove up to Baraga last year to look for Floyd before they went to British Columbia to see the glacier. I don't know the whole story because neither Donald nor K will talk about it. The trouble with Donald and Floyd started when they were children. They disliked each other from the start and were always fighting. Floyd was a logger's son and as big as Donald though ungainly and not much of an athlete. Anyway, I think it was in the seventh grade when Donald's terrier mongrel had a litter and Donald was try-ing to sell the pups door to door and one got loose on the side-walk and Floyd kicked the puppy and killed it. Anyway I heard the police came because though they were only twelve these were big boys and adults couldn't break up the fight. The police stopped Donald from dragging Floyd down to Lake Superior, where he was going to drown him. Boys and men used to fight a lot around here but now it's largely out of fashion though you hear about it taking place in the more backwoods communities and among young men who take crystal meth, which is a real problem up here. Well, luckily in the ninth grade Floyd punched a teacher and got kicked out of school and the family moved farther west in the U.P. but not before Donald put Floyd in the

hospital with a body check in a hockey game. But the grudge
over the puppy never ended. K arrived the other day and his
mother, Polly, is pissed off because K has a Mohawk haircut,
which is a stripe down the center of his head with the rest bald.
I, however, am pleased because I got to sleep a whole night. In
a week or so our children are coming home and David is returning from Mexico, where his ex-lover Vernice joined him. Now
that K is here looking like some sort of extravagant faux Indian
and I got a full night's sleep I thought this rest would create a
miracle. Instead it caused more consciousness and it became
unimaginable that my lover of thirty years will die. I sat there at
the kitchen table studying my coffee and cereal as if they would
reveal some sort of answer for my brain, which had begun to
swirl in the face of the inevitable. I had just turned fourteen and
Donald was midway through his fifteenth year when we first
became close though in most respects we were old for our age.
Of course I had met him a number of times because his father,
Clarence, worked for my parents but I knew him only slightly
because my parents were quite formal and it would have been
unthinkable for Clarence to have his son hanging around the
property. Now it's thirty years later and I'm forty-four and my
daughter, Clare, tells me that I better sort things out because I'm
likely to live a long time without the love of my life. That morning
so long ago Clarence had Donald help him digging out in the
hard soil behind the garage because the garage and Jesse's
apartment above were tilting a bit. My father was standing in
one of his stupidly expensive summer suits waiting for Jesse to
back out the car to drive him three blocks downtown. My father
was leering as usual at my friend Laurie, who was sunning with
me on the lawn in her admittedly tiny bikini. I was just really fig-

uring out the power a girl's body had over men and boys. When my brother David said hello to Laurie in her bikini it looked like he'd break out in hives. Anyway, my father and Jesse left and Laurie and I made Clarence and Donald lemonade because the wind was from the south and it was a very hot June morning. Donald was down in the hole when I stooped to hand him his lemonade, his head only at my knee level. He said, "Thanks" but he was staring downward. I said, "Why won't you look at me to say thanks?" and he said, "I don't want to" and his father laughed. At the time I never knew a man like Clarence who lived so much in the center of reality. Donald drank his lemonade and handed me the glass with his back half turned. His hair and body were wet with sweat. His shirt was off and sweat trickled down his back, and then he turned and looked straight up at my body, not my face, and said, "Thanks" again. His body smelled as sweet as the earth he was digging. I felt a buzzy sensation in my whole body. He was smooth and brown with these Finnish-Indian cheekbones. Now K comes into the kitchen and says Donald is awake and wants to talk. K puts his hand on my shoulder because I'm crying as I gather up my notebook and pens. He hands me some tissues. Donald is embarrassed when I cry as if he's a burden. C.]

Well, Clarence and his wife, Sally, were pretty happy out there on their small farm southwest of Negaunee. Their little son, Clarence, who was my grandfather, was born with a hair on his ass by which I mean he was a real wild boy. It's said he shot his first deer at age seven with a .22. They had game laws back then and he got caught but the authorities couldn't very well put a seven-year-old in jail. The family had ups and downs especially when Sally got sick from

an infection and back then just like for many people now
there was no health insurance. Sally was in the hospital in
Marquette for a month but Clarence's credit was good though
it took him years to work off the debt. It was the need for
money that drove Clarence to do a wrong thing so the story
goes. Also anger. He had lost three out of a litter of five pig-
lets to a bear, which represented lost money for his family
and his debt to a hospital. You have to add on that now
Clarence was over fifty and he wasn't used to being responsible for a wife and son. That's my own thought anyway as
I've noticed men that have real late children always seem
tired out. What happened was that the son of the Milwaukee brewer whose horse farm Clarence had worked on
telegrammed Clarence and said he would pay five hundred
dollars, which was about what a man could make in a year
in those days, if Clarence would guide him to a big bear he
could shoot so he could be photographed with the bear for
a beer advertisement. They say the man was a drunken
womanizer and he wanted to do something manly like the
American hero Teddy Roosevelt. Clarence knew the whole
thing was wrong but he went ahead anyway. The man
showed up in a private railroad car and Clarence took him
into the million acres the Longyears owned north of the
McCormick Tract in the Huron Mountains. Clarence hunted
there in the fall and trapped in the winter and knew the territory of an especially large female bear. It wasn't much of
a hunting camp as the man had some playboy friends with
him plus a photographer and some servants to set up tents
with rugs on the floors, and also a cook, who brought along
liquor and wine. Clarence was disgusted and camped about

a mile away, where he shot a deer to bait the bear and built a blind for the man to hide in. Well, the man hurt his ankle and Clarence had to carry him to the blind. The bear was shot with Clarence shooting at the same time to make sure he got his money.

Clarence knew this was the worst thing he had done in his life. He looked on it as a curse because he loved bears. There were pictures in the Marquette and Milwaukee papers and in a sporting magazine. "Brewery King Shoots Monster Bear," the article read, and though he paid his debts and bought more pigs Clarence never got over this action. It's the old problem of what men will do for money and the answer is just about anything. Clarence took to drink for a month, which was full of bear nightmares. When he sobered up he realized that the bear had a cub he might save but when he found the mother's den the cub was already dead of starvation. This was a sad tale and Clarence never hunted or trapped again because his dreams told him this was his penance.

Meanwhile everyone called Clarence's son Little Clarence. He was shorter but real wide in the shoulders. He tried to sign up for World War I when he was only twelve but someone recognized him at the recruitment center. Little Clarence always had money he made as the youngest bareknuckle fighter and also shooting deer for rich hunters for five bucks a head. Little Clarence was the despair of his parents because he was always in trouble with the law. Nothing could subdue this young man but then when he was sixteen he fell in love with this pretty Finn girl. The girl was the daughter of a commercial fisherman who was a friend

of Clarence's. The man wasn't against his daughter being
in love with a young man who was mostly Indian but he
wouldn't put up with Little Clarence's behavior. This Finn
family were religious folks of the Lutheran faith. Little
Clarence had already begun to see the light when he had
done thirty days in jail for knocking out a policeman in
downtown Marquette and had terribly missed seeing his
girlfriend, who became my grandmother Nelmi.

Things went well for about five years. You might say
they were golden years but then things unraveled in the worst
way. First, Sally took sick again and then was bedridden.
Little Clarence and his wife, Nelmi, had a son who was to
become my father. One stormy late October day Little
Clarence and his father-in-law were lost off Standard Rock
in a gale, which sad to say was not a rare event for commercial fishermen. The survivors on shore were heartbroken.
Sally got even sicker and after a year the widow Nelmi re-
married a miner over by Republic. This man didn't like Indians so that Clarence and Sally rarely got to see their grandson,
my father. Sally died in 1925 and Clarence somehow got her
casket up to Hollow Water in Manitoba, which was the place
of her people and where she wanted to be buried. Clarence
never returned to the United States. He was last seen early
in the Depression in 1933 up north of Flin Flon, which is way
up there. He was living in a cabin on an island in the middle
of a remote lake. A local trapper told the police that Clarence
lived with two bears and it was supposed that the bears ate
him after he died. No one knows but no body was found.
Clarence was in his seventies then and with his up-and-down
life it wasn't a bad way to go. I ate some bear stew when I

was about twelve and it gave me bad dreams. I asked my dad about it and he said it only meant I shouldn't eat the meat unless for some reason I wanted bear dreams.

Once when I was fifteen a bunch of us were driving around one night near Skandia drinking beer and I scooped up a bear cub near the road. I was hanging out of the car with a friend holding me by the belt. It was June and the cub was real little. It cried like a baby and I rocked it and it quit crying and stared at me under the dome light of the car. I felt real eerie and then ashamed of myself. The mother was roaring around in the bushes and when I put the cub back on the road's shoulder it scooted back to its mom. K says that bears are distantly related to pigs. I can believe this because before my mother was taken away and we lived beyond the edge of town we raised some pigs. Holding a piglet is like holding a bear cub. You scratch their tummies and they calm down and look at you as if you might somehow belong together. When our daughter Clare was a baby and had colic and I rocked her there was this same feeling. There are bears all over the Upper Peninsula and people are never sure about their feelings for them. However, the traditional Chippewa are real specific about bears. I won't go into this because it's religious. I saw this evangelist on television and it embarrassed me that this man could talk about God as if he was a buddy next door. Before my mother was taken away to the Newberry State Hospital she told me it was best to talk to God in whispers or in your silent interior speech. She had trouble with sounds. She thought sounds were somehow alive. For instance, she could handle a screen door slamming or the hum of the hand-cranked cream separator. We had a cow when I was young. But a truck passing out on Route 28 or an airplane could make her eyes fearful. We had a black-and-white TV but the sound could never be on. She was uneducated but she liked classical music just like Cynthia. I admit I like Mozart myself because if I have a problem the music will take me away from it. My mother amazed my friends because she could do an exact imitation of a cow mooing or a dog barking. You couldn't tell the difference. When she got worse she would moo or bark in the middle of the night or do frog croaks. Dad said her disease short-circuited her and she lost power over her behavior. Her own mother died when my mom was a little girl down near Bark River. My mom took to wandering out in the swamp thinking she might find her own mother. On their honeymoon my parents drove all the way to Detroit to see the Tigers play baseball. They had a roast beef dinner at a restaurant with a black couple they met at the ball game. They kept in touch but the man was killed by a random bullet during the Detroit race riot in the sixties. You can't really understand dying by a random bullet.

My dad always regretted that he didn't get to know his grandpa Clarence very well all because of his own stepfather's prejudices against Indian people especially when it's known that the Finnish people are a type of Indian themselves. Cynthia quotes this poet as saying we were all Indians once by which the poet means well back in history. In grade school we were taught that America was a "melting pot," which was hard to understand when you were a kid because out in a shed we had a huge pot that was used for scalding pigs so that you could scrape off the hair.

My dad had a hard time with his emotions after Mother was gone off to Newberry. He took all of her clothes and stuff and gave it to her cousins over near Munising. He started living by the clock working for the Burketts and repairing boats in the evening and sometimes running a trapline in winter. He was saving for me to go to college, which never happened because we got married early though Cynthia later got her bachelor's and master's because she wanted to teach. I just liked to work hard but now I wish I had learned more about how the world works. There's way too much I don't understand.

One thing I can't get my head around is that no one seems to be equipped to understand the passage of time. When my son Herald was home for Christmas we talked this over and he said, "No one understands that sort of thing, Dad." Herald says that one thing he loves about mathematics is that there's no emotional content. Herald's girlfriend jilted him when he was a senior in high school and he never got over it. She wanted to get married after graduation and he wanted to go to college. Clare told Cynthia that in Los Angeles Herald sees this young woman who is Mexican and works as a stripper in a nightclub. This information knocked our socks off. Clare said that Herald even flew down to Hermosillo and met her parents. I loved hearing this because for a long time it seemed to me that my son actually liked being lonely. It seemed to me that Herald was similar to a bunch of drunks I have known who seemed to want to be lonely and misunderstood. They had a secret gripe against the world that could only be drowned out by alcohol. Herald's grief over this girl Sonia could only be healed by mathematics.

Drunks seem to want to cut themselves off from others. I'm not an authority on this because I've never been a drunk. Cynthia says it's partly because I'm large and it takes too much to get me cranked up. She's real leery about alcohol because of her parents. Her mother, whom I learned to love, became okay when she left her husband, who was truly an awful man in so many ways that just thinking about him confuses you. He sold his son David's cabin out from under him when David was down in Chicago with Polly studying religion.

I'm all over the place. Alcohol doesn't run much in my family. My dad said he had trouble when he returned from the Korean War. He stopped drinking because he knew he would lose my mother if he didn't. He had tried to drown himself but changed his mind when he got to the bottom of the lake off the pier. One thing that truly bothered him was cutting open an enemy soldier's stomach to stick his feet in to keep them from freezing. You look at Korea on the map and you see it's real far north and they experience a hard winter just like we do in the U.P. Men are always quick to go to war and if it doesn't kill them it kicks the shit out of them. Some of them recover and some don't and who knows why. I knew a fellow pretty well who had a hard time in Vietnam and one day he drove his motorcycle off the end of a half-built bridge at a hundred miles an hour. He told his friends he was going to do it and some of them watched. They built a fire and had hot dogs and beer for his last meal and off he went. After many years of not wanting to think about her father Cynthia checked out his war record, then went down to Mexico and talked to her father's old buddy and employee Jesse, who was retired down there with his own people. Anyway, Cynthia found out that early in the war on some South Pacific island, I forget which, her dad was an officer and after a battle ninety-three of his hundred men came up dead. I knew Jesse's daughter Vera, who was a real peach.

This was a real hard time and even now so many years later I know it's hard for Cynthia to listen to but I want Clare and Herald to know my own feelings on the matter. One of the truest things I've ever heard is that the evil men do lives after them. David Sr. was always the talk of the town in the way that working folk can be amazed at the behavior of rich people. He had what some call a "drinking problem" but in fact was just a mean-minded drunk with a hankering for girls that were too young for sex. His right-hand man Jesse, who everyone in town liked, brought his twelve-year-old daughter Vera up from Mexico so she could learn English. She was beautiful and she and Cynthia's brother got an instant crush on each other but he knew it was wrong to touch her unlike his father who raped poor Vera when he was drunk. That was the end of the family. Cynthia and I ran away together. Her mother Marjorie took off for Chicago. The father, who wasn't even arrested, moved over to Duluth and no one laid eyes on him for years. David stayed home in this big house with Mrs. Plunkett looking after him. Jesse took Vera back to Mexico the day after the rape where she had a baby, a boy that was never quite right in the head though part of it might have been when he got hit by a car while he was riding his bicycle. Who knows what came first, the chicken or the egg? Anyway, years later, right after Cynthia's

mother died young David was stupid enough to go down to
Mexico with his dad where a coffee farm was owned jointly
by these two old men. Jesse and the dad had a drunken
squabble and fight and Vera's son steps in with a machete.
David and his dad were pushed out in the Gulf of Mexico
in a rowboat and since the old man was about dead anyway
David shoved his father overboard. Strange to say I didn't
feel bad when at his ex-wife's funeral this man wouldn't
recognize me or shake my hand. And here I was the father
of his grandchildren. [This story isn't hard in me. The story is as
dead as my father. I'm just thankful to whatever gods there might
be that my mother recovered after leaving him. C.]

So my own father's solution for the hard knocks of life
was to work too hard and that's also been a downfall of my
own. It used to drive Cynthia crazy in the summer when I'd
have two crews working two shifts and I'd sometimes put in
a sixteen-hour day. Cynthia did my bookkeeping. She was a
soft touch and made sure my men were paid well and had
health insurance. Maybe the worst point in our marriage is
that I didn't want us living on the money that was left to her
from her mother's family and, later on, money left from the
sale of her dad's land. Our compromise was all of our camping trips though sometimes on them I'd fish from dawn to
dark, which often in the summer was sixteen hours. Once I
took Clare a couple hundred miles west to fish the Middle
Branch of the Ontonagon near Bruce Crossing. We dropped
Herald off in Marquette, where he was going to stay with his
uncle David and hear an important mathematician speak at
the university. We got delayed over near Sidnaw when two
old ladies in a Chrysler up ahead of us hit a doe and mangled

it up pretty well. Clare was about seventeen at the time but she had a real calming influence on people just like her mother. While she settled down the ladies, I carved two backstraps, the loins, out of the deer and put them on ice to eat the following day. Just like beef or pork, venison is not at its best when it's freshest. We made camp just before dark and because there was a big moon we fished at night knowing that the next day might be slow if the fish were able to feed all night. It was warm and buggy so Clare did better with her fly-fishing than I did with bait. I built a fire about three a.m. and when the coals were right I fried up a nice mess of brook trout in some bacon grease mixed with butter so I could get the iron skillet red hot. We ate our fish with just bread and salt and then had some blueberry cobbler Cynthia had sent along. We took a short swim and laid out our sleeping bags, both of us deciding to skip the tent in favor of the big moon. We were freshened up by our swim and started talking about this and that, including how to get Herald over his grief about losing his girlfriend Sonia. We took a couple of hits from a small bottle of schnapps and I asked Clare why she had had so many boyfriends. She said, "I like affection," which meant she took after her mother, then she said that Cynthia and I were lucky we had this great romantic love for each other to carry us through life, adding that most people aren't so fortunate and that's why there's so much divorce. Love will carry you through the hard parts. We were made silent by our thoughts and watched the small rapids out in the river that caught the moon just right so the moon jiggled and wavered. We were being hypnotized by the moon in the water.

I told Clare a couple of stories about Night Flying
Woman that she already knew and then a funny story about
two friends of mine when I was thirteen who tried to hypno-
tize girls. These boys were both homely and small and the
school principal called them urchins. One of them, Melvin
by name, was a good fishing buddy and never seemed to eat
anything but doughnuts. The other, Carl, was the son of a
professor at college and snuck around after dark with Melvin
in tow peeking in windows trying to see nude women or girls.
Carl was goofy but smart and had a notebook of the best
places to see "skin" as he called it. The police had caught them
twice, once way up a fir tree outside this cheerleader's second-
story window. Anyway, they ordered a book on hypnotism
from a men's magazine. I wasn't interested because I was an
athlete, which meant I had no shortage of girlfriends. They
practiced hypnotism out of the book and one cool October
day down at the beach they practiced on me and I pretended
I was hypnotized and walked right into icy Lake Superior up
to my neck. They were pretty excited and started walking
around at school in dark clothes pretending they had secret
powers. Girls are often bigger than boys at that age and they
were both aiming at this Finnish girl with monster breasts.
She wasn't very happy and was always slugging her schoolmates, often knocking them to the ground. Carl thought of
her as a trial balloon for his real ambition, which was to see
our really pretty history teacher naked. Carl and Melvin gave
this Finnish girl five bucks to go out to a thicket on Presque
Isle and take part in an experiment. She pretended she was
hypnotized and Melvin, who was the most daring, reached
out to touch her breast though it was a cold day and she was

wearing a coat. She slapped the shit out of both of them, blackening one of Carl's eyes.

Clare thought this was real funny but then talked about how sex drives young people crazy. The moon in the river current took over our thoughts again and then suddenly it was the first light of dawn, when a river begins to smell even sweeter for some reason. Clare always has her binoculars to check out birds and way downstream in the mist she discovered a bobcat hunting frogs in a slough. The bobcat caught a good-sized frog and carried it to a dry place, walking in a proud gait, flopped down, played with the frog a minute or so, and then ate it.

Now in the den talking these stories to Cynthia I'm thinking about this old nature documentary I saw on television. On television nature is most often presented as a threat to us. I suppose this is to keep our attention. On this old black-and-white documentary a jaguar and a huge snake called an anaconda were fighting on a riverbank somewhere in South America. I was sure it was going to be a fight to the death but they finally moved off very tired in different directions. I thought time would be over for one of them but it wasn't, but then after at dinner I realized it was an old film and both of these creatures were likely dead as doornails. I thought of the day that two young men on my cement crew were arguing about our bowling league tournament the night before and started fist-fighting right in the middle of lunch hour. They were both good punchers but it was a cold March day and they had stiff hands and I knew they were likely to hurt themselves. I didn't stop the fight right away because they had to work things out and I knew their hearts weren't in the fight. It wasn't like me and Floyd and the dead puppy. Sure enough they both broke bones in their hands. I sent them off to the doctor's telling them to say it was work-related and not a fight or insurance wouldn't pay up.

[Donald took a two-day break to ride around the country-side with K. I had ordered a new SUV with a special seat so Donald could be comfortable. He was upset about the expense and I had no alternative but to ignore him except to say that the money came from my mother and she would want him to be comfortable. How could he argue with a dead woman? The real problem is that he has come to the part of his story where he feels he has to admit some bad things about himself. Donald is a good person without being overwhelmed by daily ethical or moral concerns in any formal religious sense. I think that certain germinal, if peculiar, aspects of his character came from his two months with his father's cousin Flower, who believed that people must be careful to live in complete harmony with their natural surroundings. There are also somewhat mystifying notions of people as totally interlocking and that to separate yourself is to be doomed. For instance Donald was always concerned by the way my brother David purposely isolated himself. I think that in Donald's view the only people who legitimately isolate them-selves, men or women, are *medicine* people like this shaman character he knows up in Canada. These people are said to set themselves apart in order to commune with spirits and that sort of thing. I've wondered if Donald's tribal feelings might be ge-netic in nature because you don't see these feelings in our cul-ture. However, Donald has always insisted that he's "just an American." Way back when I started teaching grade school he suggested that maybe I shouldn't teach the old *melting pot* notions as they might scare kids. I teased that not every kid had a pig scalding pot in the back shed and an out-of-control imagination to go with it. I think the main problem he saw in my brother David is that David always seemed to be at war with himself. An amusing part of our marriage is talking about our dreams at breakfast when we have dreams of any interest. I used to envy all of Donald's animal dreams but then he's quite familiar with wild animals. When he was upset with something at work he would walk it off and if you walk a long ways up here you're bound to encounter animals because so much of the countryside is at least semiwild. For instance just before Donald got sick his favorite young worker got sent to prison for three years for selling marijuana that he had grown at the back of his parents' farm over near Rudyard. Donald felt very bad about this partly, I think, because he's claustrophobic and couldn't imagine three years in a prison cell, and also because the young man was similar in character to K, that is, impetuous to the point of being a little crazy. Well, after the trial on Friday Donald took his canteen, some crackers, and sardines, and called the next afternoon saying his feet hurt. He had walked through the night over forty miles from Paradise to Muskallonge Lake down the empty shore of Lake Superior. That's what I mean by his *walking it off*. C.]

I'm getting to the end of my story but there are a number of bad things I've done that puzzle me. Such things nag at you the way you can't keep your tongue away from the hole left by a pulled tooth. My dad said that just because you've done a few bad things doesn't mean you're a bad person. And some things are right in the middle. For instance it bothered him that he knew Jesse embezzled money from Mr. Burkett after the rape of Jesse's daughter. My dad couldn't figure out what to do about the crime of stealing so he did nothing. He also said that in Korea he made love to hungry girls for candy bars, which most of the soldiers did, but then it wasn't right to take advantage of hunger. But then it's amazing what will be done for sex. I knew a guy from Iron River that made love to a cop's wife even though he figured he'd probably get shot if the cop found out. Well the cop did find out and this guy got his kneecap blasted off all for sex.

The first bad thing I did was sort of in the middle. Melvin, Carl, and me were brook trout fishing a few miles south of town. We were trespassing on this rich guy's place and we were sneaky and quiet because the guy had a German shepherd guard dog. Melvin was carrying his dad's pistol but he didn't have any bullets so I couldn't figure out the point. Boys can be very dumb. Anyway, Carl let out a yelp when he caught a big brook trout about twelve inches and the guard dog came running. Nothing's fair and the guard dog grabbed Melvin by the leg when he tried to climb a white pine. I went after the dog and faked it out with my left arm. The dog grabbed my coat but I reached over its head and got hold of its collar and swung it around hard and slammed it into a tree. Well, I went too far and the dog just lay there with fear in its eyes so I petted it and then its eyes went still though they remained open. Melvin had to have stitches in his ankle where the dog grabbed him but to this day I wonder if there wasn't a better way to handle the matter than killing the dog. Carl wondered what the rich man was protecting if he had to have a dog that bit people. Melvin had to pay his own doctor bill out of his paper route.

His parents were a strange couple in that the dad drank too much and the mother was real religious. She was fine at baked goods and if we wanted a piece of pie or peanut butter cookies we had to pray with her on our knees right there in the kitchen. It seemed like a fair trade though Carl always made crazy faces during prayer. Melvin's mom told me I was a heathen headed for hell. This scared me at the time but when I told my dad he joked that since I was only half Indian heathen maybe only half of me would go to hell. He wasn't too impressed by Christian people in that Catholics, Lutherans, and Baptists seemed to all act the same. It embarrassed him when Jesse was on vacation in old Mexico and he had to drive the Burketts to the Episcopal church in that big Packard. The question was why they couldn't walk a couple of blocks. Mr. Burkett had so many drunken driving tickets the authorities wouldn't allow him behind the wheel.

Dad said that people make terrible messes pretending they're perfect. He knew the Bible preached against self-righteousness and people still went ahead and drowned in it. When Cynthia and I got caught making love on the Burketts' living room floor and my dad got fired because of it I went crazy for twenty hours or so and then suddenly things returned to normal but not before I did some stupid things. First I drank too much beer down in Skandia during a poker game and lost the filly draft horse my dad gave me for my birthday. He had a mare he skidded logs with and had bred her to a stallion owned by a Mennonite over by Germfask. I had a full house but this guy from Trenary had a straight flush and there went my filly. This experience set me forever against gambling and is the main reason we left Sugar Island and the Soo area. I know the huge casino helped the tribe but gambling just set my nerves on edge. It's the stupid hope of getting something for nothing that corrupts people, but then after we moved to Bay Mills a small casino was also started there though there were plans for a bigger one. Cynthia told me to get off my high horse because the casino had helped finance education projects and get Indians indoor plumbing. If you're old and it's thirty below zero with lots of snowdrifts it's hard to walk outside to a privy.

Anyway, after I lost the filly I was spoiling for trouble and Melvin said let's drive down to Escanaba. Melvin had just had his sixteenth birthday and was still a virgin and this bothered him. Carl had told him to stop being so dirty-mouthed around girls and to wear clean clothes but Melvin's mother had taken off to Missouri to join this religious cult and their house was a mess. Melvin said, "No, it's only because I'm ugly." The upshot was that Melvin had heard that there was this woman that worked at a strip club in Escanaba that would screw a fellow for twenty-five dollars. Carl would drive because he was fairly sober because if he drank more than two beers he would puke due to stomach problems. Carl's dad was a big deal at the college and we were driving a newer-model Chevy. The beer was kept in the trunk so we had to slow down and drive off on a log road when we wanted one.

We got to Escanaba and of course Melvin didn't know which of the three strip clubs was where this professional woman worked. None of the clubs would let us in anyway because we didn't have identification and we weren't old enough. By the third club Melvin was pissed off and had become obnoxious pretending he was big and strong rather than small. This is what beer can do to man. Well, Carl became smart-mouthed and the bouncers shoved him away from the door and then little Melvin threw a punch about a foot wide of the mark and the bouncer backhanded him across the sidewalk into a car. I had to step in though I figured the bouncer to be about two-eighty to my two-thirty. He had a fair amount of fat around the waist, though, and I guessed he probably got winded pretty fast. Boxers know you have to build up your wind with roadwork or you can't put meat in your punches. Well, I ran on the track team so wind wasn't the problem. We boxed and I forced him to wrestle some to wear him out. I took a pretty good haymaker to an ear, which made my head ring like a church bell. By now a crowd had grouped around us and people were betting. The bouncer rushed me and got me half up on a car hood but I got my legs around his chest in a scissors and squeezed out what breath he had left. The bouncer was leaning up against the car when I started hammering him mostly to the body because that way you don't hurt your hands and it takes the will to continue out of your opponent. I hesitated before I threw my last punch because the bouncer's eyes looked like the German shepherd's a few years before. I hit him once more anyway and that's what I truly regret. I should never have thrown that last punch but I was angry about the filly and my dad getting fired by the Burketts for my behavior with Cynthia. Well, we heard a siren so Melvin, Carl, and me ran off down an alley and sat in a dark vacant lot for about an hour and then Carl snuck around and got the car. We didn't get back to town until daylight. Dad was making breakfast and told me that Mr. Burkett had called him in the evening and hired him back. He made an ice compress for the side of my face which was swollen up. He said that my body had far outgrown my brain. I've regretted that last punch a thousand times. These days men don't fight so much and it's a good thing. Cynthia's parents told her that she could never see me again but that afternoon we met up at Flower's near Au Train. Cynthia only had a learner's permit but she swiped her mother's car and drove out to meet me anyway. She couldn't have been an easy girl to raise. [I suppose I wasn't. C.] I was pleased that Flower and Cynthia liked each other. When Cynthia said something bad about her parents Flower said, "White people try to keep their children young. You're a grown-up. You can always move on." She wasn't preaching. She said it flatly, like "Try my homemade ketchup with your potatoes." I was always proud that our son Herald never got in a fight except during his hockey games when it's more or less expected. Herald never liked winter except for hockey. Once he got his B.A. at the University of Michigan with a straight four-point he headed for Caltech for graduate school. When we talk on the phone I begin with "You warm enough, Herald?" and he always says, "Sure am, Dad."

The other day K took me for a ride up to Big Bay but the day didn't turn out quite as well as I hoped. Big Bay made me think about murder again and then I couldn't swallow the hamburger K bought me at the bar and it smelled so good. I thought, "Look at me, I can't even eat a hamburger and in my working days I'd sometimes eat five for lunch." I thought

about murder in Big Bay because I remembered watching
this famous movie made in the area many years ago. [He's
talking about the movie *Anatomy of a Murder* with James Stewart,
Ben Gazzara, and Lee Remick, part of which was shot in the
Big Bay area. C.] I think I was about ten at the time and
watched it with my dad, who treated me like a grown-up
man at that time because I could do a man's work. It had
been two years since Mother had gone away and he had
pretty much got his sense of humor back, which could be
pretty rough. For instance at school a lot of kids called me
Donny Injun and some of them not in a nice way. All my
dad had to say was "You'll have to live with it." Once he
had to come to school to see the principal because I had
gotten in a couple of fights over being called Donny Injun.
He bawled me out, saying, "You can't fight over someone
calling you a name. Only if they punch you." I was upset
because I didn't think he understood me because being a
little more than a quarter he could pass for an ordinary white
person. My darker skin and bigger nose and cheekbones
came from my mother, who was three-quarters pure-blood.
It was hard also at this time because of Floyd booting the
puppy to death.

Anyway, I was sitting there in the fancy car Cynthia
bought in the parking lot of the bar waiting for K and thinking about the murder movie. The woman in it was a real peach
but then my thoughts went back to Floyd again. Sometimes
you can't control your thinking, and then this little girl came
up to the open car window and asked, "Are you a real Indian?" and I said, "About half," and she said, "How can
anyone be half?" And then her dad, who was talking to

someone in front of the bar for directions because he was a
tourist, came trotting over, grabbed his daughter, and yelled
at me, "Don't talk to my daughter," like I was a pervert.
People are set on scaring the shit out of their kids these days.
Well, K was just coming to the car with a sack of burgers and
with his other hand twisted the guy's ear and said, "Get the
fuck out of here." The guy was terrified of K and his funny
haircut and took off with his poor kid. It was unpleasant.

I'm slow to get to the worst thing about me. Last year
before I lost most of my strength to this disease I had K drive
me up to Baraga because I planned on killing Floyd. For
years I thought that if I was dying of a dread disease I'd take
Floyd along. I had to be dying because I couldn't stand the
idea of being locked into a prison. I can't even sleep with
tight covers or in a zipped-up sleeping bag. When I was real
little and out of hand my mother would shut me up in a
broom closet but not for real long. She said that if I didn't
behave a ghost that was half bear would eat me up in this
closet. And then when I was in the second grade the teacher
taped my mouth and shut me in a janitor's closet. At recess
Melvin had been pestering these older girls and they jumped
him, took off his pants, and threw them in the pond. Melvin
was real short so I had to wade in and get his pants, and I
was punished because we weren't supposed to go in the
pond. It was fenced off because a kid had drowned there
years before when he fell through the ice at recess. Well, the
teacher forgot to let me out of the janitor's closet and when
Dad came home from work at the Burketts' and I wasn't
there he went to the school. The principal was still in his
office and when he found me in the janitor's closet he was

angry at the teacher but nothing came of it except she was nicer after the incident. I was embarrassed because I'd been in there about five hours and had peed my pants. Melvin played an old-fashioned Halloween trick on this teacher where you put a paper sack full of dog shit on the porch, light it on fire, ring the doorbell, and run for it. The teacher came out and stomped the little fire getting her shoe covered with dog shit. I suppose it's not too funny but Melvin wanted vengeance on this teacher. Melvin had a bad end on the Seney stretch, which is fifty miles of straight highway between Seney and Shingleton. Melvin quit high school when I ran off with Cynthia. He became a pretty good mechanic and drove in demolition derbies, where they get about thirty old cars ramming into each other to see who lasts. They draw pretty big crowds though I didn't like them because of the noise. Melvin was liquored up and drove his hot Pontiac Trans Am about a hundred miles an hour down the Seney stretch with the state police giving chase. They said Melvin swerved to miss a deer and rolled the car about a dozen times including end over end near the Driggs River turnoff.

So K drove me up to Baraga last August so I could kick Floyd to death like he did to my puppy. Nothing about the day was what I expected. First of all it was real hot with a south wind and I had imagined killing Floyd on a cool day. We stopped at a gas station and convenience store outside of Baraga for directions and K bought a twelve-pack of beer saying that Floyd might want it as a last meal. We drove down this gravel road a few miles with my anger rising so that the edges of my sight were blurred. Floyd's place was

Depression brick, that fake brick made out of tar paper, the
whole house tilted a bit to the south from a weak foundation and north winds. There was what we call a car garden
with a half dozen old cars and pickups sitting in a wild raspberry patch. Floyd was sitting on the front porch next to a
big electric fan with an orange extension cord coming out
of the house window. Three old, fat dogs got up and barked
once when we pulled up and then the dogs lay back down
near Floyd's wheelchair. Floyd yelled out, "Donny Injun"
and started laughing as if this was a social visit. There were
no steps up to the porch but a sheet of plywood so he could
get his motorized wheelchair up and down. K sat down on a
rickety porch swing and petted the old dogs. He put the
twelve-pack on the table, on which there was a big package
of sweet rolls and bottles of Floyd's medications. You couldn't
imagine a man my age in worse disrepair than Floyd. He had
a bad case of the bloat and I guessed him to be well over
three hundred. He had so much fat around his neck that you
couldn't have strangled him. I was leaning against a porch
post because I was feeling dizzy. He said he'd heard through
a cousin in Marquette that I was sick and was sorry about
it. I was losing my anger but said in a rush that I had come
to kill him and he laughed and said, "Why bother?" I had
to move because the fan was blowing my way and Floyd
smelled bad. He drank three of the beers in no time at all.
He talked baby talk to the dogs and showed us how they
would all roll over in unison after which he gave them each
a piece of sweet roll. Floyd leaned over and turned off a
country music station so we could hear a group of sandhill
cranes squawking in a field full of big stumps to the west of

the house. I couldn't collect my thoughts. Floyd opened his fourth beer and said he was sorry about the puppy and that dogs were his favorite things. The county welfare people wanted him to move down to the VA hospital in Iron Mountain but he couldn't live without his *women.* All the dogs were female. One put her chin near the stump of his missing right leg and he gave her another piece of sweet roll and then to be democratic he had to give another piece to the other dogs. He asked me if I had a pistol because he had always thought someone might shoot him. I said no and that I was going to kick him to death like he did the puppy. He closed his eyes and said he was sorry about the puppy and then he said, "Everyone was always afraid of you, Donny." Suddenly I was embarrassed. K couldn't take it anymore and vaulted over the porch railing and took a little walk. The dogs went with him. Dogs like K. We sat there for a while talking about Melvin and also Carl, who was a GP doctor down on the outskirts of Chicago. I was itching to get out of there but was too hot and dizzy to move. Floyd said that in June a bunch of the young sandhill cranes walked into the yard and scared the hell out of the dogs. Finally K came back with the dogs and we left after asking Floyd if we could make a grocery run for him. He said no that he just ate canned food because he couldn't chew with only a couple of teeth. He seemed worried that K was going to take the rest of the beer. There was crusty stuff in the corners of his eyes and his dogs stood up to bid us good-bye.

    [A week later Donald was still quite distressed about this trip to murder Floyd. Donald also had his most severe seizure to date. He said his whole body felt like his foot did when he dropped a cement block on it, which he did a couple of times in his working life. He became so low that I was frantic and suggested that if he still intended to see a glacier he better get started. It was mid-August and K would leave to go back to Ann Arbor in a month. Right now what I remember most is my tears when they left. I was not totally confident that I'd see Donald again. When you've been married a long time you simply know the nature of your lover's thoughts and I knew he was thinking about suicide. Luckily there was a remission and he made it through the winter, which is a somewhat dormant period in the Great North, where people are mostly eager to discuss the latest blizzard and how far out Lake Superior would freeze, if not all the way across to Canada. C.]

I got down in the dumps after our Floyd visit mostly because I wondered what kind of piece of shit a man could become before he cracked. Floyd was no more than a character in one of those zombie movies I used to watch on television with Herald and Clare. At the doctor's office that week when I asked Cynthia to go out in the waiting room I tried to talk the doctor into giving me some pills for when I figured I might want to cash out. The doctor said no, that it was illegal. I said I didn't want to make a mess using a pistol or deer rifle. The doctor said, "Let me think it over." I have no intention of becoming too much of a burden to my family. Also, it's my life to end if I wish to end it.

It seemed to be time to see a glacier if I was ever going to see one. The trip turned out to be quite a joke because I never told K my true intentions and we spent damn near two weeks and a lot of driving and went to the wrong kind of glacier. Back in the seventh grade a man came to our school assembly with a film about the farthest north and Arctic country. Maybe it's the best thing I've ever seen on film. The man was in a boat in this area where there were more than a million birds — I think they were named puffins — that lived in cliffs and flew down to the ocean to eat fish. Down the shore there was a glacier as high as a mountain it seemed and this glacier was moving so slow you couldn't see it move and finally huge pieces of it would drop off into the sea with a crash like thunder. Well, when I got sick I developed this dream that a good way to die would be to be camped up on top of this glacier and ride a piece of ice as big as a house a thousand feet down to the sea. Well, I never told K this fantasy but then he wanted to head northwest to British Columbia because he had read a book about some Indians up there called the Koyukon. It turned out K was off a few hundred miles about where these Indians were. I had an old camper top and we put a mattress in the back so I could ride laying down when need be. We took a cooler, sleeping bags, a tent in case it rained, and fishing gear though K has never been much of an angler. He took a university course dealing with rivers and he mostly hikes and studies how rivers are shaped. He loves the Peshekee over in the Huron Mountains because it has quite a drop. I had also carved a hole inside a book in David's library. The book was called *The Indians of Lake Superior* and the hole contained mostly veterinary pills for pain from when our last dog, a part-malamute mongrel named Sally, got old and died. There were about thirty of these pills and I figured they might do the job for me. I only asked the doctor because I knew he'd have something more guaranteed to get me on the ghost road.

Off we went on our joke trip after Cynthia fried us up
a pan of eggs and side pork. In my condition you don't worry
anymore about cholesterol. You have to know that K is not
a normal person. He has built himself into a different kind
of person. For instance he might stay awake a few days and
nights and then sleep and read for a day and night. I used
to think he must take pep pills but Clare said no, he won't
even take an aspirin. Anyway, we headed over into Minnesota, then north toward Winnipeg, where we caught the
main western artery, Route 16. I wanted to detour up to
Hollow Water in Manitoba to see where the first Clarence's
wife, Sally, hailed from but it was too far out of the way.
Many people don't know that Canadian cities are mostly like
our own but the big empty places between cities are larger
than ours. K has a heavy foot and we drove forty-eight hours
in a row until we camped beside a fine river near Hinton,
Alberta. While K slept I caught a nice mess of trout to cook
for dinner. A game warden stopped to see if I had a fishing
license but then he looked at me closely and said it didn't
matter because even though I was American I was a First
Citizen. I started to fall down but he was a big fellow and
caught me. I was embarrassed and told him I had Lou
Gehrig's disease. He said he had a second cousin down in
Calgary with the problem. *First Citizen* is the official term
for what they call Indians in Canada.

Well, we finally made Smithers up in British Columbia and I wasn't feeling too good. K had called ahead and
when we got to the airport a helicopter was ready to take
us out to this glacier. He was to drop us off and pick us up
the next afternoon. K had given me a pill to calm my nerves

and I felt a little like the first time I smoked pot back in junior high school. The helicopter ride was quite a thrill. I kept thinking of a passage Cynthia read me once from a book where there was a Cheyenne Indian character named One Who Sees as a Bird who was an actual person in history. I don't have any faith in what they call reincarnation but if I was to return to earth in the form of another creature it would be nice if it was a bird, a raven to be exact. Once when I was night fishing in the fall with my dad on the Escanaba River down near Arnold he pointed up into the darkness at the big moon to where you could see birds like little pieces of black confetti flying south.

Well, when we were dropped off at the glacier I started laughing and rolling on the ground. These laughing or crying fits can be a symptom of my disease but this one was different. There was no ocean near this glacier. K was puzzled so I explained to him my suicide dream and he said, "Cool," which he says when he really likes something. We had a wonderful time camped there on that glacier with the light of a quarter moon glistening off the ice. I've always loved snow and ice and for a while I lay on it stark naked thinking that life can be quite glorious. When we were young Cynthia and I made love outdoors a lot mostly because we had no other place to go but then we came to like it. This included in a rowboat out on a lake where she had me rowing into the shine of the moon on the water. You can't beat these times in life.

I wasn't in too good shape when we got back in September but they had just brought out this new drug that helped some, called Rilutek. Talking with Cynthia I found

out I had a raw memory that had kept itself hidden. About
a year after they took my mom away and I lived with Flower
I got to missing my mom and I couldn't believe my dad when
he said we couldn't see her. One summer morning when my
dad went off to work at dawn, about five a.m. I got on my
bicycle and headed toward that Newberry mental hospital,
which was one hundred and thirty miles away. I figured I
could reach it by nightfall and then sleep out in the yard and
I could see my mom in the morning. My bicycle chain broke
twice and I didn't reach Newberry until midnight, nineteen
hours after I started. A night watchman caught me out in
the yard of the hospital and called the police. Meanwhile a
doctor who was on night duty had them fix me something
to eat. The doctor explained to me that my mother was in a
bad way and they had sent her downstate to Ypsilanti, which
he said was four hundred miles to the south. He said she
wouldn't recognize anyone except people she knew as a child
down near Bark River. I fell asleep in the office and my dad
picked me up after three a.m. and on the way home we
stopped near Seney and fished the Fox River. I caught my
biggest brook trout ever, about two pounds, and that helped
in this hard time. We stopped to see Flower in Au Train and
I ate fried chicken and two pieces of blackberry pie with
cream. Flower told me that she was now my mother and
when I needed her she was free to help me.

Despite my bad intentions I was sort of proud I didn't
kill Floyd. Or relieved. We were both in the prisons of our
bodies and the trip to the glacier wiped out a lot of my low
feelings. All winter long I watched these VCR tapes Cynthia
got me. As I've said my dyslexia is bad so I read too slow

but these tapes were a real education of sorts. The subjects were the types of Indian societies all over the world, including Indonesia, South America, Siberia, and Africa. I still have that book Cynthia's uncle Fred loaned me over in Grand Marais so many years ago. It's about black Indians down in the southern parts of the United States. Throughout the world none of these people got a fair shake. Some of those tribes died out completely. During the winter I liked to sit by the window and watch it snow. If I felt good enough Cynthia would help me get bundled up and I'd sit on a chair in the backyard and let it snow on me.

Herald and Clare arrived this evening from Los Angeles via Chicago. Polly picked them up at the airport. She said David would get here tomorrow from Mexico, where he's been helping poor folks move north. It's strange how he and Polly are divorced and live in different houses but still see each other a lot when he's here. Cynthia says her brother can only be taken in small doses but K says his mother, Polly, is just as difficult. Herald burst into tears when he saw me, I suppose because I've shrunk so much. Clare sat up all night with me and we had a good time talking about the old days, which are not so long ago. At dawn she said, "Dad, I know what you are going to do and I can't say I blame you," and then she fell asleep in her chair.

For about a half hour I was seeing things in the corners and at the tops of my eyes under the lids. I began to wonder where dreams were stored because the things I was seeing were blurred but they were sure enough combinations of animals. The female bear that had hung around the hill near me had sprouted great big raven wings, and there was also an otter with Clare's face.

I called out and Cynthia came down the stairs and sent Clare off to bed. I said I was sorry to disturb her but my mind was playing tricks. She teased me by saying what I had said years ago, "Whoever we are isn't for certain." We had been out on the porch of our darkened house near Bay Mills looking at stars all bundled up on a cold late fall night and that's what I'd said.

I now decided to say a little about my three days and nights on the hillside. I shouldn't be keeping all of my religious feelings from my family. I have to hold some things to myself, where they belong. They are too strange for me to understand and might be a burden to my family when they read this. I told my teacher up there but then such things are his calling. He told me that a few nights a year he "flies" out to Sisseton in South Dakota for a few minutes to poke fun at this woman who turned him down years ago. He admitted he shouldn't be doing this but nobody's perfect.

It's an ordinary thing to sit in a thicket on a hillside for three days. Everything is ordinary but more so, as if the thicket was a thousand times a thicket. Your life comes to a stop and some of the moments became hours by the third night.

The nights close to the summer solstice are pretty short, only truly dark from about eleven in the evening to before five in the morning. Of course I didn't take my watch. My dad, Clarence, used to joke that you don't tell time anything because it never wanted to hear from us, it just rushes past leaving us high and dry. The nights were pretty clear except for a brief thunderstorm the second night and I was lucky my children had taught me the stars. During and after the thunderstorm it helped me to be large. I noticed how shivering warms you up. I admit I was scared when the lightning struck the granite outcrop a hundred yards up the hill behind me. You could smell the lightning. I had seen the storm coming from the southwest across Lake Superior but nothing about seeing it prepared me for its violence.

A female bear, not real large but about my weight, came around on the second evening. I was dozing but smelled her nearness and opened my eyes. Bears can smell pretty strong depending on what they've been eating. She made some threatening noises and I wondered if she intended to kill me. This is rare but you're a fool if you don't think it happens. She went away but then came back at dawn and I got the idea that she was courting me. She flounced around outside the thicket about thirty feet away. Maybe she had lost a cub and wanted to start over. After a few minutes she gave up and wandered off, probably looking for a fawn to eat, likely her favorite meal.

Around noon the second day a flock of ravens began checking me out. I got this idea that the ravens hung around because they have spare time and were wondering what I was doing sitting still in their general home, which was where I was. Animals spend a lot of time being still so when we do too they lose their logical mistrust of us. At midmorning on the third day these three big ravens stood right outside of the thicket looking in at me. Ravens don't stand on the ground unless they're sure of themselves. Only once have I seen one

dead by the road and it was pretty young. Deer and many
other animals haven't figured out cars but ravens have. Anyway, it was plain to me that these three ravens wanted to
know why I was sitting there. I wasn't so sure myself but I
told them that the first day I had had a real short vision that
I was going to get sick and die. This was more than two years
before I got diagnosed. I told them I wasn't too much bothered by my coming death because it's what happens to all
living things sooner or later. Later would be better but it's
not for me to decide. I also told these ravens about a funeral
of their kind I had seen a few miles inland from Whitefish
Point a few years back. A real old raven had fallen slowly
down through the branches of a hemlock tree over a period
of two hours, grabbing hold of a branch now and then with
his or her last strength, while around the bird about three
dozen of his family were whirling. I heard the soft sound
when he finally hit the ground. I got the feeling that one of
the three ravens had been there as it was less than a hundred miles away. They showed no signs of leaving so I also
told them of my vision of my mother and father sitting beside a creek with a sleeping bear beside them as if it were a
pet dog. My mother and father looked wonderful and they
said, "Don't be afraid to come home, son."

In my three days I was able to see how creatures including insects looked at me rather than just how I saw
them. I became the garter snake that tested the air beside
my left knee and the two chickadees that landed on my
head. I was lucky enough to have my body fly over the
countries of earth and also to walk the bottom of the oceans,
which I'd always been curious about. I was scared at one

point when I descended into the earth and when I came up I was no longer there.

When I came down the hill and drove to the Soo with my teacher I saw one of the same ravens just north of the city. I doubt if my experience was much different than anyone else who spent three days up there. It was good to finally know that the spirit is everywhere rather than a separate thing. I've been lucky to spend a life pretty close to the earth up here in the north. I learned in those three days that the earth is so much more than I ever thought it was. It was a gift indeed to see all sides of everything at once. This makes it real hard to say good-bye. My family will be with me just like that old raven falling slowly down through the tree.

Part II

K

JUNE 14, 1995

Jesus Christ. Mosquitoes. I'm camped on a semisecret pond about a dozen miles northwest of town. I'd say it's about midnight though I've misplaced my pocket watch and I've just finished reading Donald's story by the light of my Coleman lantern. Cynthia gave it to me this morning. I think the story would be better without Cynthia's glosses but then if you're going to say something critical to Cynthia you better have your ammunition stockpiled. She doesn't get angry but she always has a dozen reasons why she's right compared to the one or two contentions you might have that she's wrong. It doesn't really matter because Donald's story is limited to family use.

I usually stay in a back bedroom at my mom Polly's house but I picked up a girl I vaguely knew at the Verling the other night and she puked on the back sidewalk. I forgot to hose off the sidewalk in the morning and Polly became a witch. Her voice pattern changes when she's pissed. It becomes terse and clipped. I remember this voice pattern very clearly from before my father died and they argued about his motorcycles. He claimed he needed motorcycles to "let off steam." I was about ten at the time and didn't understand the term and when I did it occurred to me that my father didn't have any particular steam. His was a case of a man who had kept the lid screwed on tight for so long that there was nothing left in the jar. He never took me for a ride on a motorcycle, saying it was too dangerous, which it eventually was for him. Every Saturday morning when weather was permissible he would roar off with four or five friends. Like my mother he was an elementary school teacher on the South Side of Chicago. He and his motorcycle friends were all Vietnam veterans and all singularly marked by that conflict.

Yesterday I was reading to Donald in the backyard from Schoolcraft's *Narrative Journal.* Schoolcraft was in this area in the 1820s and Donald likes what he calls the "old-timey" feel of the book. After about fifteen minutes Donald fell asleep on the old sofa that I'd hauled up through the cellar door into the yard. The little pound mongrel Clare brought in from Los Angeles lay curled up near Donald's neck. The dog is named Betty and is not very likable. When she arrived with Clare a few days ago she examined all of us and seemed to decide we were a bad lot except Donald. We don't know her background but Betty is an irritable creature. She caught a fledgling robin under a bush the other day and ate it before Clare could get it away from her. I told Clare that she looked attractive in her blue shorts, crawling around under the bushes trying to catch her dog with half a robin sticking out of its mouth. Clare screeched, "Fuck you," which Donald thought was funny.

I've come to think of Donald as a tugboat. Last year during semester break in the winter I house-sat an apartment in New York City owned by the old aunt of an ex-girlfriend. This woman, who was in her seventies, was paranoid about her art collection. We had stayed with her during a brief trip to New York and she had developed an affection for me that survived my breakup with her niece. Though this woman was Jewish she reminded me of Marlene Dietrich in the old movies I used to be addicted to. I still think Dietrich's left thigh in *The Blue Angel* is sexier than any photo I've ever seen in *Penthouse* or *Playboy*. Of course, the film had the advantage of her voice. Anyway this wonderful old lady has a voice like Jeanne Moreau's (the French actress). I spent a confining ten days in her apartment while she was off attending a trial in Frankfurt attempting to recover some of her family paintings that had been "misplaced" by the Nazis in World War II. Most of the paintings were now in the possession of an Alsatian sausage king who was unwilling to relinquish them. I got five grand for two weeks sitting in this spacious apartment guarding some Kandinskys, Tchelitchews, and Bakst stage drawings, etc., also a stimulating Mary Cassatt. I had full use of an improbable collection of take-out menus, on which she had made notations, and each day I was spelled at five for three hours by the doorman's thuggish brother, during which I walked because my sanity depends on that and my bicycle (an old balloon-tired Schwinn), which I hadn't brought to New York for fear it might be stolen. So

sitting in this huge apartment leafing through the thousands
of art books and ignoring a semester paper on Wittgenstein
as a possible source of the deconstructionists I also spent
hours with an antique telescope looking out the parlor's bay
window at the East River and the passing craft, big ships,
little ships, sailboats, and suchlike. Which reminds me of a
tugboat, their dense weight and immense power, slow to
achieve speed but with an irresistible surge of power. To care
for Donald in his present state is to finally understand that
there are no miracles except that we exist. Like his ances-
tor the first Clarence, we ride a big horse to the east and then
it's over.

Waking at dawn to the drone of mosquitoes. In June the
U.P. is a semitropical bug farm. I juice my skin with mosquito dope for a hike, trying to figure out a sentence from a
dream, "Before I was born I was water." I decided it was
mostly a neural image evolving from a book I was reading,
Fluvial Processes in Geomorphology. I'm sort of a professional
student and am allowed to take many different courses usually limited to majors because I'm also a handyman for a
big-deal dean's household. This freedom comes from my
expertise at fixing faucets, among other things.

    I make it to the haunted house by breakfast time. When
we moved to Marquette when I was eleven my new friends
always referred to Cynthia's family home as the "haunted
house" and I can't shake this early perception. When I arrive Clare has picked up her uncle David from the early
plane from Chicago. David and I eat breakfast in the den

with Donald, who can only manage his coffee and then egg-nog through a straw. Donald is amused by David's story about a crush he developed on a waitress in the Red Garter Club at the O'Hare Hilton. Cynthia says that with women David is a benign version of their father. Each new woman is an undiscovered country, but then he has learned nothing from the other countries he has visited. She added that he is always loaning them money to start a new life. Of course I already knew this. At breakfast David says that teaching in Mexico for several years has taught him "the banality of Eros." What can you say about a man that says such things? Donald wants a clear explanation. David hems and haws, saying that the problems of the poor are so overwhelming that one's sexuality drifts away. Donald says, "Bullshit" and that all of his working crew were involved in love and sex to such a crazy degree that it reminded him of the worst country music. David said that he meant that he had become less sexually motivated while teaching the poor. "You don't fall in love down there?" Donald asked and David said, "Well, occasionally" and we laughed. When Clare comes into the den and picks up our dishes she points out that though David's shoes are the same make and model, one is dirty gray and one is beige. "How could this happen?" he asks, a little irritated by her laughter. She says, "Finish your eggs," which he does with a frown, clearly not wanting to finish his eggs. She kisses his forehead and he blushes. She told me that when he comes home a couple of times a year he'll go down to Getz's clothing store and buy a half dozen of the same shirt so he won't have to decide what to wear. She thinks her uncle is "goofy" but she likes him very

much. Her dog Betty comes into the den, jumps up on the
bed with Donald, and growls at David. "Nice dog," he says.
In David you see the inevitable melancholy of the mix of
high intelligence and unearned income. It can't be much fun
to always feel vaguely unworthy. Clare has observed that
there is always a tinge of the homeless to her uncle, almost
unbelievable but true. She says that he never seems quite
comfortable except when he's sitting on the rickety porch
of his remote cabin over near Grand Marais. I once offered
to repair this porch and he delaminated as if I were intent
on modernizing a cathedral.

Clare and I take Donald out to Presque Isle but he falls
asleep in the easy chair I've hauled along. Donald likes to
sit under a tree near the graves of Chief Kawbawgam and
his daughter. This man's life spanned three centuries, from
1798 to 1901. Donald sits there and stares at Lake Superior as if it is an enormous puzzle and his puzzlement puts
him to sleep. It's a windy day and the crashing of the surf
against the rock promontory is repetitively loud. Clare is
upset as we're having a little picnic and the milk shake she
bought her father is turning to soup. Donald can manage
only liquids. He wanted me to make some pork barbecue
the other day just so he could smell it. Clare said that it's
strange to think that his body is at war with itself. After
breakfast this morning she sat out near a grove of lilacs near
the garage and read Donald's story. I was at the workbench
in the garage and saw her out the window. She would lift
her eyes and look at the lilacs, then go back to reading. Now

she wipes her father's drooling mouth with a handkerchief and he smiles in his sleep.

"Do you still own any bib overalls?" I asked. Clare imitated her father's dress until she was in her early teens.

"Yes, of course. I have four pairs, though they're too short. And I still have my favorite hammer and shovel."

"I know what he's going to do," I said, nodding at Donald and chewing on my corned beef sandwich as if mortality were a fiction.

"I do, too. I sat beside him in the middle of the night and he told me. I didn't say much. It's up to him. It's not like you can hold out any hope. People are always talking about the war against cancer but with this one the military metaphor doesn't work. You're dead with the diagnosis. The night Mom called last year I contacted a friend at UCLA medical school and got the information. Herald and I stayed up until dawn talking. As you know, when Herald is nervous he cooks something if he's near a kitchen. He's a thoroughly mediocre cook. Anyway, in the middle of the night he's cooking chili and he weighs the cubed chuck because the recipe calls for two pounds. He pushes the extra two ounces of meat off to the side and for once I didn't tease him, and then he said, 'There aren't very many people like my father anymore,' and then we both fell apart. That's what I was thinking this morning when I read about the three Clarences. These kind of people are gone forever."

"Well, I thought that too, but then I supposed that if you went far enough off the interstate you'd find some people with similarities. Also I thought of people in other parts of the world, what educated people blithely call the

Third World and then turn up the Bach or Springsteen and drink a two-dollar bottle of water, which is the daily food budget for families in ninety percent of the world population just as an American car costs fifty times the annual income of eighty percent—"

"Oh stop it, you fucking ninny." Clare rolled her eyes so far upward they were nearly all white, which she also did during orgasm when we were lovers. This stopped about five years ago, when I was nineteen and she eighteen, at which point she had perceived that my desire was greater for her mother, Cynthia. I thought that she broke it off because we were cousins and I said, "You love my mother more than you do me," and that was that. Clare never drifts. When you're with her you're always walking along the cornice of a tall building. When she says something withering you actually wither.

"The water is so beautiful it's hard to believe my great-grandpa died out there. Yours was taken underground and mine at sea." Donald gestured and Clare handed him his warm milk shake. He was talking about my grandpa, Polly's father, who was injured in an iron mine in his early thirties. He didn't die but forever after scuttled like a crab when he tried to walk freely. I was a difficult boy and my grandma would come down to Chicago in early June when school was out and retrieve me to spend a month in Iron Mountain. We would travel on a Greyhound bus because a plane was beyond her comprehension. I didn't want to go but once I reached Iron Mountain it was fine and I think of those summers as the best part of my childhood. I mean, my father would occasionally take me to a Chicago Cubs game but his lack of real interest in baseball was infectious. He would stare off at the field but you knew he wasn't seeing anything. I liked it best when we would visit a friend of his from the Marines, an Italian auto mechanic with a big family. The whole family was always eating, shouting, and laughing. They had a daughter named Gaspara who was my age but was much stronger. She would throw me on a couch and kiss me and sometimes just get me in a stranglehold and hold me tight while she read a comic. Once she demanded to see my penis and when I showed it to her she literally laughed until she cried. Still I loved her. When she helped her mother serve dinner she would give me an extra meatball and if her brother teased her she would start pounding him, throwing real punches, which her parents would ignore. This was the opposite of our house, where my parents often corrected school papers during dinner. My wayward sister later said, "They were always out to lunch." This wasn't quite a fair assessment because Polly is one of those overconscientious people, a dawn-to-midnight worker. My father, however, in his vain attempt to create what he thought was a normal life after Vietnam, simply excluded what most of us think of as reality. Years later in my mid-teens, when Polly thought that I was old enough, she told me that she had felt "sucker punched" by my father, and that after being married to David she had craved an ordinary, nonneurotic man only to gradually learn that my father had "painted himself by numbers." He was a highly intelligent man who utterly rejected his intelligence, just wanting to be a regular guy. His father taught economics at the University of Chicago and his mother translated from central European languages. They were austere and fustian academic people and I only saw them a few times when I was little. I thought they smelled strange, an odor I found out later was sherry. They moved to London before my dad was killed in the motor-cycle accident and didn't come back for the funeral. When I was in London on a college trip Polly made me look them up and they were cool and formal. The older woman that I thought was wonderful was David's mother, Marjorie. She and Polly were friends despite the divorce from David. She gave me and my sister a charge account at Kroch's & Brentano's so we could have all of the books we wanted. She would take us to the Cape Cod Room at the Drake, where we would eat lobster. Naturally my dad didn't like her—it was a matter of wavelength, his desire to keep every-thing in the discreet middle.

When Clare and I first spent any time around each other I was twelve and she was eleven. She was taller than me and wore blue-and-white bib overalls. Within minutes of a silent walk down to the St. Marys River with her dogs she said, "You're an odd duck." Polly had taken me and my sister over to Sugar Island, near the Soo, to visit Donald and Cynthia, Herald and Clare, and also to see a Chippewa powwow the next day. We were fairly fresh out of Chicago and the pow-wow was what the kids nowadays call a mind-fuck. It wasn't because I was small but these Indians looked real big because they were real big. Some of them rode up in Harleys, went into the school locker room with satchels, and then came out in full regalia. There were drum groups and several hundred

Indians dancing in a hot dusty circle. I didn't know what to think. My sister, who was ten, started to cry and Polly took her back to the car to explain things. Some people danced in street clothes, including Donald and Clare. Herald worked at a stand making hamburgers and hot dogs, which didn't taste good like they did in Chicago. Cynthia was taking care of a bunch of babies and young kids so their mothers could dance. My sister calmed down and Cynthia asked us to help her out. I held two babies at once, small brown babies. I thought Cynthia was beautiful. She had given birth to both Herald and Clare by the time she was twenty and at the time was only in her early thirties. Late in the afternoon when it was still hot I went down to the river with Herald and Clare and a few other young people and went skinny-dipping. They all teased me because I wouldn't take off my underpants. I was in a different world. Everyone seemed poor but more vivid than my life in Chicago except for my dad's Italian friends. At the time I actually wondered if Indians and Italians might be related.

Clare fed our leftover sandwiches to a stray mutt, who didn't chew the proper thirty-two times. I half lifted Donald into the car, where he promptly fell back to sleep. Clare told me I looked thicker and I said I had gone to the gym five days a week in Ann Arbor in anticipation of my chores with Donald.

"You're a good person," she said.

"But you said I was an odd duck."

"Oh for Christ's sake, that was forever ago."

"I could have said you have pointy tits."

"Of course, I was only eleven. You didn't even take off your underpants."

"I was afraid I would get a boner."

"Now men are always worried they won't get a boner."

"I always had a boner for you."

"I seem to remember that. But also for my mom."

"But I never came close."

"Of course you didn't. Did you try?"

"Never, for God's sake."

"But you had lust in your heart, odd duck."

She gave me the first close hug in five years. Her body felt so slightly fuller and my heart actually raced. I allowed my hand to slide down to her bottom.

"No necking in front of Dad," she said, pushing away, leaving my hand to touch air.

Back at the haunted house after I get Donald settled David waves me into the empty kitchen, where he's cooking what I sense will be a mediocre spaghetti sauce. Like Herald, he has no knack. He shows me a book from the den library, opens it, and there is a bottle of veterinary pills marked "Gretchen. 2 a day with meals." Gretchen was an ordinary mongrel with severe arthritis, her only talent being that she would catch fish, which the other two dogs would take from her. She didn't care. Being a finicky eater, she only wanted to catch them. The malamute named Bob would eat a five-pound sucker in a couple of convulsive bites.

"I think Donald has questionable intentions," David said, holding the obvious mystery of the pills in one hand and the hollowed-out book in the other.

"It's up to him." I turned off his sauce, which smelled like scorched tomato juice, and guided him out the back door for a walk.

It's hard to believe that David and Cynthia, with their radical differences of character, are brother and sister, but then this is true though to a lesser extent of Clare and Herald and my sister and I. The notion of personality holds mostly question marks. In the backyard headed toward the alley David started mumbling about having missed his late-morning nap, having been concerned about the pills. He takes three naps a day to get a "fresh start," though Cynthia teases him that he's the same person and it's the same world before and after his naps. David can walk all day in the woods surrounding his cabin but in Marquette he weaves a bit as if struggling to get his mind and body on the same track. Out near the garage he enters the big grove of lilacs and stands in the center, telling me for the twentieth time that this was one of his main hideouts as a child and young man. He also jokes that it was a good place from which to watch Cynthia's friend Laurie do gymnastic exercises in her bikini. I love this man whom I count as one of my fathers and have studied him carefully. Early on I found him mystifying. Right after we moved to Marquette from Chicago he bought me an expensive racing bicycle, I think for the absurd price of seven hundred dollars. I sold it to this rich kid at the college and bought a balloon-tired Schwinn in fine shape at a

yard sale for thirty bucks, hiding all my extra money in case
I wanted to run away to my grandpa's in Iron Mountain. I
needed a bike I could ride on gravel roads and dirt trails in
the woods and you didn't see mountain bikes locally in those
days. I was very worried about what David might think about
my transaction but he never noticed. He saw me on my paper
route on my Schwinn and was so pleased I liked the bike.

At the time I kept badgering Polly about all the bad
rumors I heard from my schoolmates about David's family.
The world isn't perceptually organized for seventh graders.
There are big empty places concerning sex and death, alcohol and divorce, war and world political mayhem. Kids over-
hear their parents' conversations in bits and pieces and try
to construct a reality however clumsy and malformed. Finally when I must have been about fourteen Polly sat me
down and told me about the Burkett family though she was
a little evasive about the sexual perversion of David's father.
She made much of the fact that David and Cynthia were
heroic to have escaped the influence of their father though
I already could see that David's success at this was less than
complete. Kids can have some pretty accurate insights but
they tend to come from a sharp angle and aren't very broad.
I also had heard a lot from my grandpa in Iron Mountain,
whose crippling injury had come about in a mine in which
the Burkett family had a financial interest. In the ensuing
workmen's compensation suit it was determined that the
mining equipment that crushed his legs was faulty and
shabbily repaired. Consequently, grandpa's opinions on
the Burketts did not center on sexual perversion, alcohol,
or business crime, which he referred to as "chicken shit

stuff," but on the Burketts' long-term malfeasance in the mining and logging industries.

David and I walked down to the harbor and looked at boats for an hour or so without really seeing them. David was involved in one of those "on the one hand and on the other hand" disquisitions on suicide. This man is a maddening expert on not very meaningful alternatives. My own contention was that in Donald's case it could not be considered suicide. It was a matter of being under a death sentence and deciding to push the date ahead.

"I wish it were me, not Donald," he said, staring at a gull as if it was a rare bird.

"But it's not you, for Christ's sake." I felt like unloading on this specific absurdity but then Herald walked up saying that he had spotted us from the hilltop through binoculars from an upstairs bedroom window. We paused to watch a pretty girl bending over on the deck of a sailboat and neatly coiling rope. From suicide to sex in a moment. David put a hand on Herald's shoulder. "We're pretty sure that you're father is thinking about suicide."

Herald was still looking at the girl but burst into tears. I was startled because I had never before seen him cry. He turned around and looked straight up into the sky.

"After you two left I sat with him for a while. His whole body was convulsed with cramps. I thought of suffocating him."

Herald quickly walked away and we hurried to follow, with David lagging behind because of his bad ankle.

We ended up having a drink at the Verling. I admitted
that I had brought up some pills from Ann Arbor at Donald's
request. We were all in our own peculiar knots with Herald
making a vain attempt to be coldly logical. Our emotional
stalemate was broken when a young woman came over to say
hello, the same one who had puked on Polly's back sidewalk.
She was quite attractive though her edges were blurred. It's
amazing how many young women drink too much these
days when they used to settle for marijuana. David pulled
up a chair for her. Despite long resistance he has his father's
aggressive weakness for women though not those who are
considered too young in our society. When Cynthia, however, is snide about her brother and women I correct her
by saying that I've never met a man so "generally" interested
in women. A few years ago I saw him embracing a rather
dumpy librarian out on Presque Isle who had to be in her
late fifties or early sixties. He saw me in the distance and
waved and later told me that he had had a crush on this
woman in his teens and still found her attractive. He added
that a woman's intelligence was her main erotic component.

   This did not quite explain his rapt attentiveness to the
young woman I had found to be a handsome little dipshit
with a faulty stomach. She had a sense of reality that was
alien to any perceptions that I had ever had. Herald got up
and left in a state of puzzled disgust. I followed him out onto
the sidewalk.

   "We shouldn't try to stop Dad from doing as he wishes,"
Herald said, taking a left rather than a right that would have
brought him toward home. He was headed toward the big
Catholic church to sit for a while. The Mexican girl he was

involved with in Los Angeles had asked him to consider becoming Catholic. This startled me and Herald grinned and said that he didn't have a religious impulse in his body, only ethical concerns. I walked with him the few blocks to the church feeling quite uncomfortable. I mean it's a beautiful, huge domed church but I'd had an experience there that had rather violently changed my life.

It was early in the spring of the year I was in the tenth grade. My closest friend and I were on the track team, both running the half mile. It irritated the coach when we would finish a race in a dead heat. We were sort of big shots at the time, what with me being the president of the class and he a star halfback on the football team not because he was so fast but because he was an extremely evasive runner with lateral movements that made defensive players look silly. He was very handsome and there was always a group of girls cooing around his locker between classes. Tenth-grade girls went out with senior boys and tenth-grade boys often went out with eighth- or ninth-grade girls though there was a code that you didn't go "all the way" with these younger girls, you settled for necking and heavy petting. Well, my dear friend made love to an eighth grader in his dad's pickup while they were drinking peppermint schnapps. He claimed to me that he wasn't going to put it in but she sat on it. She came up pregnant. Her parents were right-wing religious and filed a complaint with an eager assistant prosecutor, who charged my friend with statutory rape. He thought he would be kicked out of school and that his life was over. He swiped his dad's pickup and took off. The whole school was agog over their golden boy gone wrong. Some of us boys were

stupidly excited over his clean escape. Two nights after he
left he called me from Duluth to say that he had found a job
as a busboy and was staying in a cheap merchant seamen's
motel over across the harbor in Superior, Wisconsin. I wasn't
supposed to tell anybody and I didn't. A week later his body
was found in Duluth Harbor. An old man had seen him jump
from a bridge but didn't call the police for several days because he couldn't believe his eyes. A fisherman said there
was blood on some drift ice in the harbor, an unendurable
detail in the local newspaper.

The funeral mass had been held in the church, and
when I watched Herald walk in, the whole day from nine
years before came back to me. The pregnant girl and her
parents came to the mass and I started yelling at them inside the church in front of hundreds of people. Some men
wrestled me out the front door. I got on my bicycle and rode
all the way to Sault Ste. Marie and Sugar Island in the cold
rain. I stayed with Donald and Cynthia and wouldn't come
back to finish the school year despite my mother, Polly,
calling every day though later in the summer I took make-
up exams. Polly pulled this off because she was a teacher in
the school system. I intended never to go to school again but
I wasn't quite enough of an asshole to see my mother's heart
broken yet again after dad died when I was ten. David and
Polly drove over to see me but I ran out the back door and
hid. Clare knew I was hiding down in the bushes where we
skinny-dipped but wouldn't tell anyone where I was. Late
one night Cynthia caught Clare and me necking in our underpants. She didn't say anything but only rolled her eyes. I
worked for three months up to twelve hours a day for

Donald's construction crew, which helped consume my anger though I was never able to return to what people think of as a normal young man. Donald became half my father and half my friend.

It was late afternoon before I returned to the house. I had run into two old Finnish drunks I knew and one had touched my Mohawk haircut and said, "I bet the girls like to rub their butts on it." They were both in their seventies and drank whiskey heavily the week after their Social Security checks came in and after that did yard work to keep in beer money. They steadfastly refused any help from social services.

The household was upset because Donald had rejected an oxygen unit some medical personnel had brought over. Cynthia's eyes were red from crying. She and Clare sat wordlessly beside Donald, who was sleeping with an arm around Betty the dog, who growled when I waved from the front door. In the kitchen David was in a slight huff because Herald had tossed out his pasta sauce and had started a new batch. You could still smell the acrid odor of scorched tomatoes in the kitchen. Watching the two of them I thought how hard it is for any of us to understand that life is different for everyone. In my understanding of the disease, Donald's mind remains clear while his body is becoming a desiccated roadkill. Herald and David must be the only two people outside of academics who would quarrel about the human genome while cooking. David is enamored by the idea that the essential nature of the flea is nearly as complicated as our own. Herald says, "I find your generalities repellent,"

and David attacks science's fear of the "big picture," saying, "Einstein said that scientists who drill dozens of holes
in a thin piece of board aren't admirable." Clare comes into
the kitchen, tastes the sauce, but is noncommittal. "It needs
something," she says, putting an arm around my shoulder.
Cynthia comes into the kitchen, tastes the sauce, and also
says, "It needs something." She quickly fine-chops several
cloves of garlic and shreds more basil, tossing it all in the
pot and stirring. Herald wouldn't put up with any of us
touching his sauce but he can't withstand his mother. No
one can as far as I know. When the doctor stopped by the
other day Cynthia made him sweat under her questioning.
Clare whispers that she wants to go for a ride.

In my shabby pickup Clare fiddles with the music, quickly
switching from the Grateful Dead to Los Lobos and settling
on a Pink Floyd tape we used to listen to together.

"I'm buying you a new truck for Christmas."

"I don't want a new truck." This conversation has been
going on for years.

"I'm quitting the wardrobe business. I don't want to
dress people for a movie I won't like."

"What are you going to do?"

"If Herald gets married I'll go to graduate school in
Berkeley in the fall. Uncle David got me interested in human
geography years ago. I want to know why people are where
they are throughout the world. Herald can't manage alone."

"No more movies?"

"You gave up before I did."

I start thinking of my former obsession with movies, which Clare took part in when we were in our teens soon after the suicide of my friend, in other words a period of great instability. It started with my mother, Polly. When I was young, at any given moment she could explain my father to me. I envied this clarity. For some reason when I returned home late in the summer from Donald and Cynthia's my mind only felt clear when I watched movies, either at theaters or at home. No movie was too specious for me. I could watch Roy Rogers singing to Indians in warpaint and after that screen Bergman's *Virgin Spring* or *The Magician,* which cranked my mind around severely. Actors as varied as Gary Cooper, Robert Ryan, Jack Nicholson, and Robert De Niro always had a look on their faces that told me they knew what they were doing under the direst circumstances. This was a relief from being clubbed to death by question marks over my friend's death. I had always been curious about everything under the sun but the movies served to vastly broaden the dimensions of my curiosity. Clare and I were writing letters, mostly about movies, several times a week and when I ran short of money for rentals she would send cash. Herald and Clare got an allowance for "educational purposes" from their grandmother Marjorie's will and since Cynthia never nagged at them about this money they tended to be responsible. Clare and I often didn't agree on films and I remember the way we quarreled about Joel Coen's *Raising Arizona* and Bertolucci's *The Last Emperor.* I loved John Huston's *The Dead* and Kaufman's *The Unbearable Lightness of Being,* while Clare disliked both. She tended toward movies that featured clothes, like *Dangerous Liaisons.*

Meanwhile Polly and David, an off-again, on-again
couple, were worried about my obsession. At the time I
looked at them as childish in their refusal to accept that life
was chaotic and inconclusive. Life is slow and I watched
movies to know immediately what happened next. I even
made notes on what the characters might be doing during
scenes in their lives that weren't in the movies. Parents often
only see what they wish to see. Polly never knew that my
sister Rachel and a girlfriend had sold nude Polaroids of
themselves for money to buy marijuana. Clare sent me some
money and I managed to buy the photos back from a half
dozen boys. With two of them it took money and physical
threats. My sister thought of herself as a free spirit and
couldn't care less. She asked me, "Why are boys always
embarrassed when you give them what they want?" A solid
question, I think.

I suppose I became a bit peculiar and probably still am.
When I was a sophomore at the University of Michigan I had
a teacher, a graduate student finishing a Ph.D. in anthropology who was in the top five of the most unhealthy people I
have ever met. He had many "substance issues," which is a
euphemism people use for drug and alcohol problems. He
was a brilliant man in his early thirties whom students referred to as "the blob." He always smelled like licorice because he drank a bottle of Ricard pastis every day. He only
ate doughnuts and cheeseburgers. He could talk for hours
on the mystery of personality and how among billions of
people on earth no voice prints or appearances were exactly
the same. A Hitler and a St. Teresa of Avila could come from
the same genetic background. Once when we were having

a drink at Flood's I told him about my movie obsession and how it had etiolated into my only being able to watch Spanish, French, and Mexican films that were undubbed and had no subtitles. He said that the visuals in life could be wonderful but the sound track was unacceptable.

When Clare and I made our way down a trail to my campsite we ran into a half dozen people who were a crossbreed between econinnies and body Nazis with their cute outfits, fanny packs, and water bottles. The two in the lead were furious with exertion and seemed to ignore the aesthetics of nature. When we stepped aside Clare laughed and they all frowned as if she were an unworthy creature. When we reached my campsite and took a dip in the pond Clare caught a largish water snake and waved it at me as if it were a baton. It was angry and wrapped around her forearm but she somehow soothed the snake and then let it swim away.

We put on mosquito dope and made love in the overwarm tent, the first time in five years. She cried for a long while about her father and then we made love again, after which we began to talk about sex and death and then quickly dropped the subject. A friend who was an intern at the medical school at U of M had told me that surgical nurses were especially sexual but he had drawn no conclusions on the matter. Clare had become much more aggressive and I wondered idly who her lovers had been.

"Remember when you couldn't stand anything but the previews of coming attractions?"

I had done some sweeping up at a theater in Marquette in order to just see the previews. The owner thought I was daffy. I wore an old fatigue jacket from my father's military service and smoked unfiltered cigarettes. This was my senior year in high school and Polly was impatient with me though I got all A's and had won a National Merit Scholarship. I had decided on the University of Michigan because it was close to Detroit and I had become addicted to both Mexican music and the blues and Detroit had large black and Mexican music scenes.

"Why don't you come to Berkeley and live with me? Then you won't have to work so hard to support yourself."

I was thinking this over when she fell asleep, snoring softly because of her allergies. She had never clearly understood that all of my jobs had kept me grounded in actual life whereas simply sitting in my room with my studies tended to make me unstable. Besides, I didn't work as hard as she thought. For instance I took a man in his fifties who was confined to a wheelchair to all of the home Wolverine football and basketball games. I'd pick up sandwiches at Zingerman's and off we'd go. He made a lot of money in the stock market and I got a hundred bucks per game. On the way back to his grand home in the specially outfitted vehicle he would ask me about my latest sexual adventures. This could have been slightly creepy so I only told him stories I made up, and one about a professor's wife ran like a serial for nearly a year. It was as if I was describing a movie I had invented rather than a short story or novel. He liked the visuals. "Her hair was reddish and she limped a bit." Donald's story didn't need much embellishment because it had actual content. It was what William Faulkner called "the raw meat on the floor."

Staring at Clare I thought of our contact since our preteens and the idea that I may have had too much influence on her. Once I told her that her uncle and my semi-stepfather, David, was still tied to his dead father with a thousand ropes, and then one night when we were all at a restaurant together Clare was irked at David and right in front of everyone she told him that he was still tied to his father with a thousand ropes. Polly said, "Clare, that's bitchy." Cynthia said, "Clare, don't act like me." David covered his face with his hands for a long while. Donald lightened it up by saying he thought the apple had fallen a long way from the tree. You could see that David was grateful.

After my movie obsession waned I came to think that my main business was to check out everything to make sure reality was what I thought it was. For some reason I enjoyed correcting myself. I realized that the landscape changes depending on which way you're traveling the road. I simply had to accept the fact that bad things happen to good people and good things happen to bad people. Not that I wasn't still childish. I hurt Polly by refusing to go to my high school graduation. That morning I was in the grocery store buying supplies for a solo camping trip into the Huron Mountains and suddenly there was the girl my friend had made pregnant with a lovely baby she said was a year and a half. The baby reached for me and I held her between the grocery aisles. The baby had my friend's green eyes and I was falling apart inside. The girl said that her family had moved to Newberry after the funeral mass. She said her family didn't believe in abortion and they couldn't give up the baby for adoption because it might have gone to an unchristian family. She said she was still sorry every single day. "Now I have all of him that's left in my Sandra." I looked at her and down at the baby in my

arms, who was fondling my pretentious Tibetan prayer necklace. "I knew you was so close as friends." Her bad grammar
made it all more unbearable. I impulsively said that if she ever
wanted to get away from her family I'd support her and the
baby. She never called.

　　When I returned from the Hurons I rode my Schwinn
way over to Sugar Island to work for Donald for the summer. David had given me a car for graduation, a red Vega,
but I wasn't quite ready for a car. My mental health depended on the physical exhaustion of the bicycle. That summer my sister and her friends were stoned and beered up,
swiped the car, and wrecked it over near Champion. David
replaced it but I traded the new car in on a Honda pickup
before leaving for Ann Arbor. When David saw the pickup
he was puzzled but made no comment.

　　Soon after I started working for Donald that summer
Clare and I became lovers. Cynthia had fixed me up a nice
little room in Donald's toolshed in back of the house. It had
a woodstove for cool nights and mornings. At this latitude
it's hard for gardeners to have a reliable tomato crop. Once
while visiting David near Grand Marais I noted a trace of
snowflakes during the Fourth of July fireworks. Clare would
sneak out to the toolshed after she thought her parents were
asleep. I was eighteen and she seventeen but we were precocious in the varieties of lovemaking. Clare has her mother's
"matter-of-factness" and researched the subject as if she
were writing a term paper. Not very well hidden under my
mattress were instructional volumes like *The Joy of Sex* and
other manuals with bases in India and the Orient. Unfor-
tunately Clare fell asleep one night and didn't return to the

house and Donald discovered us when he woke me at dawn, about five a.m., for work. He bellowed, "I can't believe this! You're cousins!" I must say I felt a little fearful. Clare covered her head with a sheet and said nothing. Donald left the room and drove off in his pickup. Clare went inside to talk to Cynthia and Herald brought me out a cup of coffee. "Boy, you got your asses in a sling," he said, laughing. Clare and I drove off to Grand Marais in Clare's car and stayed in a tourist cabin, with Clare spending a lot of time in the phone booth next to the gas station. We visited her uncle David at his cabin way back in the woods next to the river. One of his girlfriends was there, a skinny poet named Vernice who had been living in Europe. I liked her a lot though she had a more acerbic tongue than Cynthia. I made myself useful by fixing a couple of leaks in David's roof and greasing his pump handle, which made a maddening squeak. Vernice was the first time I ever met anyone who was a good cook. I think she was skinny because she had some sort of disease but she never said what. David sensed something was wrong about Clare and me being there but he never pried. Sometimes people can't seem to overlook his eccentricities but he's a fascinating man. My mother has done everything to interrupt his brooding. A few years ago during her spring vacation from teaching she made him take her to Hawaii but he loathed the place. "People who have meaningless work take meaningless vacations," he told me. Finally after three days of suspense Cynthia showed up and said that Donald had calmed down. She asked us to keep the sexual nature of our relationship secret because Donald was an informal elder in the community and even though we weren't blood

cousins it would look like incest to some. We drove back and
Donald had decided to act like nothing had happened. We
kept the secret and never so much as held hands in public.

When we returned to the house from the campsite Herald was
in a snit because we had missed dinner. Clare nuked two
portions and we listened to David's analysis of the sauce.
He's a poor cook himself but likes to reread aloud portions
of McGee's book on the science of cooking. Everyone seemed
reasonably happy because Donald was playing tug-of-war
with the dog, his laughter a croak because of throat constric-
tions. Herald said that their uncle Fred had called from the
Zendo in Hawaii and wanted to come for a visit before Donald
died but Cynthia had said, "Please don't," not wanting to add
to the general stew. While Clare ate she scratched her many
mosquito bites. Cynthia brought some calamine lotion and
teased that we must have been "thrashing in the ferns like the
old days." Clare was displeased and shrieked "Mother!"
Cynthia has always ignored ordinary proprieties. I mean, she
behaves like a lady of high birth like her mother but in a restaurant she might push away her plate and tell the waitress
the food tasted like dog poop. Cynthia draws me aside and
says we have to talk. Immediately my stomach sinks. The odor
of Clare's mosquito-bite lotion reminds me of my grandmother in Iron Mountain who covered me with the stuff.

We walk down the hill to the old Coast Guard station near
the harbor's breakwall. We sit down on a bench and have a

cigarette. Cynthia only smokes three a day, one after each meal. My throat constricts a bit when I'm alone with her and I can't quite manage my normal voice. This has been going on since after my father's funeral when I was ten and she hugged me for a long time. It was then that I decided I loved her, with the total romantic irrationality of a ten-year-old boy.

We talk about what she calls "the plan," which is drawing painfully close. She spends most of the night with Donald and he talks best in the darkness. He is almost ready. Donald thinks that God is in every living creature, people, bugs, birds, animals, microbes, and that the earth and its mountains, plains, lakes, and rivers are part of His body. The rivers and creeks are like blood vessels. He asked me once if I had noticed that lightning bolts are shaped like river systems. I actually had noticed this. Consequently Donald wants to be buried naked in the earth with no casket. Of course this is illegal but who cares? Another slight problem is that he needs to be buried in Canada north of the Soo where he spent the three days and nights without food, water, or shelter. I was with him when he chose the grave site, about a half mile from the place of his "vigil." He won't say the Anishinabe name for it. He suggested I might try it sometime but I said I'm just a white guy. He said, "You're human" and laughed.

Cynthia talks logistics and I calm her down as much as possible. Herald and I will go up a day ahead and dig the grave and she can follow with David, Clare, and Donald. Polly doesn't think she should go even though she's been very close to Donald and Cynthia since she moved back north with us.

It's nearly dark about eleven in the evening this near
the solstice. Lake Superior is dead calm and the few sailboats have to motor into the harbor. We haven't spoken for
a long time and she holds my hand, which makes my poor
brain itch. I'm embarrassed at the inappropriateness of my
feelings to the point that I begin to feel my head sweat. She
senses my thoughts and takes her hand away. Her voice is
hard.

"Why do you love me? I find it irritating. Why can't
you just love Clare?"

I can say nothing. She walks across the street and up
the hill, disappearing into the large-mouthed tunnel of darkness made by the shade trees. I'm very tired and doze on
the bench but am suddenly awake when I remember how
my sister got to ride on the motorcycle with my dad. She
started screaming and wouldn't stop until he took her for a
ride around the block, proving the value of screaming. She
was like that with our parents. Go for the throat.

I walked a block along the water to Polly's house but
David's car was parked there. I didn't want to interrupt
whatever they had in mind. Through the yellow rectangle
of light in the dining room I could see them sitting at the
table having a drink. That's what I needed. I walked up the
hill but the big house was totally dark except for a dim light
in the den, where I could see Cynthia sitting beside Donald's
bed. I went through the yard to where my pickup was parked
in the alley in a bower of lilacs. There was a note on my windshield and I went into the dark workshop, where Clare was
asleep on the ancient leather couch. My eyes gradually ad-
justed to the darkness and there was a little light coming in

a window from a neighbor's yard light. I decide to let her sleep for a while. There's a trim little apartment upstairs but it's never been used since Mr. Burkett's aide Jesse, who was a Mexican, left for good. Clare told me part of the story about how Jesse's young daughter was raped by her grandfather. I saw a photo of this beautiful woman, Vera, at Cynthia's house years ago. Clare said that when she and Herald were in their early teens they went with Cynthia one spring vacation to Veracruz to visit Vera. Clare said she had been a little ill with flu but Herald loved the place and the trip was probably why Herald only feels affection for Mexican girls. Clare said that though it was hot in Veracruz she had chills from her fever and what she liked best was sitting on a hotel balcony and watching huge ships coming in and out of the harbor.

Sitting there in the darkness I'm upset that I love Cynthia more than Clare. My, how fate loves to jest, people used to say. It would be better otherwise. It's easy to feel anger at the randomness of love. I saw it in my mother when she told me in detail about her marriage to David. How can people continue to love someone who makes them so unhappy? Last year David told me that when he and Polly were married she had said that it was like being married to five people at once.

I figured I have had four fathers. My first, who died in the accident, and then my grandpa, who is eighty-five in a nursing home in Iron Mountain and no longer recognizes me, and Donald, who is near disappearing from earth. The last being David, who actually was there before Donald but had no effective influence until I cracked up as a university sophomore. He saw himself as a master of depression and I suppose he is. I was a very capable student but it had struck me that all my courses dealt with tiny corners of subjects and my emotions craved a complete picture. Why study seventeenth-century English literature when Chinese T'ang dynasty poetry was much better? That sort of thing. My worldview was a ten-thousand-piece beige jigsaw puzzle. David looked at my torment from a radically different point of view. He came down to Ann Arbor to where I had sat in my little off-campus room immovably for a couple of weeks. He knocked on the door and then said, "This room is a shithole" and left. An hour later he had found me a big south-facing room in this old lady's house. She was a professor's widow and the rent was expensive even though my help maintaining the house was part of the deal. We moved my few belongings and then drove to the Detroit airport and flew to Tucson. Well, we walked in the Cabeza Prieta, a vast area of the Sonoran Desert down near Ajo, and then in the wooded mountains farther east along the Mexican border for a total of ten days. At the beginning my vision was that of looking through a tunnel, which is typical of depression, and by the end it was relatively stereoscopic. We even visited a small village named Portal, where David said the writer Vladimir Nabokov used to spend summers chasing butterflies. Nabokov was a reading passion David had got from his girlfriend Vernice. This taste boggled me as it seemed so unlike David but he said he loved to read Nabokov because he was from another world and when his own became stuffy Nabokov, like James Joyce, presented an escape.

David didn't say all that much about depression. He thought that one of the central diseases of our culture was that meaningful work was available to so few. He said it was obvious that I didn't think my university studies were meaningful work but there were certainly ways of making them so if I followed my own curiosities rather than the prescribed university programs toward making me fodder for the economy. He also thought I should walk a couple of hours a day because the primitive rhythm of walking tended to *delight* the mind. Strangely, when I totally emerged from this slump I couldn't comprehend how I had almost drowned in it. However, I neglected a clue to other minor slumps to follow when on the plane home from Tucson to Detroit David advised that as much as possible I should avoid the *junk* of our culture. He said it was hard enough to live with what we know without drowning in this junk. It was a year later, when I visited a friend in Los Angeles, that I began to understand what David had said. In defense of L.A. it is essentially no junkier than the rest of our urban centers, it's just more on the surface. In New York City the endless blocks of huge buildings say to us, I'm serious and within me serious people are doing serious things, even though five thousand people in a building might only be playing with the market edge. In L.A. they've largely dispensed with the delusion of seriousness. In a rather radical economics seminar at the university we collectively decided that ninety-nine percent of the products of the culture were junk and this included books, movies, television, art, new food products, political speech. This was temporarily distressing because all of the twelve students were deeply immersed in this junk, and were perhaps doomed to earn our livelihoods buying and selling junk. Our young professor, a gay princeling from Harvard, thought it all quite funny and disappeared into Europe after a year at the University of Michigan. When I went north that June to spend the summer working for Donald, a job on which my sanity depended, the bleakness disappeared in the exhaustion of manual labor, but not the overwhelming sense that everything was a generic mistake. When David sent me to France and Spain as a graduation present the following year I felt sorry for the young intellectuals I met because the option of manual labor over there was unthinkable for the educated class. For better or worse, I was the only one who knew how to build a house. I fixed a number of faucets, toilets, and sink traps for Sorbonne students that summer.

I sat there over an hour watching Clare sleep and thinking my unproductive thoughts. I felt sexed up and impatient. I tiptoed over, knelt before her, and pushed up her skirt. I began to sing "Moon River," a song she hated, and she awoke with a shriek of laughter and pushed me over backward with a foot.

"Not here. Let's go to a motel. I don't want any more mosquitoes at your fucking campsite." She flicked on the overhead light and we looked at the assortment of the immaculate tools of Clarence, long dead, kept on the walls and at the back of the workbench, which was stained with oil. The edge of a hoe still gleamed with sharpness. Donald had given the same care to his tools as his father, Clarence. When he got sick he gave his tools and business to his favorite employee, Clyde, a grouchy Finlander who wouldn't stop working during the midmorning coffee break.

When we turned off the light and left the workshop we groped at each other to keep from stumbling in the dark and then started necking. We made love like dogs on the grass and Clare didn't stop laughing. I didn't last long and she said she hoped I'd last longer at the motel. Clare readily admits she's lucky because she never fails to be orgasmic. Afterward she often falls asleep for a few minutes and wakes up quite happy and girlish.

Herald's warmed-over spaghetti didn't do the job so on the way to the motel we stopped at a bar and had a hamburger and a beer. The bartender was cleaning the grill and hesitated in irritation but Clare offered him an extra twenty bucks, saying she was starving. "All you young fuckers get stoned and then you have to have a hamburger," the bartender said, refusing Clare's twenty. "You can buy me a drink." He poured himself half a water glass of bourbon and gulped it down. "The Tigers and Braves suck. Everything sucks except my girlfriend." It occurred to me that the bartender was two years ahead of me in high school, which would make him about twenty-six. He was a fine basketball guard and now he's fat and sallow.

At the motel Clare examined the grass stains on her knees from our love bout. She began to talk about my grandfather in Iron Mountain, which certainly delayed more sex. When I took Clare over to meet my grandparents I was startled at how much Ted, Polly's father, liked Clare. Because of his crippling mine injury he was the orneriest man

I've ever known though his wife, Nelmi, insisted he had a good start on ornery before the accident. He was courtly with Clare except for a single verbal binge against David's newspaper essay on his family and the history of mining and logging. His point was how could David know a goddamned thing if he had never been down in a mine or cut a tree? David had clearly always had "his head up his ass." Old Ted still referred to Polly as "my little girl." Clare had spent hours with him looking at his rock and mineral collection. She had done well at her geology courses at the University of Michigan in Ann Arbor, where she and Herald had taken undergraduate degrees.

Now in the motel in her alluring panties and bra she scratched her grass-stained knees and decided she wanted to visit Ted in the nursing home even though I said he wouldn't recognize her. She wasn't convinced of this.

"I'm hoping to get pregnant," she said, looking away from me to a print of a sad-eyed donkey wearing a garland of flowers on the wall.

"With me?" I almost hissed, unbalanced.

"Who else?" She smiled.

"You could have asked for my consent." I was struggling for an appropriate attitude.

"Why? You're not the main thing. I told Dad this afternoon and it made him so happy he cried. I mean I don't know if I'm pregnant but I said I was. He always wanted grandchildren. I said if it's a boy I'll name him Clarence after his father, and if it's a girl we'll have another Cynthia in the world."

"Jesus Christ, he won't even see the baby."

"Yes, he will. In his religion you stay on the ghost road for a year or so and then we have a ceremony and throw tobacco in the bonfire and let his spirit go to the other world. He said that we could still love him but we had to let him go."

"I don't know what to say." My mind had become a bucket of mud. Clare was the least maternal woman I knew.

"I'm not asking you to marry me. I'm honoring the wishes of my father."

I sat on the edge of the bed with a sense of absolute depletion in body and mind. I thought I knew her completely but now could see that her surface didn't reveal everything, which made me wonder what else might be underneath.

"Does Cynthia know about this?"

"It's none of her business. It's ours and maybe it's not yours the way you sound. I have my own money. I can go it alone. Maybe you should go over to the hospital emergency and be treated for shock."

She pushed me aside and got into bed. I turned off the light and took her place in the chair, sitting there nakedly and noting the way the mercury vapor light in the motel parking lot shone through the Venetian blinds casting light stripes across Clare's body. It was warm and she had slipped out of her bra and panties and there was a light stripe across one of her nipples and her pubic hair which normally would have been an evocative vision. I sat there quite paralyzed.

"I'm trying to get pregnant. Aren't you coming to bed?" she tried to joke.

"Of course, dear, when I finish balancing life on my nose." I was confused by two memories, one good and one bad with the bad one often returning during bad moments.

I was a spindly boy of twelve. It was August in Iron Mountain and my grandpa and I drove over to a lake adjoining the
city park in Crystal Falls, where he kept a decrepit wooden
rowboat. He liked to fish for panfish here and I rowed the
boat. After he parked the pickup I'd get his walker out of
the pickup bed and I would carry the fish poles, a can of
worms, and a small plastic tackle box and he would follow
slowly in the walker. The county welfare people tried to give
Ted one of those motorized wheelchairs but Ted wouldn't
accept it. He said he wasn't "that much of a cripple" but he
was. His legs sort of flopped from being squashed between
two tramcars full of iron ore. That day he stumbled trying
to get into the boat, banging his forehead on the boat gun-
wale and rolling backward into the water. Blood came out
of his left eyebrow and he started yelling, "My goddamned
cigarettes are wet. My goddamned cigarettes are wet. Go
get me some." So I ran across the park and downtown to a
small grocery store but the young woman cashier wouldn't
sell me a pack of cigarettes because I was too young. Naturally I started crying. An old man asked me what was wrong.
He had just bought a pack of chewing tobacco. I explained
the situation and he said, "So you're Teddy's grandson?" He
bought me a pack of cigarettes and a plastic lighter, taking
the money out of one of those little rubber coin purses that
opens like a vulva. The cashier said, "That's against the law"
and he squawked, "Fuck you and the train you rode in on."
I ran back to the boat and Ted said, "What took you so
long?" He always drank a six-pack while fishing but this
time he gave me one of the cans of Goebel. It made me dizzy.
Ted's left eye was swollen almost shut. We only caught five

small fish, which Nelmi fried up when we got back to Iron Mountain. Ted talked about the great Labor Day union picnic on this very lake while we fished that day. Every time a fish would bite and he missed the hookup he'd yell, "God-dammit" and his voice would roll across the still lake.

The good memory is easy. When I was in my mid-teens Polly and I went over to Bay Mills for a few days over Christmas. My sister didn't come along because she was in a home for troubled teens with "substance-abuse problems" for a couple of months. She would have come home for Christmas but she was angry at Mother. On our second day in Bay Mills a blizzard began with a gale out of the northwest across Lake Superior. I was helping Donald rewire a tiny house for an old Indian lady who mostly spoke Anishinabe. It was pretty exotic. Donald spoke some of the language. She was smart and wanted to know the precise nature of electricity. Clare stopped by and said we were needed at the day-care center Cynthia had started a few years before. Many mothers who worked in the Soo were going to be late getting back because of the snowstorm. The two women who worked at the day-care center were afraid of the storm and wanted to go home to their families. When we got there Herald had started a wood fire in the stove in case the electricity went off, which it finally did, but Donald waded through the snow and got Coleman lanterns from home, some sacks of candy, and hamburger and ground venison from the freezer. Polly hacked the meat into pieces and fried it on top of the woodstove. We had about twenty kids between the ages of two and five and they were quite a handful. Donald lay out on the floor and a half dozen of the kids jumped up and down on him. It was a mixed bunch of pure-bloods and half-breeds and a few white kids. Clare and Cynthia got them singing Christmas carols and it was interesting to me how they sang loudly with no real idea what the words meant. By midnight all but two little boys had been retrieved and we took them back to the house, where they wanted to sleep with Clare. We sat around the kitchen table in the light of a lantern and each had a shot of peppermint schnapps. In the morning the wind had settled down and there was thirty inches of fresh snow.

Soon after I crawled in bed Clare began to cry. At first I thought that it was because for the first time I was physically incapable of making love. I was dead meat at the idea of fathering a child. I dozed off and on and she continued to cry. This was a girl who never cried. I even heard her whisper "Daddy," which she never called Donald. It was either "Dad" or "Father." I held her but it was like I wasn't there. Her pillow was actually wet. I became desperate at my uselessness. My mind smelled the flowers at my dad's funeral. My sister had insisted on sitting on my lap and she'd worn some of Polly's perfume. By predawn and the first birdcalls Clare was still crying so I finally said that maybe we should go out to my campsite and take a hike or something. She turned on the light, got out of bed, and stood above me naked. I reached out for her and she pushed my hand away. She made weak coffee on the little room machine and spilled most of hers on the floor without seeming to notice.

After a strange night it was also a strange dawn with the slightest breeze from the south in the warm close air. There was faint thunder but the clouds were so dense you couldn't tell from which direction. I turned on the radio to catch the weather but she turned it off.

"I dreamt I was pregnant."

"I didn't know you slept."

"I read that you can dream in seconds, you know, little neural pictures. I was big as a cow at your campsite."

"Was I there?"

"I don't know. It was too fast. Are you coming to Berkeley?"

"What would I do?"

"Sign up for a few courses and take care of the baby. Cook dinner. Just plain *be*, like anyone else."

I reflected that she was becoming her mother when we parked near the trailhead to the campsite and she left the pickup door open. Donald was always closing doors after Cynthia. Clare looked up into the heavy mantle of trees at the loudness of the songbirds. I said that the clouds were so low that all of the sound descended but Clare was already off on the trail. At one point she took a wrong turn and I let her walk a hundred yards before I called out. I tried to suppress my irritation with her because I knew that her near hysteria was due to her father's impending death.

As I neared the campsite I could instantly see something was wrong. Someone had stolen my cookstove, also my medicine kit, which contained the mosquito repellent. Nothing else was missing except a bag of peanuts and a couple of candy bars. The mosquitoes came at us in horrendous clouds so I quickly built a smudge fire close to the tent flaps, adding green leaves, ferns, and also cedar branches for their delicious burning odor. Clare got in the sleeping bag with only her head sticking out. From under a tree I dug up my hidden cache, which contained bottled water, also a bottle of Calvados, a taste acquired on my graduation trip to France. I scarcely ever touch hard liquor but Calvados smells like an apple orchard in October. I got in the sleeping bag with both of us coughing from the smoke and sipping the liquor. We began to make love hearing violent thunderstorms approach from the south and the roar of the wind accompanying the storm. When the storm hit, the rain came down in bellowing sheets and soon there were a number of rivulets of water entering the tent from several directions and beginning to soak the sleeping bag. This didn't much matter as it was still warm and we were making love strenuously as if Clare expected my body to absorb her grief. Before we fell asleep we stared at a chickadee who had entered the tent mouth to get out of the still-raging squall. The tiny bird was only a foot away from our faces and regarded us with curiosity. I had one of those nearly imperceptible flashes, realizing I had never fully comprehended birds. Maybe one evening far back in prehistory all nine thousand or so types of birds had arrived on a cloud from the heavens.

When I awoke an hour or so later Clare was smiling in her sleep but shivering against me. The strong wind had clocked around to the north and I could hear the distant roar of Lake Superior, which had sunk the temperature to the mid-forties from the warmth of dawn. Not much more than a month before the lake had had a lid of ice. Now the air was clear and glittery with mother birds shrieking over their young blown fatally from their nests. Clare got up abruptly, dressed herself in wet clothes, and ran down the trail for the warmth of the truck heater. I broke camp dragging the wet tent behind me.

At the house the doctor's forbidding car was parked in front. I dropped Clare off and drove over to my mother's and hung the tent and sleeping bag over the clothesline. Mom came out the back door and we walked down the street to the old Coast Guard station to watch the huge white-capped waves slamming against the breakwall. We've always loved storms and made this walk even in the dead of winter to watch a norther, but then on a still night of twenty below zero Superior will begin to freeze and you have to wait until spring to see the grand waves again. The wind, perhaps fifty knots, was too loud for talk and I began to shiver in my wet clothes.

Polly made breakfast and while I was in the steamy shower I prepared for what might be coming. She tends to limit her lectures of disapproval to a couple of times a year. On our cold, windy walk I could see by her stiff lips something was coming. She and Clare were friendly and I hoped Clare hadn't mentioned her intentions of getting pregnant, which might precipitate a major inquisition. I always got straight A's in high school and at the University of Michigan, kept my room clean and orderly, earned scholarships and my own money except for what David slid my way. Once on a cool morning in Arizona when we were hiking David found four one-hundred-dollar bills in his pocket. He

looked at the money in puzzlement as if the parka had cre-
ated the cash. Not knowing what else to do he gave me two
of the bills.

At breakfast with a forkful of egg and fried potatoes
halfway to my mouth the hammer dropped.

"What you intend to do is illegal," she said.

"I know it." I wanted to say something smart like "No
shit, Sherlock."

"You could get in serious trouble. All of you."

"I think of death as beyond paltry legalities. Donald
should die in the way he chooses. I simply don't care what
happens afterward." The idea of civil authorities interfer-
ing knotted my stomach and I pushed my plate away. I could
understand where Polly was coming from. Her family was
relatively poor, the kind of people you see standing in lines
everywhere at Social Security offices, emergency rooms at
hospitals, and suchlike. She'd told me that if her father's
disability check was a day late her parents would become
desperate with worry. Such people have an extreme fear of
laws, rules, regulations, which at any time might destroy the
meager life they've cobbled together. Her mother, Nelmi,
worked at everything, with jobs as a grocery store clerk,
cleaning woman, and a nurse's aide, and when we would
come up at Christmas she would be out shoveling the snow
off the walk before daylight.

"I just don't want you to go to jail." Now she was rising to anger at the world in general. "They can always find
a reason to arrest a person. Maybe the Canadian authorities will catch you in the act. Remember you can't take a
pistol into Canada."

"For Christ's sake no one even owns a pistol. We're going to the place Donald wishes to die. When he dies we'll bury him. That's all. Of course it's illegal but fuck everyone."

"Don't use that word in front of your mother."

"Sorry. Anyway, David has talked to their family lawyer, who naturally advises against it. You have to register a death both here and in Canada and you can't just bury anyone where you might wish but since Donald's an enrolled member of the tribe here he's called a First Citizen in Canada and the civil law thus becomes mushy. First Citizens have different rights."

"But the rest of you aren't Indians. You have to be half." Polly's voice had become quavery.

"Who gives a shit!" I barked.

"Ssh. David's asleep on the sofa." But then David appeared at the kitchen door and poured himself a cup of coffee, his eyes more widely open than usual. David is that rare type who on waking from a night's sleep or his multiple daily naps has to reconstitute the world. Last year he told me that he has cognitive problems wherein on waking he's not sure the world actually exists. He's unsure until he consciously rehearses his senses. Once while the three of us were fishing out on the Deadstream Donald said he was jealous of David's dreaming, which includes bears, wolves, the beginning or the end of the world, a landscape of female butts, whatever. When David saw the wildly colored Hubble galactic photos he said, "I knew it. I saw them in my dreams."

Now he sat down next to Polly, hugged her, and began to eat my plate of tepid eggs and potatoes first sprinkling Tabasco liberally. "I heard part of your conversation. Don't

worry. It can be skewed so I can take full responsibility. Civil
authorities never want to charge five people when they can
charge one. Polly hates the word but this is that rare case
where you can say fuck the government." She pinched his
stomach. He winced and laughed. It was clear they were still
lovers. After my dad died and some of his friends would stop
over when we were packing to leave Chicago I was upset at
the way these men would look at Polly. She had a way of
actually listening to men's complaints that they construed
as affection. Some of his motorcycle group were tough guys
who made much of their toughness in the manner of ex-
servicemen. However, when we moved north I didn't much
mind David looking at Polly with desire. Of course I knew
they had once been married but most of all it was David's
kindness. We didn't have the money and he convinced her
to accept a down payment for a house. At age eleven I
couldn't figure it out because David looked ratty and people
in Chicago who had money looked like they had money.

There was a rap at the back door and Cynthia came in
looking haggard, her hair blown into a bird's nest and her
eyes reddish. She had been up all night with Donald, who
had developed pleurisy, his lungs filling with fluid. The
doctor had come twice and then she had finally persuaded
Donald to be hooked up to a portable inhaler. He agreed
but on the condition that Friday be his last day on earth.
Herald would accept this but not Clare, who became hysterical when she came home from her night with me. Now
Cynthia wanted a day or so with just the four of them together. This was Tuesday so there would be time to get ready
for the trip on Thursday. She wanted to see the collapsible

stretcher I had bought in Detroit to make sure it was strong enough. I retrieved it from my room and put one end on a chair and David laid on it. I sprung it up and down and it seemed plenty strong. David weighs about one-ninety and Donald about thirty pounds more but well down from his pre-illness two-eighty. It was understandable that Cynthia would fix on details when the complete picture was unbearable. When she stood up to leave she and David embraced and I thought of brothers and sisters and wished mightily that my own sister didn't keep herself so remote. I suddenly intended when Donald passed on to visit Rachel in New York City. She recently consented to speak to Polly once a week on the phone, which Polly viewed as a major breakthrough.

When Cynthia left there was a nearly interminable silence as if we three were willingly lost in our universe.

"God damn life," David finally whispered.

"Don't say that," Polly hissed, covering her face with her hands. In the past year she had started going to Catholic mass again having dropped the habit late in her teens.

David and I walked down to the breakwall and then decided to drive over to Grand Marais to see a wolf den he had discovered late last October before going to Mexico. He said it might still be occupied and we could spend the night at his cabin, which a friend had recently opened up for him. We went back to the house and quickly packed. David invited Polly but she said she wished to be alone. On the way out of town we dropped her off at church. I was curious on what terms she had begun to talk to God. She was an odd mixture. Her Finnish mother had become Catholic when she married Ted at his Italian and Irish parents' insistence. It took years for my grandma Nelmi's Lutheran family to forgive her. Consequently Nelmi never missed mass while Ted wouldn't go at gunpoint saying that the Catholic Church had always sided with the "powers that be" rather than the workingman. People used to take religious denominations very seriously. Maybe they still do. It's not something you'd notice at the University of Michigan.

On the way out of town David stopped at a butcher shop and bought two extra-large porterhouses and some bacon saying two things he'd missed in Mexico were fatty steaks and fatty bacon.

"Anything else?" I teased.

"No. I mean I think I love my country but I don't miss white people, white food, white cars, that sort of thing. And I'm of no particular use here except maybe teaching in inner cities and I find big cities too disorienting. Down there I'm in demand and I feel of at least minimal value to others."

David had written a pamphlet, in Spanish of course, about thirty-three things you need to know if you make it to the United States. Since many of the potential migrants were very poor and totally illiterate he traveled around a lot for a charity organization speaking in churches and town squares.

"How do you feel about your essay seven years later?" David had self-published a long essay on his family connection to economic predation in the history of the Upper Peninsula in a dozen newspapers up here.

"I don't think about it anymore. Donald's criticism was best. I connected my family's logging and mining to the land but gave short shrift to the people. It was unbalanced. I have to ask you this because no one really explained it to me but why does Donald have to be buried in this exact spot in Canada?"

"It's near where he spent three days without food, shelter, or water. It's an Anishinabe thing and I didn't pry into it very far. He had some sort of vision about the true nature of life there and it's the location from which he wishes to leave the earth."

"It would be good to know everything he saw. He wasn't clear!"

"That's not likely. You're supposed to have your own vision, which is more likely if you're in the right spot. Donald tried this several times before he made the whole three days. He told me he got scared out."

We dropped the groceries off at the cabin and drove on a two-track to within a mile or so of the wolf den before we began walking. It was seven hours before we got back to the cabin and without the car. There's a local euphemism in the U.P. that you're not lost, you just can't find your vehicle. Throughout this improbably arduous and uncomfortable hike my brain delivered little snippets from a course I had taken in the history of theater, everything from the Lord of Misrule, comic relief, berserk Puck, the fortunate fall, to the surprise ending. Both David and I are very experienced in the woods but we broke all the rules because our minds were elsewhere. David figured the walk to the wolf den and back would require about an hour and a half at most so we

didn't think about taking a compass, matches, collapsible tin
cups, water, halazone tablets, insect repellent, all of which
are de rigueur in this area, where the nearest people are at
least a dozen miles away.

Our first mistake was not figuring out a relatively new
log road that wiped out a familiar old trail. The new log road
was shaped like a horseshoe and only led to an eighty-acre
pulped area and returned us near to where we began. The
wind was still cool and strong from the north so we had to
make a big half circle in order to approach the wolf den from
downwind so if the animals were there they wouldn't scent
us. Rather than making the half circle through an easy open
area of dogwood and chokecherry we opted for the deep
woods. Since the clouds were dense enough to thoroughly
conceal the sun we ended up too far east, on the shore of
one of the Barfield Lakes. This meant that we were nearly
two miles off course. While David was resting his bad ankle,
injured in his teens, I could hear above the wind a faint stac-
cato roaring. I pointed to the west and David turned his head
the better to hear out of the wind. He said the noise had to
be two male bears in a quarrel about territory, or a female
defending her cubs from a rogue male. Since the bears were
in the direction of our intended shortcut to be back on course
we decided it was prudent to backtrack and virtually start
over. When we reached the open area we were three hours
into our hike and upset when we saw that the sky was clearing to both the west and north. This meant the cool wind
that drove the insects away would stop and the air become
warm. We would become more thirsty than we already were.
We thought of bagging the project as we sat under a dog-

wood on a bed of desiccated flower petals. When you're in this area in late May there's at least a thousand acres of blooming trees. David rubbed his ankle and said we shouldn't quit now because we would just go back to the cabin and talk and think about Donald or go to the Dunes Saloon and get drunk to avoid thinking about Donald.

We set out again in a half circle to the south with the sun warming us and swarms of noxious blackflies following us when we neared a creek to the west. I followed David to avoid walking too fast for his pace. He shambled rather than walked, tilting this way and that to angle his direction on the easiest route for his ankle across the lumpy ground. Every now and then he'd examine an enormous white pine stump as if it were a religious site. Finally from a half mile away we could see the lightning tree on a knoll from which David said we could see the wolf den in a clump of trees at the end of a long valley. Native peoples tend to think that lightning trees signal the approach of the gods, a place where their power directly touched earth. When I examined this charred and blasted white pine I was pleased I hadn't been there when the lightning had struck. Sitting on the knoll we couldn't see much because the binoculars had been left on the dashboard of the car. We stared at the end of the gulley until our eyes blurred, then walked slowly toward the den. It had been abandoned though there were a few deer bones in the grass and a slight sweet smell of decay in the now windless air. We sat down and laughed that our quest had ended this way. We examined the trackless dirt at the mouth of the den and David speculated that the den had probably been abandoned the previous November when deer hunters had come too close.

Now we were a good five hours into a stroll though with the sun slightly visible it was possible to use David's pocket watch as a vaguely accurate compass. We reached a long-unused log road and David said the car wasn't where it was supposed to be. This seemed funny as there weren't any car thieves in this spavined wilderness. He said we'd pick up the car in the morning and set out on a cross-country route toward the river and the cabin, pleased to reach the east end of the gulley that held his mother-of-all-stumps, which he'd shown me back in my early teens. I peeked through the roots at the roomy interior and when I looked up David was giving the stump a kiss.

In another half hour we stumbled into the cabin clearing and I ran toward the pump. We drank water until we were bilious. We slumped on the porch swing in the twilight. It was just after ten in the evening but still warmish and I took off my clothes, which were crusty with drying sweat, and took a dip in the cold river, floating south and swimming back in an eddy. David started a grill fire for the steaks out of oak kindling, which is best for meat because of the intense heat its coals generate. David mumbled that the lettuce for salad and the bread were still in the car. He retrieved a bottle of cloudy whiskey that his friend Mike, the saloon owner, had left behind. We had brought along two bottles of wine but they were also in the car as was a bag of ice in a cooler. In the cabin I put a dishpan of water on the propane stove so David could soak his wretched ankle and then mixed drinks with the whiskey and well water, which was full of tannin from an upstream swamp and iron from the ground. David drank his in three gulps and I made him another. I went out and got some wood and cedar branches, which sweeten the odor of a musty cabin, and built a fire in the fireplace for the cold night that was surely coming. David dozed in an easy chair surrounded by stacks of books. He had given his research collection to Northern Michigan University but then got lonely for the books and built another collection of Upper Peninsula history out of a local store aptly called Snowbound Books. David was a bona fide book neurotic even shipping cartons of duplicates to Mexico.

I heated a can of beans of questionable age, a bit wary because in the cold June last year a garter snake had made its way through the logs and established a home coiled around the pilot light. Garter snakes are harmless but startling when they ooze out of the stove when you're putting on your morning coffee. I woke David before I put on the steaks.

"Why do I ever leave this place?" A question to which the answer could be obvious to most though I loved it myself.

We didn't realize how hungry we were until we began eating. It was the fastest job I had ever done on a big steak and the beans were made passable drenched in hot sauce. David was waving a steak bone and talking about local native history and how in the eighteenth century east of here the Ojibway had repelled the Iroquois invasion. I was only half listening reflecting on how a tribe that had lived on Grand Island off present-day Munising had been pressured into going to war against the Sioux. The island tribe was totally inexperienced in warfare and all of the men were wiped out, thus ending a small culture that had existed for

hundreds of years. David, now thoroughly boozed, read a
passage from Charles Cleland that I already knew: "Michigan Indians, like other native people of the Great Lakes
region, have withstood and survived a biological and cultural assault that has now lasted for eight generations. The
scourge of smallpox, generations of intense warfare, the total
disruption of communities, alcohol and drunkenness, poverty, and the loss of their land and many cultural traditions
have come upon them without their choosing. It is almost
beyond belief that they have endured at all . . ." and then
more words about the miracle of survival.

"Remember when Donald carried me?" He dropped
the book to the floor and his chin was now on his chest. He
was referring to an evening when we had brook trout caught
in a beaver pond to the south, near the empty wolf den.
David was wading in his boots and had stepped into a beaver path under the surface and went in over his head, twist-
ing his bad ankle on tree roots when he scrambled to shore.
Donald had carried him piggyback through the woods a mile
back to the car.

"Yes. We caught some nice fish," I said. He was now
fully asleep and I dragged him to his spartan single bed in
the corner. On an end table were small framed photos of
his poet girlfriend Vernice, and a youngish photo of the
Mexican girl Vera. I mixed myself a nightcap not looking
at the glass while I drank because the water turned the
whiskey into a fecal brown. I went out and turned off the
Yamaha generator letting my eyes adjust to the total dark so
as not to stumble on my way to the cabin. The sky was nearly
creamy with stars this far from ambient light. I thought I

heard a wolf far in the distance but maybe not. I had heard them there before.

I was awakened just before dawn by the first birds and David's resonant snoring, also a dream that verged on nightmare. My grandpa Ted used to like to tell woeful stories about his family while we looked through a pile of scrapbooks. In the dream an old photo talked in a language I couldn't understand. It was Ted's great-uncle Alberto, who drowned in a mine when the Michigamme River poured into the Mansfield shaft over near Crystal Falls way back when. It happened in late September and Alberto, who hated the cold, had intended to return with his savings to his home ground in Emilia-Romagna in Italy to start a trattoria. Ted liked to end his stories with often inappropriate morals. "Alberto's story shows a man that if you want to do something you better get your ass in gear." The dream made me wonder what language the dead speak. A local politician rejecting foreign languages in a school budget had said, "If English was good enough for Jesus Christ it's good enough for our kids."

I trotted the two miles or so down a log trail to fetch the car, pausing only for a baby skunk who came out of the ferns ahead of me. He stopped. I stopped. He sat down. I sat down. I was likely his first human. I described my recent life and he seemed to doze, then walked off under the mantle of the ferns.

When I reached David's car I realized I had forgotten to search his pockets for the keys but luckily they were in

the ignition. I chewed on a crust of bread and for a still
moment I understood clearly what was happening to everyone I loved.

We had a morose breakfast in Grand Marais and David
decided to take the back way to Munising, a matter of fifty
miles of lumpy road. When we passed Au Sable Lake he
pointed out a distant sandbar across the lake where he had
"lost" his virginity to Laurie, a friend of Cynthia's who had
died of breast cancer at what he described as "the unacceptable age of twenty-five." I joined David on his obligatory
midmorning nap, this one on a dock near Munising where
boats departed for Grand Island, the scene of the disappeared tribe that had failed at war.

When we reached the house at midafternoon Cynthia and
Clare were opening a big Fed Ex carton on the front porch.
It was a Styrofoam cooler from Mississippi full of sweet
corn, peas, and tomatoes. Both Cynthia and Clare are provi-
dent about money but there are certain indulgences.

"You guys look like shit," Clare said with a broad smile.
"You could shuck the corn. We'll do the peas inside."

"We misplaced the car." David picked up an ear of corn
and studied its inherent mystery. "There are always an odd
number of corn rows on the cob, never even."

Cynthia stood up and looked down the steps at us. It was
plain to see that she was struggling for the right words and
looking up into the oak tree bordering the sidewalk for help.

"This morning Donald said that it's real good that you
love me but it's time to let me go." She turned to go into the

house and then paused to look in the dining room window where Donald was propped up in a chair staring blankly out at us. Herald stood there with a hand on Donald's shoulder to steady him. And that was that.

Polly came over for dinner after which she was driving to Iron Mountain to see her parents. We had a mid-August meal in June with a pot roast, corn, peas, and sliced tomatoes. Herald had moved Donald's electric hospital bed into the end of the dining room so he could be with us. Cynthia told me that this expensive bed had precipitated their last little quarrel two months before. She'd reassured him that the bed could be given to one of the hundreds of infirm locals who had no health insurance. Donald was always interested in value rather than mere cost. In the summer he wouldn't drink soda pop, which he said had gone up five hundred percent in his lifetime, packing along iced coffee in a thermos instead. When hamburgers went up a quarter at a local Soo diner he inquired and the owner, who was a friend, showed Donald his books and explained the price rise, but economics were a lacuna for him. I once tried to explain the nature of inflation but he thought it as pathetic as daylight savings time.

Far in the back of the cupboard Cynthia had found her baby dish with her name on the border. The dish had compartments and Cynthia fed Donald a few spoonfuls of corn, peas, and tomatoes she had pureed. He closed his eyes and smiled at these memories of earth. Clare put on Donald's favorite piece of music of Jim Pepper, which is a chant of the names of dozens of Indian tribes, and then a number of marvelous jazz compositions.

Herald and I stayed up late at the kitchen table making lists and plans. The mathematician in Herald rose to the surface and I was startled at the completeness of his lists, with everything from pickaxes, shovels, camping gear, water, bug dope, and fishing equipment. Canadian customs was usually easy but to make a plan fail-safe it had to appear that both cars contained people off on an Ontario fishing expedition up near Hawk Junction, north of Wawa. We weren't going that far but the idea was to have no problems at customs. My Toyota pickup didn't have four-wheel drive so we were using David's old Subaru. Herald would take it in early the next morning for a tune-up and new tires. I had watched from the kitchen window when David had cleaned out his junk and covered it with a tarp. It had taken him over an hour because he had to stop and examine passages in the dozens of books in bags in the back.

I had to go out to the workshop in the garage to get the two hypodermics I had hidden there. Just before I left Ann Arbor Cynthia had called to say that it was questionable whether Donald could swallow a handful of pills and she had rejected his not joking idea that we shoot him in the head like a sick dog. I was in a panic and explained the situation to the crippled big-shot stockbroker I drove to sporting contests at the University of Michigan. He was far to the right but was also an absolute right-to-die advocate. He got the two hypodermics full of Nembutal and God knows what else from a horse farm over near Metamora. This mixture was used to "put down" sick or badly injured horses. He said that was what he'd use for himself. Anyway, Herald said that we would hide one in each car. He examined his father's death potions with the bleak look of a man intent on suicide. We were planning on leaving before dawn on Friday. Cynthia, Donald, Clare, and David would follow at noon, which would give us time to dig an appropriate grave. I had dug well pits in a day's time and with Herald's help I figured we could dig a grave in four or five hours.

We had a whiskey nightcap, which loosened up Herald ever so slightly. He retrieved a Detroit Tigers ball cap from his room and put it on my head to cover up my "silly" Mohawk haircut, which he was sure would attract negative attention at Canadian customs. I tend to avoid mirrors and remembered my haircut only when it drew the attention of older people in Marquette. Younger ones would say "cool" if anything. Herald said that his dad liked the idea of dying on the day of the summer solstice. When she and Donald had eloped Cynthia had swiped her father's expensive telescope, a Questar, from his big closet of unused equipment. Cynthia loved the night sky and Donald quickly adopted her obsession. Sometimes at work in the daytime I'd see him squint up at the sky as if he thought he might be missing something. When Herald went off to Caltech he sent back large blow-ups of distant galaxies taken by the Hubble telescope and Donald tacked them up on the walls of his workshop.

It was nearly midnight when I had a small, second nightcap figuring I'd quit this nonsense when the current time passed. Normally I don't like my mind to feel blurred or

muted. A large part of my life is to check out reality and make
sure it is what I think it is and normally I enjoy the extrem-
ist reaches my mind wishes to take me to.

Herald was sleepily explaining chaos theory in modern physics when we heard Donald moaning and thrashing
in the severest body cramps. Cynthia slept on a single bed
next to his and began softly singing nursery rhymes, which
seemed to best calm him. Herald burst into tears when we
heard the strains of "Bobby Shafto's gone to sea." I gave
Herald a hug and fled the house.

It was a hard night. I woke at four a.m. and thought,
"Twenty-four hours until zero hour." I had dreamt about
my father fixing his motorcycle in our tiny yard in Chicago.
This had awakened me and I began thinking about fathers
and how Donald had helped straighten out my wild kinks
in high school when David, who acted as my stepfather
(though Polly wouldn't remarry him), was lost in his own
desolate space after finishing his twenty-five-year project.
I recalled one evening when Herald, Clare, and I had gone
over to the Canadian Soo to visit some French-Canadian
friends who were mixed-breed Ojibway. We went to a dance
out on the edge of the city and most people spoke pidgin
English at best. We danced all night to a French-Indian band
that had come down from Montreal. It was the most fun I've
ever had dancing before or since. During intermission I
talked to an old man who used to cut pulp over near Iron
Mountain who said he had met my grandfather Ted and his
family back in the forties. He said that the French-Canadians
wouldn't go down in the mines because they were death
traps. I asked him if he had read Émile Zola, whose *Germinal*

we were reading in high school. He laughed and said he couldn't read or write. He was in his late seventies and still worked in the woods. He said he had fathered nine children who were all doing pretty well.

At first light I went for a walk and a mile down the beach I ran into Clare. Oddly enough she was writing an immense version of her name on the smooth sand left by the storm two days before. The beach doesn't get much traffic in June, when Lake Superior is still too cold for swimming. Clare was a little embarrassed to be caught writing her own name. It had been a real hard night and Herald was now sitting with Donald so Cynthia could get some sleep. I asked if she needed to again go over the road and topographical maps north of the Canadian Soo. She said no, and that she remembered the gas station near the turnoff from our fishing trip years before where we had bought some fine smoked whitefish.

"I'm not saying you should marry me if I'm pregnant." She sat down on the sand in the middle of the first letter of her name.

"I will if you want to."

"I mean I don't need two kids at once."

"You sound like your mother. People say I'm the most mature young man in the U.S." I sat beside her and kissed her knee.

She laughed and then said that they were doing a trial run with Donald by driving him over near Au Train so he could say good-bye to his aunt Flower. I reminded her to take along several jars of a particular Jewish pickled herring Cynthia had ordered from Chicago. Flower had glaucoma

and her license had been lifted after she tailgated a squad car
in Munising. She didn't want more than two jars of this herring at once for fear of ruining the pleasure. Cynthia had
supported Flower for quite some time though an anthropologist from Kalamazoo College would also stop by now and then
with sacks of groceries and blackberry brandy of which she
drank a single ounce a day. I had stopped to see her on my
way up from Ann Arbor and she was sad that her "little boy
Donald" was sick and that she had told Donald that they
would take many walks in the far corners of the earth when
they entered the spirit world. She was particularly interested
in the Yakut and Sami natives of far northern Scandinavia
and Russia. The anthropologist told her about these people
and she trusted that they would like each other. Strangely
enough, I had no doubt that Flower would accomplish this.
I didn't know all that much about Anishinabe religion but
in contemporary terms you couldn't have more mojo than
Flower. If anyone was a true Night Flying Woman it was
Flower.

   "Where are you?" Clare pinched my stomach.

   "I was thinking about Flower. Remember when we
were there and she talked to that bear when we were out
picking berries?" The bear had rubbed against Flower before going away, ignoring the rest of us.

   "That's not the kind of thing you forget." Clare gave
me a chaste kiss, got up, and walked back toward home.

It was a day of the comforting mindlessness of errands, lists,
sporting goods and hardware stores, selecting new tires for

David's car, eating a fried whitefish sandwich with Herald
at the Verling, where we talked about David's obsession
with Mexico. Herald made the point that Mexico was more
vivid. Life was more reduced to its essentials and both the
good and bad were more clearly visible than in the U.S. I
reflected aloud that David had spent his life nearly suffo-
cated by ambiguities and Mexico likely offered the tonic he
needed. It was that and the fact that he felt useful down
there. Herald and I were both a little smitten by our large
Finnish waitress, who refused to flirt. You never get away
from this sort of thing. Nelmi said that despite Grandpa
Ted's dementia he still flirts with the nurses.

I barbecued pork ribs for dinner to go with the rest of the
Mississippi vegetables. Donald wanted the smell so I moved
the Weber over under the den window. A family joke is how
inept Donald is at grilling outdoors. He is always in a rush
to eat the food. Once while we were camping I saw him eat
a raw pork chop doused with hot sauce but then he said there
hadn't been a case of trichinosis in Michigan since World War
II. Cynthia tried to feed him some pork she had chopped fine
with a little sauce but he couldn't swallow it. He smiled when
she wiped his chin with a kitchen towel. You could see the
visit to Flower had put him in a fine mood despite his discomfort. Flower had given him her grandfather's bear-claw
necklace, which he wore around his neck and touched now
and then.

    After dinner we sat out in the backyard with Donald
on the sofa I had moved out in the yard. David told some

stories about getting lost in the woods over the years, including once in a blizzard over near Sagola when he had walked into his pickup on a gravel road. Herald and Clare sang an absurd ditty they had performed as a duet at the talent show early in grade school. Cynthia sang the Beatles' "Yellow Submarine." I couldn't sing a song or tell a story because I had begun crying and couldn't quite stop enough to use my voice. I had begun thinking that it would be good knowing that it was your last night on earth rather than simply being hit by a car or something like that.

I spent the night in a sleeping bag in the backyard to make sure I was ready for my departure with Herald at four a.m. Clare joined me for a while but we didn't make love. We looked up at the stars and didn't talk.

I was hollow-stomached and damp from a light rain when Herald woke me in the predawn dark. We drank from a thermos of coffee and there was a strong light in the east by the time we passed through Shingleton heading east. The clouds had broken up and the sun looked too large when it rose as it often does. We ate the pot roast sandwiches Herald had made and listened to some of David's Mexican tapes. Herald translated some lines of a border *corrido* the content of which was all love, death, and the drug trade. I changed the tape to mariachi music to escape further sinking myself in my seat. Beginning when Clare left me in the night I was seeing reality as a goofy seventeen-year-old in extremis, my brain making and remaking and editing life as a movie. It was disturbing because I thought I had purged myself of this impulse. When we whizzed through Canadian customs with the agent saying, "Good luck fishing" my mind altered his line and began to view the world in black and white despite the bluish-green water of eastern Lake Superior to the left and the high, green forested hills on the right with the conifers a dense green and the hardwoods not totally leafed out this far north, their pale green normally my favorite color.

We were digging hard by seven-thirty below a granite escarpment about three miles from the lake, which was visible over the treetops. We were in a small clearing where the drainage had gathered soil over the millennia after the glaciers had passed. It was hard digging at first with many large rocks over a hundred pounds dislodged by our pickaxes but then we were lucky when a little deeper our shovels hit manageable soil. By ten in the morning we were deep enough so when I looked out at ground level I saw the lid of grass, ferns, and wildflowers covering the ground. We certainly were appropriately deep but we tacitly agreed to keep digging because we had two hours before they would arrive, and now the ground was anyway soft, and we didn't want to stand around and think so continued on until the hole was truly enormous, about eight feet by six. We had no gloves and Herald's hands were becoming blistered and smeared with little blood splotches. I told him I could square off the hole, which he ignored, but then he cussed saying he had forgotten to buy a collapsible ladder. I told him he could easily find a dead hemlock sapling we could shimmy up. A moment after I helped Herald out of the hole I was frightened to hear another voice and I scrambled upward. I heard Herald say in a quaking voice, "Don't bother us. I'm digging my dad's grave."

It was Donald's teacher, or "medicine man." I won't use the other name vulgarized by the culture. I had met him a couple times with Donald over the years. We nodded and I introduced Herald. "So Donald is passing on?" he said. He walked over and began stripping cedar branches at the edge of the clearing for the bottom of the grave. He brought several armfuls to the grave's edge and then said he would go out to the roadhead and make sure no one came through after Cynthia passed. When he left we drank from a bottle of water and Herald said, "He looks so ordinary," and I explained that he was a surveyor for a timber company in addition to his tribal function though he lived separately from other tribal members.

We were finished by noon and applying first-aid salve to Herald's hands when we heard Cynthia's car approaching in the distance. Herald put a sweaty handkerchief over the hypodermic, which I recalled was full of phenobarbital and also Dilantin to make the euthanasia run smoothly. I looked up the escarpment and imagined Donald sitting there for three days and nights and getting reassurance from the not so benign silence of the earth.

We went over to help when Cynthia pulled up. Donald wanted to try to make the twenty yards or so of rumpled ground in his walker with Clare and David on each side of him. He was smiling and I had to look away to suppress a sob and then I gave up and sobbed. Cynthia and David

helped him sit down at the edge of the hole and Cynthia sat
down beside him with her arm around his shoulders. Donald
nodded to Herald, who quickly plunged the hypodermic into
Donald's arm. Clare and I got down into the grave and helped
Donald stretch out on the bed of cedar boughs. Cynthia slid
down and lay beside Donald crooning softly. Within minutes
Donald was dead and we helped each other out of the grave.
Cynthia tossed a handful of dirt and whispered something I
couldn't hear. Cynthia and David sat down in the grass off
to the side while Herald and I filled in the grave. Clare had
been off picking wildflowers and sprinkled them on the fresh
dirt mound. And then we all drove home.

Part III

David

Carol left my cabin at first light after she threw her hair-brush across the cabin and into the kitchen counter. Her little dog Sammy retrieved the brush but then wouldn't give it back to her. She's angry because I won't take her to Mexico with me next week. I explained that I'm working down there and don't have time to be a tour guide but added that I'd give her a ticket to visit at Christmas. That wasn't good enough. "Why would you work if you don't have to?" she asks, which is a logical question from a woman who has been a waitress and barmaid for twenty years.

It's nearly four months since Donald's passing to wher-ever. The cabin floor is truly cold after the warmest sum-mer and early fall I can remember. I step on the abandoned hairbrush with a bare foot. Of course no one has a clue about an afterlife. I turn on the coffee and then light a kerosene lantern on my worktable not wanting to walk out to the shed in the cold rain to crank up the generator. Donald has been gone from the summer solstice through the autumn equinox. Cynthia's been taking care of Flower, who hurt her foot in late August. Flower works in her garden barefoot and she cut her foot and got blood poisoning. By luck Cynthia stopped by to get a couple of blueberry pies and Flower was feverish with a swollen foot. Cynthia's real motive for going over to Au Train was to get Clare out of the house. Clare has been severely depressed since her father's death and it's been nearly impossible to get her to move from her room. K told me that part of it is because Clare wanted to be pregnant but isn't. She was supposed to be at Berkeley this fall and K back to Ann Arbor but now they're going to stay at that house in Marquette for want of anything better to do. Cynthia is beside herself because she knows that Clare sleeps in her dad's bib overalls. Herald left in midsummer to go back to Caltech and to be with his girl-friend. He came in September to help for a few days but gave up saying that perhaps his sister should be committed somewhere. I talked to Clare through the door of her room but all she would say is that she couldn't understand life and death. This doesn't put her in a unique position.

Anyway, it helped Clare to go with Cynthia to Flower's in late August. They got Flower over to emergency at the Munising Hospital, where she had to be put on intravenous. At the hospital Cynthia found out that Flower was seventy-eight rather than the sixty-eight she had claimed. After three days Flower escaped the hospital in the middle of the night and walked home overland on what she described to me later as the "old Indian path to town," which she had known since childhood. She said it was easy because there was a big moon. She had to get home for the simple reason that she was obligated to make three dozen berry pies for various cottagers for the upcoming Labor Day weekend. So what helped Clare was having to help Cynthia make all of these pies while Flower sat back in her old leather chair giving instructions. I can't say that a month and a half later Clare is completely out of the woods but she is emerging. I'm not suggesting that helping to make three dozen wild berry pies is a nostrum for depression. Something else is afoot here. The flavor of wild blueberries, blackberries, raspberries, thimbleberries. The smell of pie dough for which Flower renders her own lard from pigs a neighbor raises. The ordinary act of making pies but also the eerie serenity of Flower's bare-bones little house, part tar paper and part Depression brick, but on the inside a couple of layers of pine boards with sheets of tar paper in between for insulation, and pieces of gunny sack stuffed around the windows. The woodstove is the center of the room, the cookstove also fired by wood over near the only door, her single bed in the corner. There are a number of worktables, one for carving canes and weaving porcupine quill baskets, and one that holds objects she's found on her wanderings in the woods and on the shores of Grand Island: feathers, stones, a couple of bear skulls, beaver skulls with their peculiar teeth, a painted coyote skull, a rather frightening wolf skull, arrow- and spearheads, a soapstone peace pipe in the form of a loon, her favorite bird. It is hard to imagine a house so totally *on the ground*.

Certain problems of late trying to force pieces of U.S. and world history into logical constructs. This is improbable

with the history of Mexico but perhaps only because it's
fresher in mind. I mean I'm more accepting of the chaos
of U.S. history merely because I've had it in mind for so
long. Maybe the nature of historical chaos should have
been taught in school? Anyway the pressure, the burden,
the hubris of trying to force my puny logic on the sprawl of
history has made me goofy again with the repetitive effort.
My emotional life has squeezed out the edges of this effort
so that when I wake up from my books and notes I'm disgusted. I walk out on the cabin porch and suddenly a mere
mosquito, the last one of the fall, seems far more interesting
than any of my thinking, and the presence of the river is so
overwhelming that my senses leave my thoughts well behind, where I'm beginning to think they belong. No one
appointed me a junior Toynbee.

A flash of sunlight comes through the east window and
I walk out on the porch and down the hill to my rickety
little dock, where I put a bare foot in the swift, cold water.
Heraclitus was wrong when he said you can't step in the
same river twice. You can't even step in the same river once
except for a microsecond. Life is like that Vernice would say
about anything inscrutable. My errant mind turned to her
lovely bare butt when Carol leaned over naked in the first
light to try to get her hairbrush back from her dog, who
didn't know you weren't supposed to play at dawn.

I wonder why I keep returning to this dialectic of exhaustion. My social work in Mexico has nearly gotten me
over this as a disease but when I come home for the summer, and after being okay for a couple of months in the las-
situde of this northern season, the illness of history returns.

Again, how do we manage to live with what we know? It's so apparent that governments can't learn from the previous generation let alone the distant past. Thinking of Donald I doubt whether I should have used the word *disease* but then the way his motor neurons began to die, thus destroying his musculature, my mind wanders back to my dithering obsession with the destructiveness of history.

Fifteen minutes along the river trail I remember that I've forgotten to eat breakfast and return to the cabin for a quick bite. This would never happen when I'm in Mexico and live close to the ground and like everyone else I get up at daylight and have tortillas or a roll and coffee and some fruit, a few tablespoons of loathsome yogurt. My beloved dog Carla used to remind me about breakfast because that's what she wanted on waking, preferring a nasty combination of cheddar and oatmeal. My semiadopted dogs in Mexico come around at dinnertime for food, then a nap on the patio. They arrive when they hear my ancient Subaru rattling up the trail.

As I head back on the river trail to the south I remember something about my wicked father that I hadn't recalled in years. One summer morning at the club when I was nine or so and Cynthia was seven my father was taking care of us when my mother had a bridge breakfast. Our nanny had been fired the day before because she smoked and drank, both of which my parents did in great quantity but then some rich people don't have much to do except to be exacting with their employees. Anyway, Cynthia wanted to go for a walk while my father would have preferred to play rummy and read the paper. Off we went toward a little lake perhaps a mile distant from our lodge. The trail was clearly marked but Cynthia was in her "secret Indian" mood and insisted on walking cross-country. I had to follow her because my father was in a linen suit and he would call out to us from the trail. Sometimes Cynthia would run and then purse her lips with "sshhh" and we wouldn't answer my father's yells, which were getting him angry. When we reached the lake we could see my father down the shore standing on the dock and bellowing out for us. I called back and Cynthia slapped at me wanting to further tease him, and then she took off her clothes and swam out in the lake. I gathered up her clothes and waded along the brushy shore toward my father, who hissed, "Your sister is impossible" for the thousandth time. Only Clarence the yardman received her total respect. Cynthia swam slowly toward us but then about thirty feet out from us she pretended to struggle and went under. I wasn't worried by this trick because I knew she would swim underwater until she was beneath the dock, but my father jumped in after her. The water was full of swamp tannins and iron, had a muddy bottom, and was only waist-deep where my father jumped. He lost one of his loafers though a club employee later retrieved it. Cynthia came out of the water and ran naked and laughing up the trail. Totally out of character my father began laughing and lit a half-wet cigarette, then sent me after Cynthia to get her dressed. At lunch that day I heard him tell my mother, "Far in the future I have sympathy for her husband."

I almost take a wrong turn on the trail not because I'm thinking of my father but because my neurons summoned up the visual of my barmaid friend Carol bending over to grab her dog an hour or so ago. This happened a split second after tears formed over Donald. It's a matter of how to accommodate our minds that never stop even in sleep. Of course it would have occurred to me that I had taken the wrong trail when I descended into the swamp and beaver pond where I fished with Donald for brook trout last summer when he could still walk however wobbly. Cynthia called me at the tavern last night to tell me that Clare had begun cooking dinner though she would return to her room when the meal was prepared. Cynthia and I talked over drinks with Polly about Clare's depression and Polly looked at me with amusement. "Can't you remember?" she asked because of course I've had a number of depressions, but then she went on rather brilliantly, Cynthia thought, to explain the quotient of time. There's much talk about "healing" these days before the blood is dry on the pavement. Polly has been taking a vacation from having sex with me for nearly two months. I suspect she's infatuated with a younger man, also a teacher, because twice I saw her blush in his presence at a school picnic. At one time I would have found this inconceivable because men love to think of themselves as the singular dog on the block despite the presence of others.

I'm startled when I emerge into a clearing west of Barfield Lakes. In the distance about a quarter mile off a bear stares at me and then trundles away from my upwind scent. It occurs to me that since I'm so preoccupied with things that no longer exist it's a specific tonic to see an actual bear. History always withers in the face of a raven squawking at me from the bare tamarack tree beside the pump house.

Cynthia said on the phone that Clare has taken to driving into the Yellow Dog Plains wearing the camouflage suit I sent her when she was a senior in high school. She wanders around all day packing along a tin of sardines, crackers, and a canteen of water communing as she says with the ghost of her father, whom she will not let go despite his request that she do so. Since Cynthia has failed to get Clare involved in what is known euphemistically as "professional help" she is counting on a Ghost Supper over near Brimley in the first week of November (this is a somewhat ritualized dinner after which everyone throws tobacco on the bonfire to release their beloved dead with the ascending smoke). Cynthia has hopes that the presence of so many of Donald's friends will help Clare's inability to accept her father's death. Cynthia said that the whole process was comprehensible to her because she was with Donald moment by moment from the inception of his illness and for two years until his life ended. I talked to Herald on the phone two weeks ago and he seemed fine until he said he was sure he saw his father at the crowded outdoor market in Hermosillo. For the first time in his life he had nearly fainted and his girlfriend had taken him to the bar for a couple of shots of tequila under her assumption that alcohol dispels ghosts. Herald told me not to tell Cynthia about this experience but he wanted to know what I as an "intellectual" (an antique word!) had to say about it. I wasn't able to say anything and still can't. I'm simply not equipped to talk about such things.

Right now I'm looking for my armchair stump, a white pine stump that has decayed in such a way that it has formed a semblance of a living room easy chair. It is located in a sparse grove of chokecherry and dogwood trees but every year the collected flora grows and the landscape changes somewhat. Rather than actively finding the chair I stumble into it after giving up the idea. It was at least a quarter of a mile from where I searched the hardest. This was upsetting as if a cool breeze were blowing through my brain. I remembered a line of poetry Vernice liked: "The days are stacked against who we think we are." My mind has lapsed backward to my return in early June when I read Donald's story between three and four in the morning during an insomniac night. It was a jarring experience enclosed as it was by sleeping nightmares on both sides. I tried to look at the story again as recently as yesterday but have been unable to do so. I wondered at the idea that the dissonance of mood should so strongly affect what you read and that the contents would become part of your dream life without your having completely digested them. Consequently, I keep having this image of the first Clarence riding the draft horse Sally on a cold, smoky October morning, riding toward the east where the sun is red from the vast forest fires and the Chicago fire to the south. This is somehow mixed with a childhood story about orphans in a storm. And then the next image is of the horse falling to its death from the ore dock onto the ice far below. In my mind the horse takes ever so long to fall and sometimes stops a moment in midair. Because of the nature of when I read it Donald's story has become more real to me than all but a few incidents in my own life. I see the grotesquely fat diabetic on his shabby porch drinking warm beer and feeding his dog sweet rolls. My own Carla's eyes would roll with pleasure when I'd feed her fried whitefish or lake trout skin.

I said to my uncle Fred on his brief visit this summer that we tend to live within a gray egg and rarely break through the shell to see life as it is, and he said, "No we don't, we just think we're within the egg but we're outside of it. We feel safer in there." I was irritated of course but came to no conclusions. There had been a rare heat wave and after a sweaty night we took a dip in the river at dawn. A group of noisy ravens watched us and there was distant thunder from the south. I stood in the river and said, "Right now I'm outside of the gray egg." Fred and a raven in a fir tree were staring at each other as if the bird had hypnotized the man. It took a number of cautious years for the ravens to determine if I was safe enough for them to hang out in the yard.

I had been sitting in my stump chair for about an hour when I smelled something strong and rank. I thought at first that maybe the breeze had shifted bringing the scent of a dead deer, a coyote, or some other decaying animal. But there was no breeze and my skin began to prickle and crawl with the obvious thought that there was something behind me. I certainly hadn't heard anything approach but then I had been lost in thought, a long-term habit that has gotten me into trouble a number of times. I was half encased in the stump and swiveled awkwardly until I could see behind me. The bear I had seen earlier was sitting in a sunlit glade not fifty feet away. I went from dry to sweaty in seconds, my breath shortening, while I thought of what to do. In all of my sightings and encounters in my twenty years locally I've never had a bear behave in this manner. With bears you always part company as soon as possible, usually with the animal leaving with all possible speed. No one can outrun a bear and I could see just a glint of my car parked about two hundred yards to the south off a log road. I gave up thinking, stood up and turned around and whispered a stupid "hello." I began walking toward my car with a tight ass and quivering innards and it was naturally the longest two hundred yards of my life. It was only when I opened the relative safety of the car door that I thought, "Maybe it's Donald."

I drove the ten miles or so out of the woods faster than usual with a new and peculiar itch in my brain that I figured could be dispelled only by the sight of the harbor of Lake Superior or, more likely, a cheeseburger and beer at the Dunes Saloon. It was a simple case of cowardice in the face of a new experience. I had always stuck to the idea offered by my ninth-grade science teacher that all genuine phenomena have a natural or scientific explanation and driving out of the woods my faith in this had become a bit wobbly. I hit a long puddle too fast and fishtailed then slowed until I almost became stuck and downshifted into four-wheel drive with the windshield covered with mud. I felt relieved when I finally reached the blacktop that led to the village. I reminded myself that my persistent life question, "How do we live with what we know?" didn't cover everything and that I might humorously add, "How do we live with what we don't know?"

At the bar my sometime lover of last night, Carol, at first ignored me though there were only two other customers, old Finns making a whiskey dent in their Social Security checks. She hissed at me, "You're an asshole," which the Finns thought very funny. I called Cynthia from the pay phone at our appointed time of twelve-thirty, which doesn't always work because on some days she's a substitute teacher until Polly can get her on as a regular. On this day her voice is bell clear and musical, which means her mood is good. She tells me that Clare is letting K accompany her on her way over in my direction to clean out a hundred or so bluebird houses on the Kingston Plains. She has sent along a pot roast for our dinner, which pleases me.

When my purposefully overdone cheeseburger arrives I have a confusing memory of Cynthia from when we were in our early teens. It was an early June morning in the last week of school. I was having breakfast alone and leafing through some of my mother's art books for prurient reasons. A bare-breasted Courbet woman and a series of Degas dancers always hit me the most directly. I went upstairs to get my schoolbooks with the accustomed hard-on and through the open door I could see Cynthia toweling off after a shower, a disconcerting reminder of the Degas drawings I had just stared at with lust. I averted my glance from the taboo Cynthia, who was singing a Beach Boys song, and wondered how my nasty, ugly parents could produce a girl with such a lovely shape. At the time she was reading the Brontë sisters, Jane Austen, and George Eliot and called me Squire Glum.

On the way back to the cabin after the pleasant denial in the tavern I naturally returned to Donald and the bear so that by the time I passed the village limits my discomfort had palpably returned. I was a boy again walking past a cemetery in the dark. Donald loved bears. One had visited him during his three nights without food, water, or shelter.

Bears would occasionally visit the bird feeder at the cabin because of their affection for sunflower seeds but they would leave if I rapped at the window. Years back a young one had followed me on a long hike out in the sand dunes though at a distance of a couple of hundred yards, but until this morning I had never had one approach so closely. I had nowhere to go with my unrest. I had read a dozen books on black bears but none of my knowledge was doing me any good because these books were of a scientific nature. Perhaps ten years ago I had loaned my copy of Rockwell's *Giving Voice to Bear* to Donald, who in turn loaned it to a friend, who consequently lost the book when he moved to Thunder Bay up on the north shore of Lake Superior. Donald was upset about the lost book, which dealt with various American Indian tribal attitudes toward the bear. I assured Donald that I could find another copy but I never had mostly because I felt more comfortable with a purely scientific approach to the mammal. Donald teased me about this once when we were brook trout fishing and on our long walk into the beaver pond stopped so he could inspect a large oak tree that had been blasted by lightning. These are meaningful spots to the Anishinabeg, places where the gods have touched the earth directly. Donald had noted my lack of real interest and said, "You think a bear is just a bear."

At the cabin I sat on my creaky porch swing wishing that Clare and K were already there so I wouldn't have to deal with these scattered thoughts of bears, death, and lightning trees. The oak had been large and its upper half had been shattered into scorched splinters, the green wood too damp to burn for long. I tried to decide if it would have been

good to be there when it happened as sort of an aimless
Moses to whom a burning bush was only a burning bush.

I went into the cabin and poured myself a rare midday
whiskey thinking it might allow me to take a nap after which
my perspective would be changed. A few days before on the
back porch of our house in Marquette I had been having a
drink with Cynthia and Polly and had become irritated at
their matter-of-fact confidence about absolutely everything
that was passing through their minds. Cynthia started my
eventual disintegration.

"I was thinking when I got up this morning that how
can death be bad when it's happened to every single living
creature and plant since the beginning of the earth? I said this
through the door to Clare's room but she didn't answer. Instead she turned up the volume of a Schumann record. On
the way downstairs I remembered reading that Schumann
died in an asylum at age forty-two." While Cynthia spoke she
watched with amusement at the way I gulped my highball.

"I know what you mean," Polly said. "When I was at
Iron Mountain last week I helped a nurse bathe my dad. All
the time I was growing up he made sure I never saw his bare
crippled legs. Anyway when I rubbed his legs with a warm
washcloth I thought, 'Those can't even be called legs.' I
wondered if his life had been worth it in ordinary terms. It
was nearly forty years since his legs had been mangled in
the mining accident. The question was whether his life was
worth it?"

"Did you even ask him?" I questioned stupidly.

"That's not the kind of question you ask your dad. When
I was in high school a friend drove him home from the union

hall and the both of them were truly drunk. Well, Dad fell
down in the yard and wouldn't move and his friend had
fallen asleep in the car. Dad was still pretty big then and
Mom and me couldn't move him. It was a cool May night
and Mother was afraid it might rain. She took the oilcloth
from the kitchen table and spread it out on the grass and
we rolled Dad over onto it so he wouldn't get damp. We
covered him with a few blankets and a piece of canvas tarp.
At first light Mom went off to work and out the window I
saw her standing there in the light rain with her lunch bucket
looking down at her sleeping husband. A little while later I
heard him yelling for coffee so I took out a thermos and cup.
He was staring up into the crab-apple tree, which was full
of birds, and he said, 'These goddamned birds woke me up'
but I could see he was very happy. After that he took to
sleeping outside quite a bit."

"That doesn't seem like much to carry a person." I
sipped at my ice toting up life's balance on my imaginary
board.

"Oh for Christ's sake, David. Go listen to your Coast
Guard weather report so that you can say something sensible
like 'It's windy' or 'It's cold' or something solid. Where are
you today, anyway? I mean for Christ's sake you've never
learned small measures. A hungover cripple wakes up under
a crab-apple tree and smiles at birds. Go sleep under a crab-
apple tree." Cynthia was pissed.

Of course she was partly right. I had spent basically
twenty years thinking and come up with a fifteen-page un-
distinguished essay. Now dozing on the porch swing with
its homely creak the sound of which irritates a local downy

woodpecker I am obsessed with how fragile art, literature, love, and music, even the natural world are in the presence of severe illness and inevitable death. Four months after Donald's passing we're still staring off into the middle distance even when we're facing a wall three feet away. Five years ago my life was saved by finding a dead man under a manzanita bush, and a week later seeing a photo of a dead girl, her face covered with large sun blisters. But I didn't know and love them.

When I awake Clare and K are standing in front of me in their silly-looking camouflage suits. Clare looks thin but is smiling and K is drinking a beer. This is my last day at the cabin and it's passing quickly what with mid-October sunlight being so flimsy this far north.

"I found a car for you. It's a used Subaru four-wheel drive, five years old but with only forty thousand miles on it. It's pretty ugly and needs a paint job but I know that's not what you want. A mechanic friend checked it out and says it's aces."

"Thanks. I'm glad you're here partly because I'm hungry. Cynthia said you're bringing food."

"It's only four-thirty and we walked our asses off. I want a shower and then a margarita at the bar."

Clare began stripping her clothes off on the way into the cabin. K looked a bit haggard, perhaps from the effort of trying to bring equilibrium to Clare. I was looking at him trying to think of something helpful to say in Clare's absence but then he disappeared behind the memory of a dream I

had been having on the porch swing. The dream was chaotic but began with milk cows and numbers. Around the
turn of the century, say from 1890 to 1910, when mine disasters were at their worst in terms of fatality numbers, the
victims' families in company housing were welcome to stay
in the housing but only for a month. For this time the families continued to have the use of a milk cow. I had seen old
photos of these often gaunt milk cows in rocky pastures near
the company row houses and women on stools milking the
cows into buckets often with children watching. For a moment in the dream I thought I saw Cynthia on a stool but the
woman more closely resembled my mother. Then numbers
began to appear in the landscape. Numbers often marred
my interesting dreams but in this case Donald was number
one but the number was blurred. This was an area where in
three major mines nearly two thousand men had died in a
twenty-year period. In the dream I finally understood that
death and numbers don't cohere. Everyone is "one." An
accident report might say that nine died, four of them in their
teens, but each death was "one." Each of six million Jews
was "one." With death it is a series of "ones."

I came back to ordinary consciousness when K jumped
up on the porch, an upward leap of four feet and thus beyond my immediate comprehension. He showed me a letter
he and Clare had received from Fred at his Hawaii Zendo,
which mostly described Fred's difficulties growing exotic
fruits like pomegranates and figs. This immediately made
me homesick for Mexico, where at a roadside stand in the
province of Veracruz Vernice and I had bought thirty-two
kinds of fruit. Fred concluded the letter by saying about

Donald, "I never knew anyone who so thoroughly was what he was."

K and I tried to pin this statement down into a sensible framework but then Clare came out on the porch from her shower. When I'm with K he often drives and I sit in the back seat and regularly this position causes different perceptions and emotions. Cynthia says this is because I know so few people that I rarely get to sit in a back seat. It worked better when I picked up Vernice at the Guadalajara airport a few years ago. After a fine night in a fancy hotel where we had a room service dinner on a balcony and could hear acoustic guitar music from a club below us we set out early in the morning toward Zihuatanejo with me at the wheel thinking about nights of music, love, and laughter.

"If we're heading southwest toward the coast why are we driving into the sun?" Vernice had asked quite irritably. She was quite intense over seeing the Pacific Ocean for the first time.

I had stopped on the road's shoulder and mapwork revealed I had made a wrong turn an hour before, which made Vernice even more irritable. I got in the back seat of the spiffy rental car after a little quarrel and fell promptly asleep, a habit started early when my parents quarreled loudly and I'd take to my room for a nap while Cynthia would head out the back-porch door. Anyway, I didn't wake up until four hours later, at noon, whereupon Vernice told me I had missed some gorgeous mountainous landscapes.

"You have a gift for English. Describe them," I had said.

"Fuck you," she said.

The trip was going poorly partly because I had miscalculated the nature of the roads and the time it would take to drive, and since we arrived a day late in Zihuatanejo (I had neglected to call) our plush beach hotel had rented our room. We found another place at one-tenth the price that Vernice typically liked better. It was on a five-story rooftop overlooking the harbor and closer to the poor folks downtown. It was really only a small room with a huge patio, the entire rooftop, with chairs and a table, lounge chairs, and plants. It was hot in late May and the air conditioner worked poorly so that after a good dinner of a whole roasted fish we pulled the mattress out onto the deck. Vernice still wasn't in the mood for love but when I woke up in the night she was standing naked at the roof's edge looking at the harbor and the ocean beyond the harbor's mouth and the approach of a gigantic thunderstorm from the southwest. I joined her a little queasy from two bottles of wine to "smooth" my feelings.

"I'm seeing the Pacific Ocean," she said.

I got us chairs and we sat there watching the lights on the tiny boats far out in the harbor fishing for snapper in the night. As the thunderstorm got closer the boats started heading in and I mentioned that I should drag the mattress back into the room and she said, "Please don't." There were black birds on the cornice and in palm trees nearby that I later determined to be great-tailed grackles. They had horrid voices that were wonderful. Vernice got up from her chair and sat on my lap waving her hands in the very warm liquid air. Now the approaching storm was only a few miles out near the harbor's entrance and the lightning cast a hot blue glow on the huge volcanic rocks covered with seabirds, mostly *gaviotas.* With each tremendous clap of thunder perhaps a minute apart our grackles would scream their slate-breaking calls back at the thunder. "How many millions of years have they been doing this? Just like us, arguing with thunder," Vernice said, swiveling her body so that I entered her and she was still watching the storm, and then we could hear the wind and the sheets of rain coming toward us. When the storm reached us we were literally submerged and ran for the mattress, got under the soaked sheet, and continued making love. When I was on the bottom I could see the bluish-white lightning up through the sheet. I had never felt such a warm rain and driving wind and wondered how grackles could withstand its force to keep screeching. We dragged the mattress back in the little room and flipped it over and where there was a dry spot in the middle we finished making love. Vernice began laughing in between singing phrases of the Catholic Christmas hymn "O Holy Night."

I came to consciousness from my reverie and could see Clare waving from the front window of the tavern. I tried to remember if it was Camus who wrote, "It rained so hard that even the sea was wet." I went inside and had a double whiskey, which my putative girlfriend the barmaid poured short. She had met K before but when I introduced Clare as my niece she said, "I bet. I've seen you with a lot of nieces."

"I am the asshole's niece," Clare said.

"For a while they called us *needy* but now they're back to assholes," I said to K, who was racking up the pool table for a quick game with a pulp cutter who smelled strongly of chain-saw oil and pine resin. Like miners and commercial fishermen, loggers always look older than they are. This one, Tom by name, was drunk one night and in an enraged state asked me why breakfast cereal had gone up to five dollars a box. He had four kids and a wife so large that their rusted-out compact car tilted to the passenger's side.

Clare was back at the front window looking out at the cold harbor. The wind had picked up from the north and it looked like a mid-October snow was coming.

"Mother said Vera called from Jalapa and her son did something very bad, I'm not sure what, and now he's in a place for the criminally insane. Or don't you care about your half brother?"

"I knew he was headed in that direction. Vera claims he was okay until that car hit him while he was on the bicycle. So I'm not sure. Back when I met him he was what the Mexicans call *muy malo*. They save that one up for men, and a few women, who are real bad."

"Anyway, Mother's helping Vera get him in an institution that's not so totally crummy. When I was up wandering around the Yellow Dog last week there was this one spot near a small waterfall where I sensed Dad in the river. Of course it was the last place we fished together. I was wondering if some of our spirit might stay in a place. What do you think?"

I was nonplussed. This kind of thinking was out of character. Clare tended to be as matter-of-fact as her brother Herald though, rather than mathematics, Clare leaned toward botany and the history of clothing. I certainly wasn't going to tell her about my bear experience of the morning the thought of which still gave my stomach a jiggle. I glanced at Clare, who clearly expected an answer of some sort, however lame. Once while we were fishing Clarence told me that he talked to his wife in the asylum on the phone. She was unable to speak but he said he knew "what she was saying."

"I suppose that death, especially the death of someone we love, pushes us away from all of our built-in assumptions about what life is, I mean the ready-made day-to-day life and all that we've learned about what it is supposed to be that we readily accept. Death gives us a shove into a new sort of landscape." My voice trailed off with disinterest in what I was saying, or maybe slight fear.

Clare gave me a hug and we watched an Indian fish tug bounding over the surge of waves behind the breakwall. The wind was truly picking up from the northwest so the tug had been lucky. I was irritated when Clare ordered another drink and invited my barmaid friend for dinner but then I got over it in minutes and drove down to the dock to buy a couple of whitefish to grill on a wood fire to go with the pot roast Cynthia had sent. How could I become irritated with Clare in her present state, which had more than a tinge of pathology? When I reached the dock I was struck by how closely the captain, a Chippewa named Francis, reminded

me of Donald in his prime, tall and about three hundred
pounds with a wine-barrel chest.

The evening was as far as possible from my usual last night
at the cabin, which is a maudlin affair with me sitting before the fireplace listening to the wind in a mental state best
described as muddy. Vernice has teased me about being a
solitary Romantic poet when I'm not even a poet. It has simply been a matter of balancing the world by avoiding it,
which means limiting my exposure to the woods and water
of the Upper Peninsula and for half the year or more some
of the remoter regions of Mexico, where I've found a purpose of sorts.

At the cabin we "turned loose" and had a party. We
drank, ate, and danced, and then drank, ate, and danced
some more. I'm unsure what we had in mind, mostly nothing except the impulses children have toward play. For instance, it's raining in July and a tiny creek through a vacant
lot is gathering water so four kids bust their asses building
a dam until they're exhausted, filthy, and wet, but also delighted. That kind of thing, notwithstanding the peerless
icon of death that hovered over us, and everyone else on
earth for that matter.

We started slow with K splitting some oak for the fish.
As the fire burned down we stood in the lee of the pump
shed staring at the flames as people do, also at the flames
through our amber glasses of whiskey. I agreed with K on
the addition of what is called a "space blanket" to the survival

kits I put together and distribute for Mexicans intending to migrate north. Space blankets are sheets of material used by campers to protect them from cold and dampness but I thought they could also defend against the summer heat of the ground, which reaches over one hundred and fifty degrees. These space blankets fold up into a pocket smaller than a wallet. Depending whether it was winter or the severe heat in some of the desert areas of the border the survival kit I designed included a thin but effective thermal vest, a small compass, two canteens—one for water and one for Gatorade—sunscreen, a bag of dried fruit and sunflower seeds, route maps depending on the area, and halazone tablets to purify drinking water. The packet was in a Velcro latched bag and could be attached to a waist belt and weighed a little less than five pounds. I distributed these free of charge to workers' groups and through left-leaning Catholic priests. I was opposed by many on both sides of the border for political reasons, which didn't bother me except for the legal expenses I incurred avoiding prosecution by the United States. My raison d'être was simple on the surface. Estimates of crossing deaths along the entire nineteen-hundred-mile border with Mexico went as high as two thousand a year. I had learned to be goofy rather than logically argumentative with my opponents. I'd ask, If you could prevent twenty major airline disasters each year, wouldn't you? The project costs me seven months of my time and about three-quarters of my income, which is unearned and derives from my dead mother and also my share of land I've been selling off that was owned by my father's grotesque family.

I'm an extremely imperfect person but this effort is as
close as I can come to the naive Christianity of my boyhood.
I haven't come close to a Bible in nearly thirty years except
for Stephen Mitchell's small and incisive *The Gospel According
to Jesus.* I have no interest in organized Christianity other than
the art Vernice showed me on our trip to Parma, Reggio,
Modena, and Florence. Vernice, incidentally, refers to my
project as pure "Quixote." Cynthia and Polly are all for it,
as are Clare and K. Herald, naturally, has doubts. Donald
loved it. I minimize the importance of my effort. It's not
much but it's all I can do. It started when I found the dead
man in a wilderness thicket a few miles from the border
south of Sonoita, Arizona. The man smelled like a dead deer.
Two days later in a local tavern an ex–dope pilot told me
that two hundred miles to the west over in the huge Cabeza
Prieta if he wished on moonlit nights he could navigate by
skeletons on his under-the-radar flights. Three days after
that while looking into what is euphemistically called "the
problem" I saw the photo of the nineteen-year-old girl from
Veracruz who died of thirst on the Tohono O'odham Indian
reservation just over our side of the border. Naturally I
thought of Vera. That did it. The project didn't start out well
but I'll get to that.

We roasted the fish as Vernice had taught me with dry ver-
mouth, butter, and lemon. There were three bottles of wine
left from Vernice's visit in August. Part of the name of the
wine read *"Sang des Cailloux,"* which Vernice said meant the
blood of the rock, after the steep stony slopes in the Rhône

Valley where the grapes are grown. Naturally I liked the idea of drinking the blood of the rock though K observed that the effect of the wine was pretty similar to any other alcohol. With K everything is in particular, from deftly turning the fish to talking about Donald's powers of observation that were learned from his tribal friends. K had talked to anthropologists about this matter, who in turn had referred him to a monograph written by Hallowell in the twenties saying that the "Gibwa" had thirty ways of describing a lake, in short, a high degree of specificity. K added when putting the fish on a hot platter that he had read that the Inuit had two hundred different terms for describing snow conditions.

We danced for a while between eating the fish and the pot roast. The batteries on my radio (the generator produced only direct current) were worn thin so K pulled his pickup around to the north window and cranked up the truck's stereo with Los Lobos. The wind was cold through the window so I turned up the propane heater and added big maple logs to the fireplace. The four of us jumped around to this Chicano music though I had to be careful about my weak ankle. It was wonderful to see Clare out of her mind. By common consent we didn't talk about anything more serious than the food and music, which in themselves have become more serious as I get older.

We were quite drunk by the time we collapsed before midnight except for K, who had the sense to go out and turn off the generator. Clare had never stopped dancing except for a few bites of food. K had closed the north window but we forgot to turn down the heater and with the overloaded fireplace we awoke in the middle of the night to a ninety-degree cabin and all of us stumbling around drinking cold water.

The old Finn who took care of the cabin in my absence arrived at seven in the morning to help me close up for the year. I had the worst hangover since college twenty-five years before what with the cautionary idea of my father always present, which stopped me from overdrinking. The old Finn (in his late seventies) had a cup of coffee with the remaining inch of whiskey poured into it, glancing over with appreciation at Clare and Carol, who were getting out of bed in their undies. In July he had crawled under the cabin and removed a lot of dirt, jacked up the sagging southwest corner, and laid several courses of cement blocks to bring the cabin back into plumb. He reminded me a bit of Clarence, whose Indian blood was mixed with Finnish. These were people without irony. Last October while illegally spearing salmon in front of the cabin he spoke of a trip to L.A. to visit relatives in the "tumble buggy," which was what he called an airplane. A cousin took him on a tour of L.A., which he figured had bad drainage because nearly all the land had been paved over. He had also said, "Be careful, Mr. Burkett, the world is filling up." He added that he bet "Clark Gable got more pussy than a toilet seat."

K made a breakfast hash out of the leftover pot roast and potatoes. Carol vomited in the backyard. Clare took a quick skinny-dip as her father would have done though the temperature was barely above freezing. I fell asleep at the breakfast table after I heard the old Finn say about Clare,

"That girl's got balls." When I woke up everyone was gone and I shivered staring into the nearly dead fire.

On the way back to Marquette I stopped by Flower's near Au Train. Clare and K were intending to stop there but no one was home. The door was open and there was a note from K saying that he and Clare had gone off to help Flower fetch a deer she had shot early that morning, though they were out of season. Flower in her eighth decade shot a couple of deer each October. He had added, "Try the pie," so I cut myself a piece of venison mincemeat pie. Flower had minced the meat and marinated it with dried fruit in cheap brandy and cooked it in a lard crust. It was delicious. She also pickled deer hearts and tongues, which I found interesting. I looked at a peculiar bear-claw necklace hanging above her bed but I didn't feel up to touching it. Donald had told me that Flower had religious reasons for not eating bear meat.

When I reached Marquette school was out so I stopped at the bungalow Cynthia had bought a few doors to the west of Polly's house. It was a bare-bones place, almost empty of furniture, probably a reflex against my parents' insistence on the finest furniture available and maybe the house was simply a gesture. Cynthia wasn't home yet from substitute teaching so I took my warmest coat and stocking cap from the car and sat on a lawn chair in the front yard watching Lake Superior misbehave with the wind at maybe thirty knots from the northwest and the muted roar of the water, a white noise possessing the air. I was a little astounded by how good I felt as if all the alcohol, and maybe the dancing too, had been electroshock therapy or whatever. The fast, cold clouds were leaving large patches of light out on the water and a neighbor's tattered American flag was whipping and cracking up on its pole. I was a day away from the beginning of my long drive down into Mexico on my modest mission to reduce suffering. It was five years now and I remembered wondering at the time what could possibly happen to me after my father slipped beneath the waters off Alvarado. How would I recover into a different life? What was left of me raised the question of what I was before. I hadn't weighed enough to stick to the ground, always a problem for your average ghost. I was the problem because in our time the contest is to see who can ask the biggest questions and I had become an expert.

I managed to doze off there in the windy yard and was awakened by Cynthia's laughter as she nudged the crotch of my trousers with the toe of her shoe. I had an obvious hard-on.

"Who were you dreaming about, big brother?"

"A woman I never met. There's this physicist in England who thinks our dream people that we don't know actually exist. We just haven't met them and might not ever meet them." The whole idea mystified me.

"That's what I call an unprofitable line of inquiry. Did Clare tell you our half brother is locked up, maybe for good?"

"What did he do this time?"

"Beat up two trespassers who were hunting. One was a politician from Jalapa. Who lost an eye and some teeth."

"What can Vera do?"

"Not much. I'm helping him get better accommodations. Fifty bucks a month gets him a sofa, a television in his cell, and better food. What helped is the lawyer got him a brain scan at the medical school, which showed the injury from the bicycle accident years ago. Now Vera has no one."

The fact was that Jesse had died last year and he was the only one with any control over Vera's son. I tried to imagine Vera sitting at the kitchen table of the small coffee farm, my memories of which were blurred by the violent events. In my mind's eye I could mostly see the wildflowers on the hillsides.

"Should I stop and see her?"

"I don't know. She said she would like to see you but I couldn't tell her where you were headed this time."

"Probably Zacatecas or San Luis Potosí. Maybe even Durango because I heard a mine might close there, which will mean men will try to head north. Durango has always scared me. Behind this motel where I stay there's a long wall full of bullet holes where hundreds of men were executed during the revolution."

We went inside and had coffee and I examined the piles of Russian and European novels stacked on the dining room table. Cynthia had been an obsessive reader as a girl and now with Donald gone she was resuming the habit. She felt that novels were a more "reliable" source of information than all the nonfiction I read, partly because it was less threatening.

I really couldn't understand why Cynthia was staying in Marquette but it was a raw subject and all she would say was that her decision was based on the fact that Marquette was the scene of both her worst and her best memories. I

was going to bring up the subject again but she started reading, which meant our conversation was over. Her eyes were
misty and I kissed the top of her head.

I immediately liked the rust splotches and cracked back
window of my new car, which means it will be safe from
envy in Mexico. Amid all the stuff in the old car while I'm
switching gear between the two I find Panza's collar stuffed
up under the back seat. A predictable lump arises as when
I imagine I see Carla trotting doggishly ahead of me on a
logging two-track through the forest. Panza was a big stray
female mutt I adopted during my brief months in Caborca.
She was at least part Catahoula and half Australian shepherd and wasn't a particularly pleasant lady. A neighbor told
me she had been a guard dog for some drug runners who
had flown the coop in the middle of the night. She slept in a
hole she had dug under a shed behind my little house. Friendship came through the not very secret ingredient of food,
especially a pot of boiled tripe I'd chop up and mix with
kibble. Within days she became my companion and guardian, refusing to come in the house but draping herself out
on the porch near the front door. I had a worktable and chair
on the porch and she would look at my books and writing
sad with puzzlement. If so much as a sparrow landed in the
yard she would issue a coarse rumble.
        I can't say I was comfortable in Caborca though I was
lucky to meet a local cop who had worked for two years in
the Oldsmobile plant in Lansing, Michigan. Since I had
gone to Michigan State in East Lansing this slight bond was

considered major and he would often stop by for a beer in the late afternoon. The altruism of my survival kits confused him at first and the idea that I would live in Caborca rather than anyplace else on earth boggled him. He warned me that some local "coyotes" were misunderstanding the intent of my survival kits. These coyotes are men who guide migrants into the U.S. for a high fee usually across the mountains that surround Nogales or Douglas, or through the desert to the west between Nogales and Yuma. Either route can be hellish indeed and sometimes a coyote will abandon his group if he feels the Border Patrol closing in, or for no particular reason other than dishonesty or laziness. One abandoned group of nine all died of thirst including a woman who tried to eat the Bible she carried in the derangement of impending death.

So I had been forewarned by my cop friend but couldn't quite believe that the local coyotes wouldn't understand the purity of my motives in distributing the survival kits. The cop, however, said that it might make younger male "wetbacks" think they could go it alone rather than saving for years. Anyway, one evening when I had walked downtown to have dinner one of the coyotes came past and riddled my house and car with a shotgun and far more important blew a lower left leg off Panza. Luckily it was the bony skin and I applied a tourniquet, made a phone call, and headed for Tucson, a few hours to the north. This turned out to be stupid and nearly got me jailed, because U.S. Customs wouldn't let me in the country as I didn't have vaccination papers for my dying Panza. I had to be restrained after standing there fifteen minutes bellowing, sobbing, and cursing but then one

of the customs agents called a local vet, who got up in the
middle of the night and saved Panza. She lived for three
more years much farther south. When I'd leave for the north
each May I'd find an appropriate old man to care for her
for money, unload five hundred pounds of kibble, and kiss
her big ugly face good-bye.

I left Caborca two days later. Panza was frantic while
I packed so I loaded her into the back of the car with her
bowl of beloved tripe, which smelled poorly. My cop friend
came over and we discussed my obvious need for vengeance.
I couldn't just cut and run. Even in the Upper Peninsula
someone shooting your dog is a very serious matter. The cop
advised that I shouldn't do anything personally or I might
be forced out of Mexico, which would be the end of my
mission. Instead I gave him a goodly amount of cash so that
he and his colleagues would make it hot for the coyote. I kept
in touch by phone and within a couple of months the coyote
had been forced from his hometown and eventually ended
up in prison over in Mexicali. Of course Panza because of
the way life had conditioned her never became the companion Carla was but last year when she was hit by a truck in
Durango I was bereft.

Our last evening was a bit muted. Cynthia and Polly were
amused by the fatigue felt by Clare, K, and me over the night
before. I tried to help K grill steaks in the backyard but there
was a cold hard wind that my heaviest coat didn't seem to
repel and he sent me inside. Cynthia pronounced my salad
dressing "nasty" and made another. By common consent my

cooking is poor though I eat it with relish. It is only when I go into the poorest, cheapest restaurants and find their food superior to my own do I understand my mediocrity or less. Cynthia says it's because I'm always "on the way to some- place else." It is her opinion that to cook well you have to stop time and dwell completely on the ingredients before you start.

I sit at the table with my hands joined to the hands of Cynthia and Polly. We stare over into the living room where K and Clare are half dozing and watching a video documen- tary about Bengal tigers. I sense that Polly and Cynthia are joining me in the wordless questioning of what will become of these two young people who, perhaps like myself, so obvi- ously wish more from life than life willingly offers. I wonder if their relationship isn't doomed because they started too young, and they haven't stopped being stepbrother and -sister, if this overfamiliarity doesn't prevent the mystery of love, but then I look at Polly and question if there is a mys- tery to love or mere confusion, or if the element of chance doesn't suffocate everything. I mean the chance of acciden- tal meetings: Polly at the hamburger stand in Iron Moun- tain, Vernice selling matches near the Newberry Library in Chicago, or Vera coming north from Veracruz. With Clare and K the union is perhaps too much like mine with Laurie though Clare and K are far more sophisticated. Are they able to delight each other? The thought of bald Laurie in her last days rattles my heart in its flimsy cage.

Cynthia and I walk Polly home. They are talking about the problems of Polly's daughter, off in New York City, who has an acute case of herpes, which makes it difficult for her to find "sexual partners" (Polly's phrase). I find their matter-of-factness about such matters amazing and the idea of being a partner with a dick rather clinical. Cynthia kisses me good-bye at her door and tells me not to try to see Vera without calling home first. I feel the mildest resentment over this but agree. I continue on with Polly and minutes later we're at her doorstep. I had figured that there was some chance of her inviting me in because it's Friday night and she doesn't have to teach tomorrow. No luck. At her door I get a conclusive peck on the cheek and a whispered "Take care of yourself." Of course I'm pretty confident she has another friend or "love interest" (her term). When she visited the cabin in August and spoke with "martini truth" (her term) she wondered why I kept hanging on to her when I never really wanted a wife or children and had no intention of being in the area more than half the year and with that time being spent mostly at my "depressing" cabin. Over the years Polly is the only person who has openly found the cabin depressing. She thinks the windows should be enlarged. I stand out on the street for a few moments and through the yellow square of light I can see her on the kitchen phone, probably with her daughter or boyfriend. I tend to try to hold on to what we used to be together.

On the walk up the long hill toward home it occurs to me that the wind has subsided and the three-day blow out of the northwest is over; the inland sea, Lake Superior, gradually has become a murmur rather than a steady roar. The last of the leaves from the hardwoods that line the street have fallen and are pasted against the sidewalk by rain, their bright yellows and reds turning dullish. Time to head south.

I have this sense of being a prematurely old man in a quarrel with himself over the worth of his life, a hopelessly bullshit notion. I stop under a streetlight and think about Donald and how the death of a man who was so loved seems to exhaust everyone as if they're struggling in a vacuum and not quite enough air is being pumped in for survival. There are none of my helpful little packets for this border crossing.

In the last fifty yards toward home I see that the lights are out except for up in Clare's room, and a porch light in case I return. I am relieved and then immediately wonder how much good my more than twenty years in the woods have done me. The culture pretends it admires solitude (but not too much solitude, for you might become nonproductive) but I'm swept away by the Saturday western movies that Cynthia and I watched on television as children wherein the nutcase prospector is always returning from his solitary life in the mountains and babbling at everyone in the village. After a few days and nights at the cabin and in the woods seeing no one at all and then going into the grocery or tavern my voice would sound tinny and alien to me as if speech were not the natural fact that I had assumed it to be. Of course I had read the testimony of explorers, religious devotees, or adventurers who had been lost on land or sea, or had simply withdrawn from human concourse for long periods. In their accounts you quickly learn that what we think of as ordinary reality needs the contact with and reassurances from others. Even a man and dog alone for a month become each other in ways that are ordinarily thought improbable. I pushed away the thought of Donald's time on the hillside.

I poured a large whiskey to help me sleep and tiptoed up to my room. Down the hall there was light under Clare's door and the sound of Clare either weeping or making love to K. I quickly entered my room and put a tape of Mexican music on low to drown out any noise of anguish or sex. I was completely packed except for a number of letters from my local lawyer, several of them still unopened. I never took this kind of mail to the cabin thinking business information to be blasphemous in the woods. I mean over the years I had become friends with this lawyer but that didn't mean I wanted to deal with any problems. This had been especially true of the four months since Donald's passing.

I tried to further put off the mail by calling Vernice in Iowa City but she had people over and couldn't talk. I asked if I should call later but she said it was pointless because I was stopping to see her the day after tomorrow. This was a little deflating after Polly turned me away. I took a gulp of the whiskey and read letters for fifteen minutes not so much with a sinking feeling but with a bleak confirmation of what I had already begun to suspect. I was slowly losing control of my Quixote survival-kit project to my assistant Jan, in Tucson, who had always liked to think of herself as a "facilitator," one of those contemporary words of blurred meaning. Beginning five years ago she had helped me put together the survival kits in a motel room and we kept the material in a rented storage unit. She was a senior at the University of Tucson at the time and gradually became an ardent border activist though her work for me was part-time. I basically supported her partly because she had a network of friends, some a bit shady, who easily got my kits transferred through Mexican customs to Cananea, and later Magdalena, where I picked up five hundred at a time and was on my way. I began to lose control two years ago when she felt she needed some credentials to get work after I retired from the project, which as I said I totally financed. An activist lawyer friend of hers did the pro bono job of drawing up hokum papers for a not-for-profit corporation with Jan listed as president. I never attended any of the meetings of these border activists though I largely admired their diversity of efforts, which even included distributing barrels of fresh water along the border. All I wanted to do was to be directly involved in the relief of suffering. I was ill-suited temperamentally to be part of a larger "movement" however worthy. I had come to this conclusion on independent action even before my friend and analyst Coughlin had advised that since I had done a quantitative amount of damage to myself with my obsession over my father I should proceed slowly with hands-on activity and avoid simply brooding and writing the rest of my life away. The whole problem came to the surface the autumn before when I reached Tucson and was made to feel like a delivery boy by Jan and two of her friends when we got together for several days to assemble the survival kits. On the last day they gave me maps and contact numbers of where I should take the kits and I told them that I had already made commitments to certain church groups and labor unions in central Mexico. We came to a compromise but there were some unpleasant feelings. I felt like a soldier being sent off to battle by three young women who had no knowledge or direct contact with war. They were adamantly against the Catholic Church as a capitalist tool and had no real knowledge of the liberation theologians or the movement I had been familiar with in my year at the seminary twenty-five years before.

What my lawyer was telling me is that I had effectively lost legal control of my project but should try to hang in there because Jan had on hand sixty thousand dollars of my money for gathering the equipment for this year's survival kits. There had been seventy-five but Jan and a friend had gone to two conferences on Third World poverty, one in Maui and one in San Francisco. The lawyer had asked for expense accounts and Jan had hedged saying she might send them along but was not obliged to do so.

When I finished the mail my brain felt tickled and itchy. I thought of going downstairs to get another drink but it was midnight and I hoped to leave at dawn. This was a distracting idea when I realized there was no reason to leave at that time. Americans like to say "Let's get an early start" and so they do. This "segued" (K's word) to general feelings of gibberish and garbage, both real and merely emotional. I had been dwelling on death and religion all summer and hadn't paid any attention to business as evidenced by the lawyer's letters, but before then my attention to such matters had always been scant. It was partly because the money was unearned but mostly because I had minus interest in business and numbers. Part of me was the university sophomore who reads Dostoyevsky's statement "Two plus two is the beginning of death" and never gets over it.

The tickle and itch in my brain followed me into bed and increased when I turned out the lights. I thought that what Jan was doing is the way the world works. Nothing

should be as it is without growing larger, which is the central content of business discourse. I couldn't very well blame
her for being a child of her time especially when I ignored
the warning signs and then the near mutiny last year. Jan
could never admit that there would be no migration problem if businesses in the U.S. were legally required to iden-
tify their workers but then businesses thrived on paying the
minimum wage or less to their workers. It still seemed a lot
to Mexicans who were averaging between three and five
dollars a day. If you were making five bucks a day at an
American-owned maquiladora plant in Sonoran Nogales
and stood on a hill outside your cardboard hut you could
see a Pizza Hut in American Nogales where you could
make more than five bucks an hour. It was a no-brainer
why people crossed the border.

    I dozed off for a while but awoke abruptly with a dream
of a bear I had seen at the bird feeder at the cabin. It was an
old male with patchy fur. I awoke when the bear started
talking in the dream and I didn't want to hear what it had
to say. Just before I awoke the bear had receded into a small
cavelike hole in the universe. I didn't know what to make
of this and there was an urge to call Coughlin for a psychoanalytic reading and anyway he was still in Montana likely
packing up for his return to Chicago in the late fall. He fished
and wandered out of Twin Bridges from mid-May to late
October, and then returned to Chicago, where he worked
part-time for an alcohol and drug clinic. He needed Montana but he also needed Chicago for her museums, libraries, theaters, bookstores, and most of all classical music,
which he preferred to hear live.

I woke again before daylight in a curious state near laughter. This frankly amazed me and it occurred to me it was because Jan presented an actual problem rather than one of my somewhat airy periods of obsession with sex, religion, the chaos of history, or death. I gave up. I said aloud, "I don't care." There was nothing I could do about Jan for the time being. I could always start over if I wished. Meanwhile, it was pointless to eat up my own guts.

I went downstairs and made coffee and heated my thermos with boiling water. While sipping coffee I wondered if "I don't care" was the hole that my dream bear had disappeared into. I felt wondrously light looking out the kitchen window into the darkness. Naturally I doubted if this good feeling would last but as Vernice says, "Kiss the joy as it flies."

While shivering in my packed car I remembered something Cynthia had said in passing to the effect that she knew very well that Vera didn't need any financial help for her son but that she wanted to feel that there was some sort of contact between us and our half brother. It was obviously not her son's fault the way he came into being. Cynthia had also said that it's not infrequent that someone who had experienced a closed-head injury like our brother ends up exhibiting violent behavior. I'm ignorant on the structure of the human brain but recalled reading that such niceties as the knowledge of right and wrong are in the frontal lobes and that damage to this area can cast one adrift.

"What are you doing?" K was suddenly outside the driver-side window dressed for a hike.

"I'm thinking," I said, rolling down the window.

"If you'd start the car and turn on the heater you might stop shivering," he suggested.

"Excellent idea." Five winters in Mexico had stolen my tolerance for cold weather. "Is Clare okay?"

"Of course not. She thinks her father is alive in some form but she won't say how."

"Maybe the Ghost Supper will help." I was referring to the ceremony that Cynthia was taking Clare to where you throw tobacco onto a bonfire and release the spirits of the dead you've been clinging to. The event would be held in a couple of weeks over near Bay Mills.

When I drove away K looked as if he was bearing up under too much of the weight of the world but then I reflected on my own insufferable tendencies in that direction, which Coughlin had said was a form of megalomania, of hubris, for me to think that I could do something beneficial way beyond the powers of any single human. At least K was dealing with the reality of a somewhat deranged lover. In July I had spent the afternoon with a brilliant forestry professor from Michigan Tech over in Houghton discussing the history of logging in the Upper Peninsula. At the cabin over a glass of wine he had looked at me askance and said, "Nearly all of the ill effects that you've traced to your family took place a hundred years ago or more. You're talking as if it was yesterday and still going on today and that you can do something to ameliorate the situation. You remind me of some of my save-the-world environmental students. I have great sympathy with their earnestness but such purity of heart can lead to radical self-deception. You have to learn to ignore the disastrous big picture and come down to the singular wetland or piece of forest you might wish to rescue. Of course you have to comprehend the science, the details of the whole picture, but cast your role as a screwdriver rather than a tank."

After an initial hollow stomach I found a trace of amusement in the idea that if through the miracle of time travel I had been able to murder my great-grandfather or grandfather their competitors would be ready for the same job of greed and destruction and there was the additional problem that I wouldn't exist.

I stopped near Witch Lake for a quick look at two hundred acres I was thinking of selling but came to no conclusions. Years before I had found a dead wolf in a dense thicket near a marsh and inspected the smelly carcass for gunshot wounds. There were none. It was rangier than the largest German shepherd but quite thin with a gray muzzle and bad teeth. I was relieved that it had obviously died of old age. Now I turned the car around when I saw the spot down a steep hill in the distance.

In a motel in Iowa City I looked at the journal of the first day and a half of my trip. I've learned to write down certain things I've seen rather than the banal thoughts that don't bear rereading, or when you do reread them your soul yawns in the stuffy air:

Noted that south of Witch Lake my peripheral vision has expanded doubtless because of the dream. All of the birch and hardwood and aspen leaves are gone from

the three-day northwester and there are patches of
snow in the shade beneath gigantic outcrops. The
Michigamme River is low from the fall drought and
scarcely remembers that it drowned so many miners
long ago.

Near disaster west of Iron Mountain, where I
should have headed south but was thinking of Polly so
many years ago when we were high school seniors and
on a wintry dawn I was staying in a second-floor room
at the Best Western. She visited on her walk to school.
Her knees were cold but the thigh draped across my
face was moistly warm, my first time going down. This
sexual trance causes me to go off the road near Florence, Wisconsin. Luckily the ditch isn't deep but I clip
off the right side-view mirror on a poplar tree. I churn
out of the ditch in four-wheel drive. A trucker behind
me stops to see if I'm okay and gives me a cup from his
thermos of coffee assuming I fell asleep. I don't say,
"No, I had my face in divine-memory pussy." A few
miles down the road I stop at a tourist picnic area and
doze for an hour, still shaky with my brush with injury
or worse. The sun through the windows of the car is
too weak for warmth and I wake up shivering and remembering when I fell through pond ice with Glenn
while skating but the water was only chest-deep.

At a motel just north of Davenport I stand out back
thinking of the thin scimitar shape of the new moon, also
about Jesus and all of the semitrucks roaring past on Inter-

state 80 a mile to the north of me. In reference to Jesus I couldn't quite remember the words of admonition to take care of the poor since it had been so long since I had opened the New Testament. I certainly wasn't doing an inclusive job but it was a tad better than nothing. I thought of the curious and energetic jubilance of Mexican children play-ing with their makeshift toys, something I see less of in the U.S. with our children in the highly organized play that has been devised for them by bored adults. K collects used baseballs and mitts for me to haul south and give away. K is amazingly athletic. When he visited me in Zacatecas he played in a local pickup game and jumped over the head of a stooping shortstop. The moon is moving. I can see it. Unlike in the U.P. there is a warmish wind from the south. What is ghastly is to see these Mexican children become careworn adults making three bucks a day. Two hours ago I ate an enormous pork chop called a "porkerhouse." In Torreón when I sponsored a *barbacoa* I was amazed at the amount of meat people ate, a dozen roasted *cabritos* (young goats) and a couple of beef quarters organized through a Catholic church in a very poor barrio. The girls dancing remind me painfully of the way Vera and Cynthia used to dance. After my accident this morning I kept returning all day long to the absurd power of sex. Some author won-dered at the nature of us as animals in human clothing. At a bad diner lunch while looking out the window at the Mis-sissippi River near La Crosse, Wisconsin, I nevertheless found the sallow, grumpy waitress sexy. She was extremely busy with too many tables and when she served me I could feel the heat from her body. I took three car naps and each time I awoke delighted with life on earth despite its desperately compromised nature.

Vernice came over to my Iowa City motel shortly after my arrival at midafternoon. For the first time in more than a decade she looked truly healthy. She was at her nadir a year and a half ago when I met her in Florence, Italy, for the purpose of seeing a retired doctor who had been a specialist in tropical medicine. She had been on a year's fellowship in Glasgow, Scotland, and was cold, weak, and utterly miserable. It was in mid-March and I was in Zacatecas at the time but her voice sounded so small and remote that I decided to meet her. I flew from Mexico City to Rome, which was a not altogether pleasant reminder of an earlier trip to France in search of Vernice. Most of us know that medicine is scarcely a precise science but Vernice had been lucky to meet a doctor in Glasgow who had been a colleague of the Italian doctor when they had both worked for the United Nations in Arusha in Tanzania. The Italian doctor was a sprightly old man who looked like Sigmund Freud. The first few days we stayed in an inexpensive *pensione* where if I leaned precariously out the window I could see a half inch of the Arno River. When the doctor put Vernice in the hospital for tests I moved to a nice hotel where I could get room service. Vernice had been treated previously for liver flukes she'd encountered on a budget trip to Morocco when she was living in the south of France with her lesbian partner. The Italian doctor, however, determined that she has two additional parasites, including one she had caught walking barefoot on a Jamaican beach; the third was of indeterminate tropical origin and the doctor explained to me that such parasites, though anyone can get them, are more typical in those on budget travel funds. After Florence Vernice was on the road back to health continuing her treatment with a specialist at the medical school in Ames, Iowa. Always a leftist bully she insisted I fly to Rome tourist class but after ten days in Florence and a night in Rome, when she was safely on a flight back to Glasgow, I changed my ticket to business class, proving, I suppose, that there was some of my parents left in me. Understandably in Florence our only physical contact was holding hands and it was like holding hands with a wraith.

Now in Iowa City she sipped a scant inch of a nice wine I had bought and then we were off on an arduous walk in a hilly area north of town, a densely wooded few hundred acres not at all like my preconception of Iowa. We sat down near a lovely pond with a used prophylactic in clear view and rather than being her usual schoolmarmish self telling me what to read Vernice talked about university parking problems and the iffy question of whether she was on a "tenure track," which would mean a lifetime sinecure. She was in her early forties and was fatigued with traveling between "lesser universities" as a temporary poet-in-residence.

I still felt light-headed and pleasant though I had read enough about pheromones to understand that none were present there by the pond. The feeling wasn't really similar to Polly's brisk good-bye but it was hard to see clearly the nature of the curious bond I had with Vernice, which had never recovered its original sexual intensity. Cynthia had chided me a number of times of late about my "appearance" so I had put on a clean (but old) shirt and combed my hair before Vernice had arrived at the motel. Her single night at the cabin in July on her drive from Iowa to a summer-school place in Vermont called Bread Loaf had been pathetically chaste despite my wheedling. When we stood up at the pond she allowed me to embrace her and when I slid my hand down on her buttocks she wordlessly pushed it away. On the hike back to the car I remembered when I lived near Patagonia, Arizona, near the border six years before and misdirected myself on a hike ending up in a ranch yard where a chained-up dog was barking into the distance with his back turned to me. The rancher came out of the house and gave me directions to my car and I asked him about the dog. He said that the other cow dogs were off rounding up some heifers but this dog was worthless and was always left behind. Of course it was after the rancher explained about the dog, but I felt there was an eerie sense of longing in its voice.

At Vernice's pleasant rented bungalow she told me to take my usual nap because a small group of poet friends and graduate students always came over late Sunday afternoons for an hour. Meanwhile she would put on a big capon to roast, which was my favorite, and I could take the leftover fowl on the road in the morning. I lay down on the couch in her writing room with a glass of red wine and looked at the photos above her desk thinking I hadn't really planned on leaving in the morning but then Vernice has always fixed the itinerary when we've been together. After a passing glance I averted my eyes from a photo of Carla and me at the cabin and then I fixed on it. Was I ever that young?

I felt pleasant seeing one of the last rays of the afternoon sun collide with my half glass of red wine. I closed my eyes and saw Vera getting out of the car across the street from the Emporio Hotel in Veracruz. She really said nothing except to tell me to please go away. She had my father's child. Who are the children of raped mothers? Two weeks after Donald's death Cynthia and I walked half the night in Marquette under the light of a full moon. There was a trace of madness in her talk. We were out by the ore dock near the power plant studying what the moon was doing to the water. She was saying that Clarence and Jesse were the best parts of our childhood, the only adults we truly loved. Clarence gave her his son Donald and they had had a fine life. Our father destroyed the life of Jesse's daughter. Her life became predetermined by our father's act. Cynthia walked into the water up to her knees, wriggling the moon around her. She was doing fractions with our lives. She turned to me with her face shadowed by the moon behind her and said she was sure that I had spent all of that time in Mexico the past five years because Mexico was Vera even though I didn't see her. I was probably rescuing Vera over and over trying to help people survive. I walked out in the water and put my arm around Cynthia and said, "I don't know."

Now in Vernice's writing room I felt that it was comical that I'd probably stay at the cabin the year around except that winter brought a couple of hundred inches of snow and many twenty-below-zero nights. I stay in a place because it seizes me. I go to a place because it seizes me. I doubt

if there are as many turns, corners, crossroads in our lives
as we think there are.

"Where are you?" Vernice is standing in the doorway
as if invisible. She laughs so I do too. "Come in. I can't remember that poem you gave me."

They were all sitting around the dining room table, seven
of them, and they certainly weren't discussing business. Of
the three young women one named Dora was terribly attractive, something I always feel in my tummy. None of the poets
they were talking about were authors of the books of high
quality that Vernice had given me (she was pleased with my
fascination with Wallace Stevens, whose poems like good
paintings made me want to live inside them). Instead they
were discussing, mostly scornfully, colleagues in other MFA
programs around the country. I made the mistake of saying
that when Vernice was being doctored in Florence and on our
last day she was strong enough to walk around the Uffizi for
a couple of hours she had said, "It seems cheeky for us to give
a master of fine arts in America."

Six of them looked stricken by my story but it was
applauded by a scruffy young gay man who seemed the
brightest of the lot. Vernice promptly changed the subject
by getting me to quote from a Mexican poet, well known
down there but unheard of in the U.S. and the only author
I had ever suggested to Vernice who passed her implacable
muster. His name is Francisco Hernández and he wrote of
the madness of Schumann, Hölderlin, and Trakl.

Estoy harto de todo, Robert Schumann,
de esta urbe pesarosa de torrentes plomizos

de este bello país de pordiorseros y ladrones
donte el amor es mierda de perros policías
y la piedad un tiro en parietal de niño

That was the only portion of the very long poem I could quote and I translated:

I'm tired of everything, Robert Schumann
of this mournful city of leaden rains
of this beautiful country of beggars and thieves
where love is the shit of police dogs
and pity a kid with a bullet in his brains.

That ended the little party and I was pleased when Dora gave me a not entirely chaste hug. I basically ate the capon and roasted vegetables solo because Vernice insisted the chicken was overdone, a small matter for a citizen of the northern Midwest, where the chicken is always overdone. She did, however, drink a lot of wine, which was untypical of her, right to the point where her voice slurred like Judy Garland's on talk shows. My parents absolutely hated it when Cynthia mimicked their voices slurred with alcohol and, in my mother's case, pills. For unclear reasons Vernice rehearsed the history of what she called our "friendship," another indication that we weren't going to make love. She made coffee but barely touched hers, and couldn't stop rattling on about her career and the likelihood of getting academic tenure. She failed to ask a single question about me or my family when usually she wants to hear about Cynthia. I ascribed the narrowness of her concerns to alcohol and the job worries, Vernice having taught at seven colleges and universities in ten years. She now feared that having published her little quasi-pornographic novel with a small press years before in an effort to make some money had jinxed her. She kept repeating that this was a period of political correctness in American universities, a matter I had no familiarity with except from reading newspaper items. I was relieved when by ten she showed me to her small guest bedroom with twin beds. I had had enough to drink that I didn't want to chance driving across town to my motel. The room was far too warm and she came back in her bra and panties and helped me struggle with a stuck window. Her figure was truly full for the first time in a decade but her attitude reduced me to thinking of her as a sexy photo in a magazine, the kind my friend Glenn pasted to the walls of his room with perfect knowledge that never in his life would he get to touch such a woman. She slumped down on the other bed and I tried to turn off the very modern bed lamp, which was evidently faulty because I couldn't get the light to go off. I gave up at four a.m. to Vernice's not unpleasant snores and cold wind coming through the window blowing the curtains apart. I went downstairs for a glass of water and then took a chicken leg from the fridge. I sat on the bed eating the chicken leg and feeling my dick stiffen at the sight of Vernice's sprawled body, but then her eyes opened.

"What are you doing?" she snapped, sitting up and trying to cover herself.

"I'm eating a chicken leg," I said.

She huffed out of the room so I dressed and left, driving altogether too many miles without taking a nap to Dalhart in the Texas Panhandle, arriving in a bleak twilight. I ate a mediocre Mexican supper reflecting that it was like eating in a French bistro in Missouri. If you spend a long time in Mexico you become a food critic elsewhere. I was utterly jangled from the long drive and thinking about Vera so I bought a pint of whiskey anticipating a long night. There was a wild and stupid urge to backtrack a bit and drive south to Brownsville and down the coast of Mexico to Veracruz. What stopped me, of course, was the brooding and dread I intermittently felt over what I might have to confront in Tucson to further the life of my survival-kit project. I'm the rare bird who finds Nebraska and Kansas fascinating so most of the time my worries were drawn away by the land-scape and I would whistle along to doleful country music on the radio, most of the contents of which were laments over aborted love.

It's appalling on a road trip when you fall asleep shortly after seven in the evening and are wide awake at two a.m., still in your clothes and twiddling your thumbs. On the wall there was the same print of a sad-eyed donkey wearing a garland of flowers that I had seen in a half dozen other motel rooms. On the other side of the room a new one presented itself that I hadn't noticed when I'd arrived: a sappy long-horn bull on an aqua-greenish promontory surveying the sunset, naturally, and a valley full of cows.

The room was cool but I was sweating from jumbled dreams that centered in the thickets behind the cabin. A big mother bear was concealing herself but I could only see her baby flouncing in the yard near my bird feeder. This had happened three times in twenty years and only once did I

see the mother peeking from behind the pump shed. In the
dream the moon was my mother's face and though it was
dark I could see the baby bear crying because it couldn't
locate its mother. In actuality a baby bear crying sounds like
a human baby. Somehow in the dream the baby bear was
Vera and the invisible mother bear was Donald.

I was utterly disoriented so I poured a drink of whiskey
and turned on the television to escape the dream. By happen-
stance the only movie on was one of my father's favorites with
Bing Crosby and Bob Hope somewhere in the tropics. He
owned a copy of this movie and I can remember on several
warm summer evenings him playing it on a rented projec-
tor in the backyard. There were always drinking adults but
Cynthia and I loved the occasion because the movie made my
father laugh a full-throated nonironic belly laugh.

I turned the television off and sat there on the bed's edge,
then went to the desk, where there was no room for my legs.
I got out my journal and turned on the clock radio to a Mexican station that was playing *corridos*, the contemporary peasant folk songs of the border mostly dealing with love and
death and the drug trade. The music conflicted garishly with
my memory of standing outside Dante's house in Florence
with Vernice. It was the next to the last day of our stay there
and I celebrated her diagnosis by having four glasses of
prosecco for lunch. She was wobbly for health reasons but
happy and I was wobbly from wine. Vernice has always loved
discussing the more grotesque and furtive aspects of sex and
I've never hesitated to amuse her with my own tales. Anyway, back in college I had taken an advanced course in world
literature and written my term paper on Dante. Standing

there in front of his house I babbled on about Dante and his beloved Beatrice and how at the time I was writing the paper I was living with Polly in married housing at Michigan State. It was midwinter and I was having the usual depression and though I was after Polly a couple of times a day for sex I had difficulty coming off. What worked was if I imagined Polly was Vera and then I could ejaculate. Naturally I was ashamed of myself and also more than a bit puzzled. Vernice was delighted with the half-drunken story and stood there laughing in the shady, ancient alley. Vernice knew everything about my Vera obsession minus this story and when she finished laughing she put me through a silly quiz.

"Do you think Beatrice ever stood over Dante's head on the beach when she wore only a bikini?"

"No ma'am."

"Did Beatrice ever show Dante her bare butt in the upstairs of his parents' house?"

"I doubt it."

"Would Dante have written *The Divine Comedy* if his father had raped Beatrice when she was twelve?"

The last question broke the antic mood and I stood there weeping in Dante's alley with Vernice embracing me for comfort.

Back in the motel room I thought comically that these were pretty unique memories for the donkey and the bull on the wall to witness. It was pointless to think that my father had murdered my Beatrice when she was still alive. If anything, life was outrageous in its lack of symmetry. Donald wasn't a bear. Donald was Donald. Why was my mind imagining a fresh mythology? Of course in Donald's tribe men

had become bears but that was Donald's tribe not mine. And
Vera was a Mexican girl from Veracruz. Her father, Jesse,
brought her north to learn English, where she met and loved
my wonderful family. Nearly thirty years later it was suddenly unthinkable that I allow my father's ghost to stop me
from going to Veracruz to see Vera. There are no damaged
goods when everyone is damaged goods.

Despite the nature of the night my curious sense of well-
being persisted. Coughlin had always been disappointed in
my apparent lack of a dream life, or a dream life so repellant
that my conscious life denied its existence. I couldn't very
well call him in Montana or Chicago after three a.m., or Vera
to tell her I was headed her way. I was amused to remember a quote from a sophomore course in English literature.
I loathed both the course and the quote: "In tragic life, God
wot, No villain need be! Passions spin the plot: We are be-
trayed by what is false within."

I felt this phrase to be as banal as the jingle "Fly the
friendly skies of United." Now in the motel it occurred to
me that our passions are so messy that we don't even need
a villain to fuck up our lives. I immediately gave up the
thought of what my life would have been like without my
central villain. A nitwit college roommate in my freshman
year loved to say, "There is no God but reality."

I tried to sleep for a while but my brain was constructing vivid pictures, from Vera's bare bottom to a huge coal pile
I climbed as a child out near the ore docks. In grade school I
liked to take the long way home and is this still true? So did
Cynthia in her own directions. My father had Jesse follow
me and then showed me the zigzag map. Like Cynthia I had

dozens of dog stops, places I'd stop and pet dogs because I was forbidden one. Children are hyperaware of what other adults think of their parents and I could see how people tried to avoid my father's dry and corrosive wit. Once when I was about seven he took me fishing at one of the lakes up at the club and promptly fell asleep from a hangover, draped along the width of the back seat of the rowboat. I was rowing clumsily trailing a lure from a fishing rod. In sheer luck a very large pike struck the lure and I yelled. My father rolled off the back seat and fought the fish on his knees. We had no net so I rowed to shore and he beached the fish, which was kept the rest of the day and evening on ice in a cooler on the front porch of our lodge. It was the biggest pike of the summer and many men came by to look at the fish, even men who disliked my father. Naturally he didn't say the fish was hooked while he was sleeping. Still, I was proud of the admiration he received.

I overslept but then immediately called all three numbers Cynthia had given me for Vera, reaching her on the third. "I'm coming to visit you in a week," I said. "It will be fine if you arrive," she said slowly and then we were cut off. The third number was for the small coffee farm, where the phone service is unstable with wild orchids hanging from the wires. And that was that.

Tucson was a mess as expected. There were only two hundred of my compact survival kits left. Jan and her two friends had held a fund-raiser (rock bands, etc., plus fifteen thousand of my money) and bought a new van. In September they had set off loaded with survival kits for Cananea, where they had been *pushed around* by some coyotes. They then made the mistake of driving south from Agua Prieta toward Nacozari de García, and then farther south toward Bacanora, where they didn't realize that the bad road ended. Evidently some coyotes had followed them because when they stopped to wash up in a mountain creek the van had been stolen leaving them *high and dry*. I received this information early in the morning at the Congress Hotel, which Jan thought of as the "headquarters" of our mission. Now that I was in town there was going to be a lunch of the board at the Congress at noon to see if we couldn't "jump-start" the project again. I didn't even know that we had a board of directors but Jan insisted she had written my lawyer to tell me so. We embraced and I said that I would see her at noon. I then went back to my motel, packed up, and headed east on Route 10 toward El Paso, where I would turn south toward Veracruz. I figured the drive would take four days, a small item in my life these four days, but in this case time would grow larger with each mile and the ever so gradual change in the landscape.

I don't usually drive at night in Mexico unless I'm on a well-traveled route and Route 45-49 south qualified, but then I mistrusted my level of attention on this trip. Whatever I tried to imagine about seeing Vera would doubtless prove inaccurate but that didn't stop my imagination from creating a reality that probably had the flimsiness of Hollywood movies about American Indians. In the most ideal form there was more than a tinge of silliness. I would arrive at the small coffee *finca* and stop to look at the wild orchids, which as "epiphytes" lived on air and water as they hung from the phone line. The stucco house itself was the color of a bruised rose, which merged wonderfully with the deep green hill on which it was built. I had no problem for some undetectable reason expunging the memory of my previous trip to the farm, the most physically violent event of my life. Where my father's hands were buried bore no interest to me. I suppose the lack of my missing thumb tip had been such a daily reminder that the event had lost every filament of impact. But then Vera herself had luckily not been there that day and she was now the relevant creature that appeared in the palimpsest my mind constructs with the landscape. The best thing about travel, though, is that it's difficult to be consumed by the past against the backdrop of a fresh landscape. There are so many semi-idiotic questions that you don't have time to seek answers. Where does this river I'm crossing begin? What's up that lovely canyon? When was that church built? What do people around here do for a living? That dog trotting across a barren field must have a name? Why is the waitress in the café so happy?

I made the coastal city of Tuxpan on the evening of the third day, which meant I could see Vera the following noon. I called Vera and had my sylvan fantasy destroyed. She would be in Jalapa, where she had started a clothing store in the spring. I would have known about the clothing store if I had even read any of the letters she and Cynthia had exchanged since her sudden departure nearly thirty years before. Cynthia has always teased me about my selective reality. For instance I had told Vernice when she writes me a letter to please leave out any information about men she was seeing, plural or singular. In Vera's case I had been masochistic enough to read some of the teenage mother–type letters, which were full of the usual pen-pal nonsense and once late in the evening while staying with Cynthia she had given me a lachrymose letter from Vera saying that she would never find a good husband because a raped girl with a child is ignored by gentlemen in Veracruz. The whole picture is usually beyond my ken. When I'm at the cabin and call Cynthia from the tavern in Grand Marais she teases, "How many birds and beasts have you counted today, darling?" She's referring to a visit of hers to the cabin many years ago when she spied a page of my open journal on the kitchen counter that read "12 warblers, 5 thrushes, 3 ravens, 2 deer, equals 22." But then on most days my skin is not thick enough to absorb the anguish involved in the daily life of many of the world's citizens. I'm either handing out my simple-minded survival kits or retreating to my log hideout in the woods where the sound of the river baffles the world's noise.

In Tuxpan with the waning sun behind me the lightness returned while I was staring at the sea with its overwhelming neutrality. In the last light I looked into the heart of a large tropical flower full of busy insects. I remembered that someone had written that all human life depended on a few inches of topsoil and rain. You could easily add the improbable sea. A number of people were still taking an evening stroll in the gathering dark and then suddenly streetlamps came on. An old man led a mutt by a green leash and the dog sniffed at my foot and gave me a quizzical look. I said, "Good evening, magnificent dog," and the dog looked concerned so I said, "Buenas tardes, perro magnifico" in my pidgin Spanish. The dog felt better and the old man laughed.

I sat there looking at the lights of boats way off in the water until I began to doze despite my hunger. I wondered if my expectations about Vera should be made of air, soil, and water instead of my usual somewhat neurotic fandangos where my mind in its perpetual slippage keeps constructing a future to amuse itself. On Cynthia's dresser there was a photo of Vera sitting on a horse wearing a beige riding outfit against a steep hillside of coffee bushes. She's simply smiling with no backspin. I suddenly wondered if there were any fish in the river ten miles north of her farm. I had crossed the river so long ago on the way to my father's doom. I got up and walked up a brightly lit street looking for a suitable place to eat a fried fish, remembering that when we went out for brook trout at dawn Donald would tote along a salt shaker, a small iron frying pan, a baby food jar of bacon grease, and a loaf of Cynthia's homemade bread, and we would eat the first few trout over a smudgy campfire, listening to the inevitable whine of mosquitoes and the loud early morning birds, certainly too numerous to count. I passed a street musician playing a dulcet wooden marimba with overelaborate motions as if he were dancing in one place.

At first light from the hotel window the sun rose, a bruised tangerine in the sea mist, seemingly too ovoid. "Red sky in morning sailors take warning," we used to say on Lake Superior, except the Gulf of Mexico was utterly placid, and the air out the little balcony of my room very warm. An

old man rowed past in the harbor, his dog sitting on the
back seat as if it were helping.

I had a tinge of cold feet about being there but all in all
was quite giddy at the prospect of seeing Vera, though I had
become quite convinced that nothing would be as I expected. After dinner before I called Vera I talked to Cynthia
in Marquette, who addressed my perplexity by saying, "Do
you think after nearly thirty years she's going to fall sobbing
into your arms? For Christ's sake she was twelve when she
had a crush on you." After hanging up I decided not to let
the obvious truth of this discourage me. I called Vera and she
had me write down the address of the hotel where she had
made a reservation, which rather obviously meant I wouldn't
be staying with her. She would be quite busy at her store until
eight in the evening but then we would have dinner and in
the morning drive out to the farm, which was only a dozen
miles away. The store was only three blocks from my hotel
so that when I arrived I should stop by to say hello.

I dawdled my way south from Tuxpan acting as if I
were a tourist when I stopped briefly at the Zempoala pyra-
mids, but with the kind of absurd butterflies in my tummy
I had had before a high school football game with Escanaba
which we were predicted to lose. On the outskirts of Jalapa
I actually laughed at the old saying "Don't put all your eggs
in one basket" since I have always put all my eggs in one
basket. You couldn't imagine a set of parents more lacking
in folk wisdom than my own. Cynthia had absorbed hers
from Donald and his father, Clarence.

I checked into the hotel in Jalapa and watched a boy
attendant scooping some coins out of the lobby fountain and

asked him in Spanish if he was becoming rich. He giggled and said that someday he wanted to buy a Mustang, meaning the car not a horse. The hotel itself was decorated in the 1920s time warp and the doors to the rooms and the bedsteads were hand-carved. I tried to wash my face without looking in the mirror but then dared a glance and said loudly, "You goofy fuck, what are you up to now?" No answer was forthcoming and I hummed "Moon River" into the towel though I've always loathed the song.

Vera's clothing store was more than a little startling. It was a scant block from the ominous cathedral and was full of name-brand stuff in addition to cheaper imitations: Lauren, Hilfiger, French Izod shirts, and a large section of sporting wear. I suspected her clientele would be the sons and daughters of larger coffee plantation owners, and the more prosperous students from the local university and medical school. Two niftily dressed salesgirls approached and I simply said, "Vera" and one escorted me to an office through a closed door in the back.

Vera was clearly her father's daughter. She was behind a very big desk going through bills and receipts as Jesse had done at my father's desk in the den in Marquette. She was a very attractive forty-one-year-old businesswoman wearing a beige linen suit and rimless glasses. She jumped up and hugged me but then promptly answered the phone. I could understand that she was talking to a wholesaler in Mexico City and when she hung up the phone she said, "Well?" and then the phone rang and she talked to a wholesaler in Chicago in English. When she hung up this time she said, "Jesus Christ" and I followed her out the back door into an alley,

where she lit a cigarette. I rarely smoked but had one too
and naturally felt a little dizzy. A well-dressed man came out
the office door and she said, "Not now." I guessed him to
be a suitor.

"Your boyfriend?" I asked.

"Of course. I should sell you some clothes." She laughed
when I looked down at my inelegant outfit. She took a hand
of mine in hers and looked into my eyes until I turned away.
She laughed again. Her hands were cool and dry while mine
were sweaty. The cuff of my shirt was frayed.

"How long are you staying?"

I looked off down the alley as if it bore a specific interest and shrugged. "Indefinitely."

"Cynthia told me about your survival kits. Are you
going to give me one?" She laughed again.

"We'll take two on a walk in the mountains tomorrow,"
I said, my voice lacking volume. She turned to the ringing
phone in her office.

"Take a walk. Take a nap. Go to the museum. I'll see
you at eight."

I followed her back through the office and she gave me
a peck on the cheek. Another well-dressed man, in his thirties, was waiting evidently to take her to lunch. Of course it
had never occurred to me that there would be other men in
her life. As I walked back to the hotel I wondered if I'd developed this simplemindedness as a means of self-protection
or it had merely dropped on me from the heavens like rain
or birdshit. I apparently didn't have the toehold on life processes owned by men who have wives, children, and regular jobs. I was a drifter who could spend an hour in a thicket

watching a bird called a brown thrasher feed on deerflies. Spending half my life in the woods despite all the books piled around the cabin ill-prepared me for a mating.

I ate two bowls of delicious albóndigas (meatball) soup and drifted sleepily through the museum designed by Edward Durrell Stone drawing minus reassurance from twenty-ton Olmec heads and figurines of women undergoing transfiguration into jaguars. Only I could meditate on the nature of love and sexuality staring at these immense heads of sculpted stone whose meaning was as inscrutable as love. I tried to remember what I had written about Dante and Beatrice in college but the conclusions weren't poignant enough to endure the passage of time.

I caught a taxi back to the hotel, undressed completely, and took a nap after rereading a few pages of Octavio Paz's *The Labyrinth of Solitude,* a long essay of more than biblical authority about Mexico. When I shut my eyes I could see Cynthia and Vera dancing in our living room so long ago with my father watching them like an insane ogre in a Brooks Brothers summer suit. How did I watch Vera for those six weeks? Lust and anguish, and the burgeoning of something more we never quite understand, the smallest but most ungodly powerful niche in the human genome, as meaningful as topsoil and rain.

Vera looked very tired when we had a drink in the hotel lobby but a rum and cola perked her up. She wore a pale blue dress, which made her hair even blacker. When I asked her why she worked so hard she was stumped at first.

"My father was your father's servant only so I could spend his money? I don't know. I look after the whole family like he did but I don't make them into children like he did. He could be quite mean-minded."

"Never to us," I offered.

"No, his job was to not be mean-minded about you. He was always worried about you but never had to worry about Cynthia. He was happy when she ran away with Donald. He thought Clarence was the finest man he knew in America. He thought the war had made your father a drunken beast."

"I don't see why he stayed with him."

"It was his best opportunity. Both Cynthia and I figured out he stole from your family. I'm sure you know this."

"I don't care. I never did. Jesse and Clarence were my real fathers."

"And your father stole from you and Cynthia. Our parents were thieves except your mother."

We were on our second drink and ate a light meal in the hotel. She began to cry when we talked about Donald and then her "hopeless" son. She was unmercifully beautiful when she cried. I ordered a third drink but decided not to touch it. I walked her to her apartment, which was only three blocks away in a rather elegant small building with a burly guard standing near the door. The guard gave me a hateful look as if I were responsible for Vera's tears but then smiled when she embraced me.

"Why are you here?"

"I was wondering if I still loved you. I wanted to find out." That was all I could say.

"Maybe it's good that we have no future," she said and then went in the door.

I followed her car with my own with difficulty rather early in the morning. When she stopped at the hotel she was wearing jeans and a wool sports coat against the slight chill. She was smiling as if our doleful evening hadn't happened.

At the farm I waited for the miserable thing that had happened there ten years before to revisit me. It didn't. I had exhausted it until it couldn't carry its weight. My dead father was so much less than an ordinary dead father whom others had actually loved.

The farm itself was dormant and Vera explained that coffee prices had collapsed seven years before bringing great hardship locally. Now the prices were beginning to recover and she might start again.

"This farm partly belongs to you and Cynthia," she said when we entered the house. An old woman was cooking in the kitchen and they hugged each other.

"I don't want to own anything except my cabin," I said lamely.

"Cynthia says you are an odd man. You were an odd boy and now you are an odd man. You loved books and women." She laughed and showed me to what I thought she said was "our" bedroom but then she lapsed back and forth between Spanish and English. On the way into the bedroom I had glanced at the living room floor where my father had fallen with his severed hands. No stains. Vera showed me a big shelf with dozens of books on clothing that Clare had sent her. Two more cartons had recently arrived because Clare had "lost interest."

We took an hour's walk in the hills with Vera carrying a machete in a scabbard attached to her belt. I teased about this but she said a neighbor had been bitten by a stray, mad dog. Toward the back of the modest property there was a whitewashed casita where she said an American ornithologist lived with his Mexican wife. She gave them free rent for keeping an eye on things because the old woman in the kitchen was mostly deaf. She said the ornithologist and his wife left at dawn every single day to look at birds and that they would be having lunch with us. On the walk back we saw a small poisonous snake whose name I didn't catch. She said she didn't kill it because it was "just a baby." She threw me off balance by saying she had to go to Chicago the following week to a clothes show and perhaps I would go with her? She thought that Cynthia might come down from the north.

Back at the house I sat on the living room sofa drinking cold water with a nearly unbearable tension in my heart as if I were swimming through a questionable dream.

"Why are you out there," she called from the bedroom.

I walked into the bedroom as if my feet didn't quite know what they were doing. There were tears in my eyes and I couldn't stop them. She was standing there in bra and panties holding up two outfits on hangers.

"What should I wear?" she asked.

"Why are you doing this?"

"I tried to before I should have. Now I'm trying again."

I was hoping I wouldn't die before I reached her.

Part IV

Cynthia

I checked into the Drake a few hours after David and Vera were due to arrive. I called their room and left a message, then took a walk up Michigan Avenue deciding I didn't need to look at Lake Michigan just yet having spent so much of my life gazing at Lake Superior. The air was oddly warm and still for November 15 and I was glancing at smartly dressed people rather than in store windows when I saw them coming toward me a half block away. I ducked into a store entryway suddenly wondering if I was ready to see them. This is unlike my usual manner that my kids called *confrontational,* a word rarely encountered when I was growing up.

I stood there in the glass foyer surrounded by expensive men's shoes and was amused to think of what Donald would have said about five hundred bucks for a pair of shoes. Within moments I could see Vera and David approaching through a double pane of glass, which mildly distorted them. Vera was window-shopping with a critical look and David was staring up and away as if something interesting was going on halfway up the tall buildings. He has always thought that the basic realities were within his mind's contents rather than outside of him. I wasn't quite ready and ducked through the door and let them pass. I waved away a neutrally handsome young salesman, waited a few minutes, then left turning down a side street toward Lake Michigan. When I was nearly to the lake I had a feeling of déjà vu before the polished entrance of a brownstone and realized I had been there with my parents nearly four decades ago, and that these daffy people had owned a huge collection of Lalique glass.

I turned west for a few blocks then walked through a piss-smelling pedestrian underpass, and then farther west along the beach. I sat on a park bench needing to collect my thoughts but was distracted by the story of one of my mother's friends, whose corgi named Ralph had found a shoe on the beach with a foot still in it. Chicago detectives call these *partials*. Finally I was calmed by glistening Lake Michigan, which, though it lacked the clarity of Lake Superior, was overwhelming enough to remove the thought of a severed foot.

Five months after Donald's death I still sense strongly the continuing vacuum that once was his body. Sometimes the vacuum struggles to resume his bodily shape but what is most real is the presence of the voice, and the occasional scent of raw lumber and cement, and occasionally the scent of sun on his skin. Now I can hear him say as he did farther up the beach on a park bench near Mother's house in Evanston, "I wonder if there are any fish out there in front of us?" And then he turned to the vast skyline of Chicago and said, "There must be a mile of bedrock or they couldn't raise buildings like that. They must have had a bunch of people who knew what they were doing." On our infrequent trips Donald, Herald, and Clare would eat three or four of those crappy-style Chicago hot dogs teasing me for squeamishness.

Uncle Fred wrote me a fine letter from Hawaii last week. There was a fascinating paragraph on all of the delusions the death of a loved one can bring upon those left behind. He quoted a Japanese philosopher whose name has slipped my mind: "No changing reality to suit the self." I showed the letter to Clare, who became angry and walked away. She finally admitted to me that she thinks her departed father has become a bear. I view this as insane though I know it exists in Chippewa lore. I think she spent so much time up on the Yellow Dog Plains because she was looking for Donald as a bear. The two of them used to fish the Yellow Dog when we visited Clarence in Marquette. I didn't say so to Clare but I was certainly pleased when the season for bear hibernation had arrived.

Sitting there on the park bench I abruptly thought that "No changing reality to suit the self" is too austere for the actual human condition. My dreams have to be part of reality and they aren't susceptible to rules. I'm a fairly clear-headed human and understand that despite all the diversions our culture offers us there's no escaping the pain of his death. There are no palliatives, or at least none that work for me.

Way back in college I remember an anthropology professor saying, "Primitive people think that when they talk to
God He's listening and that some sort of answer can be expected." As Herald likes to say, "I can't get my head around
this."

By absurd coincidence I can see Vera and David approaching in the distance. Actually it's logical because the
hotel is close and he's deeply claustrophobic. When we
were in Zihuatanejo we took a little panga south and walked
his favorite beach, which is fifty miles long. We saw the
coxcomb-shaped dorsal fins of passing schools of fish that
he said are called roosterfish. I keep stupidly thinking that
he could have done all of his logging and mining research
in a couple of years instead of twenty but then his head was
full of knots that no human hands would untie. Father had
to die first and then the knots apparently began to loosen.
You wonder how life can be so errantly determined but it
is. For instance, in my earliest teens I had seen Donald around
school but only as a leading member of the athletic clique.
At the time I was busy behaving poorly and reading English
novels, which were able to divert me from my life. And then
there was that hot summer morning when Clarence and his
son Donald were digging behind the garage to shore up the
tilting foundation. Laurie and I made them lemonade. I said
to Donald, "Why won't you look at me?" and then he did. I
was immediately conscious that he was the man on earth
least like my father. They're still a hundred yards away but
Vera waves. The idea of them together is so appalling that
it's acceptable, somewhat in the way ancient peoples would
have accepted Greek or Roman mythology. I laugh at this

idea. Your father Zeus rapes the girl you love but keep yourself from. You wander thirty years but after killing your
father you return to her. Something like that. How does this
story end? Who knows. I only know how my own story
ended. I'm trying to have the heart to begin again.

Vera approaches with David far behind, doubtless
thinking about the theory and practice of Lake Michigan.

"I saw you hiding in the shoe store. I didn't tell David.
You weren't ready for the carnival?" she laughed.

"Not quite yet." We embraced and turned to David,
who picked up half a dog-chewed Frisbee and put it in a
trash can. My thoughts returned to appalling love. "You
know that I told him that he should go see you. I didn't think
you'd end up in the same bed."

"Why not? I always thought of him as my first boyfriend. That book you sent me said that it's hard to live with
the unlived life." She was properly grave.

"Yes, our Episcopal priest who was mostly a nitwit used
to talk about the sins of omission and the sins of commis-
sion as if life were a bundle of meat tied up with a butcher's
string." She took my hand brushing a finger across my
wedding ring. I was errantly thinking about Thomas Hardy
and wondered if those dozens of English novels I read so
early had done my mind harm. I would confuse the fictional
vicars with the local Episcopalian priest, whose first prior-
ity was dinner. My father would send him prime beef roasts
from Pfaelzer's in Chicago. When I took Herald and Clare
to England in their teens I was daily amazed at how well
the novels had prepared me. Donald wouldn't fly. He'd
always say, "I'll hold down the fort and feed the dogs."

"That was a beautiful way for your husband to die,"
Vera said, clenching my hand.

"Yes, it was." To avoid the lump rising in my throat I
got up and walked down to the water to where David stooped
like a child with a hand swishing through the waves.

"It must be ten degrees warmer than Lake Superior."

"Ten?" I teased. He always ascribes pointlessly exact
numbers. The weather is never in the seventies but "seventy-
four" or "seventy-seven." The time is always "8:47" or "8:33,"
or "the first dawn light came at 6:08."

"How was Clare when you left this morning?"

"She drove me to the airport then was headed to Snowbound Books to pick up her fresh shipment of bear books.
She must have a hundred different titles. K is humoring her
but is upset because she has decided not to go to the Ghost
Supper. She's refusing to say good-bye to her father."

"Maybe she'll talk to Coughlin. She liked him."

"Nothing doing. She'll talk to me a little. She'll talk to
K, but mostly she drives over to Au Train to see Flower and
hear bear stories. I spoke with Coughlin and he said there's
really nowhere to go but to let her work it out over time."

We walked up to the bench and sat down on each side
of Vera. Her eyes were moist but she was smiling. She had
had our father's baby and I supposed or wondered if that
made her our stepmother? She leaned against David's shoulder. We sat there in silence and I began to half doze in the
weak sunlight. I'm not sure what sleep is anymore. It's inter-
mittent at best with a dozen novels always on the night table.
There's an incalculable rudeness to death. How much am I
meant to understand? A dark-complected young man in run-

ning clothes quickly passed us, nearly as large as Donald had been, and I felt the slightest twinge of desire, the first in a very long time.

I stayed in Chicago for three mostly pleasant days despite the weather, which became wet and blustery but not as cold as it would have been in Marquette, where, the television had said, there had been a major snowstorm that had stranded thousands of deer hunters in their tents and camps. Vera spent much of the days at the wholesale clothing convention showing lines for the coming spring. David and I bundled up and walked a great deal and had one mildly awkward conversation about being the sons and daughters of privilege. The explicit question was "What are you going to do now?" and I said "Continue teaching, I guess" though I didn't enjoy Marquette as I had the Soo or Brimley or Bay Mills, where I taught Indians, mixed breeds, and poor white kids. Prosperity rarely brings out the best in children. David was looking into an international version of the Peace Corps that had headquarters in Switzerland but had an opening in the Veracruz area for someone who could afford to work for very low pay or had the predilection to do so. Much of the work would be directed toward ensuring pure drinking water in villages since so many diseases were waterborne. This seemed oddly limited but David said with conclusiveness, "I always liked the idea of water," as if it were an idea. This conversation took place in front of the Newberry Library, where he was showing me the exact spot on the sidewalk where he had met Vernice. I looked gravely downward at this historical place and couldn't help myself and laughed at the ordinary ways lovers first meet. Donald was digging down a hole. David met Polly at a hamburger stand in Iron Mountain. And David meeting Vernice the Matchgirl, who had helped him more than anyone else but Coughlin. When Vernice was terribly ill with tropical parasites I had sent her a check and in return she had given me a double-volume set of the Russian poet Anna Akhmatova. I admit I rarely read poetry but somehow no writer had helped me as much with Donald's fatal illness as Akhmatova, who had one of the most spacious minds in human history. I had kept in touch with Vernice since meeting her in Chicago so long ago partly to have her insight into David's precarious mental condition, which Donald described succinctly: "David doesn't seem to have both oars in the water." There is a specific visual of a man rowing with one oar, or a crow trying to fly with a single wing. The psychologism in the term *depression* scarcely covers the thousands of varieties but it is always a circular infirmity.

Each of my three evenings we had dinner with Coughlin. The first one was a little iffy because we went downstairs in the Drake to the Cape Cod Room and halfway through the meal David abruptly left for the ground-floor bar, where we found him eating a cheeseburger. He explained that the Cape Cod Room was where he'd had dinner with Father the evening before the fatal trip to Mexico. Things got even rougher in the bar when the subject of war came up and I carelessly described a little research I had done on the World War II battles in the Philippines in which both my father and Vera's father, Jesse, had taken part. A martini had made

me half daft as I rambled on about the Battle of Cape Engano
and also gruesome land battles where my father lost most
of the men he commanded. Coughlin said he had met an ex–
Green Beret medic while fishing in Montana who had tried
to duct-tape together several dozen children who were in
pieces when our personnel had called in mortar fire in the
wrong place. I wasn't hearing Coughlin clearly when he
quoted some poet saying, "There's a point at which the ex-
posed heart can't recover." I was looking at the increasingly
pale face of my brother, who got up abruptly and walked
out. Vera also looked stricken and followed. Naturally I was
upset but at the same time amused that Coughlin continued
drinking with relish. I raised an eyebrow.

"In thirty-five years of practice I've heard everything.
There are no true monsters, only some people like your father who with regularity acted like a monster. It's still
episodic."

"Meaning?" I quickly drank a full glass of wine.

"Well, David managed to spend half his life research-
ing the wrongs his family visited on everyone. Long ago I
told him he should be looking into what happened to his
father during the war. You managed to do so. It never works
when you leave out even a small part of the picture. It's a
little like the doctor who failed to diagnose the reason for a
woman's stomachache but then she failed to tell him that her
husband punched her there. War can do horrible things to
men. Most recover well enough to behave well and some
can't. And some don't seem to want to as if the horrors are
encysted in their brains to be examined over and over almost
as if they deserved affection or at least loving attention

because what would be there if the horrors were taken away? In crude farmland lingo, pigs love their own shit."

"Even as a boy David never seemed to have enough skin. I mean his skin wasn't thick enough while mine was."

"Precisely. Once on the way to fish we stopped to look at a big snapping turtle crawling along the road and I said to David that it would be bright of him to take this creature as a model, you know, develop a carapace."

He paused because David returned sheepishly but with Vera looking as if she had told him an important secret. The old waiter stopped by, shaking his head at the cold hamburger, and David said he'd settle for a dozen oysters. Vera ordered a cold lobster "just in case" she had to leave again. She laughed and tickled him somewhere critical under the table.

"To close the conversation and get on to something more interesting like a beauty queen's perineum, true, I never gave my father the slightest break. Mother told me that she remembered him before the war and that's why she held on with the help of booze and pills. Let's give the dead a break today."

David raised his glass and we all followed. I felt slightly choked and Coughlin gave me a peculiar look that I get from K and used to receive from the young men on Donald's work crew. I admit I felt pleased.

Through an old friend of my mother's who is on the board of the Art Institute of Chicago I wangled two passes to visit the big Gauguin show at seven a.m., two hours before the museum officially opened. David and I were quite dumb-founded and when we left the museum in a cold, windy rain I thought of how undemocratic art was in that so few do so much while the rest of the world looks on. I recalled that when I took Herald and Clare to the Tate in London when we were on our English trip in their teens Clare had been transfixed by the Turners and asked, "How can one artist be so much better than others?" Gauguin didn't bring you happiness but consciousness.

I had a rare insomniac night that was pleasant, drifting in and out of sleep, but awoke trying to determine what was reality and what was dreaming. I called Clare at three a.m. thinking she had called me. "Mom, I'm asleep!" she hissed, but it was precipitated by a dream of a call she had made from college when distraught over a crush she had on a professor (eventually consummated). Most of the thoughts and dreams were about Donald and dealt with what he had said again only a week before he died: "You're going to have to find yourself a boyfriend." Before dinner last evening I had taken a walk with Coughlin and he had taken my hand when we crossed Wabash. I told him his hand felt strong and he laughed and said it was because he had been rowing and fly-fishing at least ten hours a day for months and now that he was back therapizing his hands would become weak again. He then spoke of a man he had been counseling for thirty years whose father had died in a building fire in Chicago. The man had been ten years old at the time, a single child, and had basically spent his bachelor life with his

mother maintaining their West Side apartment as a shrine
to the dead father. "We just do things we need to do without consciously thinking about them. But then we can become trapped if we don't finally think them over. There's
something to be said for the old European model of wearing black for a single year. Of course you lived with Donald's
death sentence for quite some time. We've been so inept and
careless about death in America and have paid big for the
consequences. Surprise! We die. That sort of thing."

"I think we're a little better than that up in the north.
I don't mean the cities of the north but the villages. Over
at the reservation death was an open book we all at least
glanced at every day."

"Well, yes, because life was slower and more rumina-
tive. Farm kids eat the animals, the pigs and cows that they
loved. Once in Italy I entered a basilica by a side door and
in the lintel above me skulls were embedded as a reminder,
a memento mori, and then there are all of those paintings
and murals clearly illustrating the end of the life process. I
must have counseled a thousand patients on this matter and
there is always a nearly mute craving for reassurance that
there's something more in the offing for their loved ones."

"And what do you say?" He had paused overlong and
we were standing there looking at wind-tossed and rumpled
Lake Michigan, a view shorn of anything comforting.

"I say I don't know." He laughed at himself. "I say that
I have no idea. I say that no one knows. Back in college in
Dublin we wise young cynics used to tease devout Catholics with the question of just where in the human body is
this soul located? We were witty smart-asses, children of

the Enlightenment, and in the postwar gloom barely past the century's halfway mark we had noted that ninety million had died under God's supposed tent in two wars. Last year I was talking to this kindly old biologist from the University of Chicago who was dying of a kidney tumor. He was nominally an Episcopalian but mostly because he loved their church music. He was neither plus nor minus about the prospects of life after death feeling it was unscientific to assert anything either way. He did point out that in terms of DNA each of our cells contains thirty-two thousand indicators of what we are, so that there's plenty of room for a soul. 'It needn't be very large. What's wrong with a nanosoul?' That's what he said to me."

I was instantly transfixed by what he said. I remembered a walk along a river over near Au Train with Flower, who told me that our departing spirits enter the bodies of our favorite animals. That meant that Donald was a bear, but then I was absurdly troubled that my own preferred animal had been the very ordinary dog. Did that mean I had no chance for a reunion with Donald? Standing there looking out at the troubled water with the cold north wind burning against my face I felt a palpable heartache. Dogs and bears don't like each other. Somehow I managed to laugh at the blatant silliness of it all. Coughlin looked at me, his face a question mark, and I couldn't explain myself so said nothing.

"Well, despite your being well-read and educated it's natural to slide toward your daughter's thoroughly irrational point of view. She's also well-read and educated. You said last evening that you'd like me to come up to Marquette

and talk to her but why should I dissuade her from thinking like her father's people? Back to being well-read and
educated. What does it offer us when someone we love dies?
We keep talking about Clare going off the 'deep end,' especially David, who's overfamiliar with that territory."

"But then what's an appropriate response to death?" I
interrupted.

"There isn't a singular response. You keep on truckin',
as that cartoonist Crumb said. You're probably having a thousand responses a day because your brain simply can't stop
trying to comprehend what has happened to you. It's the largest question mark we deal with in life and no response will
make it go away. We envy the devout who experience the pain
but have a surefire explanation. I'm curious if Donald gave
you any advice before he passed on?"

"He said, 'You can remember me but let me go.' He also
said, 'Find yourself a boyfriend.'" And then I collapsed as
if the bones inside me had dissolved. I simply crumpled and
began to sob for the first time since we buried Donald. I felt
my chest might burst from sobbing. Coughlin knelt down
on the sidewalk and cradled me in his arms. A passing jogger stopped, his face a blank.

"Is this a medical emergency?"

"No. Her husband died," Coughlin said.

"Oh Jesus Christ how awful." The jogger sped off.

The last evening in Chicago was a marvel of pleasantness. I
had the somewhat giddy feeling that everything was beyond
my control including the central problems of Clare and David

and Vera for instance. They were very happy to be at a Mexican restaurant with an odd name, Topolobampo, eating Yucatán food. To be sure they were a nearly lunatic couple launched on an affair that would be startling if you knew the total background as I did. There was a near miss with a sour note when we were talking about the relative safety of travel in different countries and Coughlin said it's hard to avoid the issue because the whole human sensorium is directed toward safety. I could tell that all of us were suddenly thinking of the same thing for a few moments, that the arena of death destroys the illusion of safety. We let it pass without comment, all sipping our margaritas in silly unison, seeking alcohol as a tranquilizer.

David thought that since I was unsure about teaching middle-class white kids in Marquette I should come to Mexico and take a three-month course in intensive Spanish and teach there. I said that I couldn't leave Clare until she achieved some sort of minimal stability. When this happened I was thinking of moving farther west to Minnesota, or farther yet, and teaching at a reservation school. I couldn't really go back to teach at the Soo or Bay Mills, where Donald would be so overwhelmingly in the landscape, a presence like the weather. Besides I'd had so much experience with the foibles and difficulties of Indian kids though perhaps I should stick with Chippewas. I had talked to a retired teacher in Sault Ste. Marie who had taught both Zuni and Hopi children and she had assured me that they are radically different cultures from the Anishinabe. I mean I could learn the differences but why not take advantage of what I already knew.

"You can't just leave Clare with K?" David wondered.

"Well, no, not for the time being. They're lovers after a fashion but they're more like quarrelsome cousins on some days. I mean they've known each other since they were ten years old. The other day before I left there was a mild wrangle about who left a book behind at a beach picnic fifteen years ago."

"Having children lasts a long time," said David, an expert in solipsisms.

"It's easier when they're in prison," Vera said. "Every day I was waiting to hear that he hurt someone new."

"They could be wrapped in banana leaves like this pork," David said, staring down at his dish.

"Pigs are easy compared to adult children. It's my profession and I'm not in full control of my mind and behavior. I'm sixty-five and in Montana this summer I became infatuated with a waitress at a diner. I even sent her flowers. A rather large local cowboy, her husband in fact, had to tell me she was spoken for. At my age I assumed I was beyond this but I wasn't. This is why I like chaos theory." Coughlin laughed so hard he nearly tipped over in his chair.

We all walked together back to the Drake. I embraced David and Vera because I was leaving in the morning. They seemed eager to be alone. I was almost envious remembering that smoky feeling I'd have before making love, a sort of letting go like diving into a lake off a rowboat. It was only ten so I invited Coughlin up for a nightcap. We couldn't help but return to the subject of Clare but he was

concise and direct saying that normally the children follow the mother's lead in the grieving process when the
father dies. Our case was an exception with Clare going
off on her own peculiar tangent. He had no idea what the
dimensions of her search would be but thought there might
be what he called "a way down and out" in her belief that
her father's soul had entered a bear. Meanwhile, no real
harm was being done. This wasn't the sort of pathology
that was full of precedents in psychoanalytic literature. He
knew a cultural anthropologist who spent a lot of time at
the Newberry Library's American Indian collection and
this man might offer some guidance on the phenomenon
for whatever it was worth. Meanwhile, I should be thinking of the millions of people who presume that on their
point of death their souls will ascend to be with Jesus
wherever. "This, in fact, is their perception of reality and
it's not subject to argument. Clare is drawn to what she
thinks was her father's perception of reality. It doesn't
matter one whit if it's part of a Chippewa system of belief.
It's what Clare believes about her dad."

I found myself looking at this dear man and wishing
he were forty-five rather than sixty-five, and then blushed
inside myself. Despite all of my reading I suddenly felt I
knew nothing. I was high and dry in Chicago at night in
November with rain spattering off the window.

"Twice seven plus three." Coughlin laughed as if he
read my feelings.

"What's that?"

"It's French folk wisdom about men and women. A man
is foolhardy to start an affair with a woman if he's more than

seventeen years older than she. I think we've missed by four
years."

I sat there woodenly thinking this over, trying without success to understand the meaning of successive years.
I recalled Polly saying she had had a "crush" on this man
years ago. It wasn't the time to wonder why he was attractive. He got up as if embarrassed, kissed my forehead, and
left.

K picked me up at the Marquette airport, fairly glum because Clare had suggested that he go back to Ann Arbor
while she "worked things out." While we waited for my
baggage he admitted that he wasn't optimistic because she
mostly hung out in her room with her hundred bear books,
and then last night she had slept out on the back porch in
her sleeping bag despite the fact that it was near zero. She
had also been visiting Flower every day for more bear stories and Flower was helping her build some sort of little hut
in the woods where she intended to spend a lot of time this
winter. Despite the coolness of the baggage area I felt sweat
popping on my forehead with this last fact along with the
image of my daughter freezing to death on a January night
when the temperature could be twenty below zero or worse.

Outside my spirits rose. To northerners there is an
ineffable sweetness to the aftermath of the first blizzard. We
had flown north in a cloud bank but now the sun was break-
ing through and glittered off two feet of fresh snow. K joked
about how the state police and game wardens were busy
finding marooned deer hunters. I recalled with some mel-

ancholy how much the four of us had enjoyed our first venison meal, with Donald at the stove inexpertly frying the meat
and Clare jumping up from the table because Donald's gravy
always curdled when he added flour and cold milk to the
pan juices and Clare shrieking, "Dad, you have to whisk it."

When we reached the house there was a note from
Clare saying only that she had gone to Flower's. K's luggage
was stacked in the hall. He was leaving after he made sandwiches for the trip to Ann Arbor and I suddenly realized I
would be left alone in the house where I had experienced
my less than glorious childhood. I shivered though the house
was warm.

"I could stay until the morning if you'd like," K said,
giving me a not totally reliable look.

"No, I'll be fine." I was watching how much hot mus-
tard he was spreading on his sandwiches and thinking what
a lithe, muscular body he had. Clare had complained to me
when she was under the influence of wine that K's lovemaking
was "overenergetic."

K dropped his sandwiches in a sack, filled his thermos
with coffee, and then I helped him carry his bags out to his
pickup. He kissed me good-bye on the lips when I was slow
to avert my face. I watched him drive off then made my way
carefully up the icy walk thinking that it might somehow
be a relief to fall flat on my ass. I lay down on the sofa and
wept for less than a minute, and then said "Fuck it," got up,
and spent several hours cleaning the house, including scrub-
bing the kitchen floor on my hands and knees despite the
fact that a cleaning woman was coming tomorrow. I thought
idly of the fiction that there is an appropriate response to

death. The only one I could think of was a modest culinary trick an Italian girl had taught me in college. Fry three eggs in an ample amount of olive oil that you've brought to nearly smoking heat. Eat with good peasant bread, which I didn't have so settled for toasting an English muffin. Death faded for ten minutes at which point I decided to reread *Love in the Time of Cholera* by García Márquez, which Clare had sent me seven years ago when she was a college freshman. Since I couldn't escape love and longing why not immerse myself in it until I drowned?

Before going to bed after reading not all that many pages of García Márquez I peeked into Clare's room, which was surprisingly neat except for the stacks of bear books on a card table below her bookshelves, which held her nature guides and large coffee table–sized books on the history of clothing. I noticed a number of fresh volumes on Ojibway customs and then backed out of the room. Married couples are daft and possibly destructive when they don't allow each other privacy in some areas. I always avoided inquiring after Donald's religious practices. When Clare was in her early teens she and Donald built a platform in a clearing in the woods well behind our house to feed ravens and crows roadkill and extra fish. I did ask about this and Donald said, "Ravens and crows aren't just ravens and crows." A little old man, a tribal elder, once dragged a deer mashed up by a semi back there. The deer was as big as he was so I helped because Donald, Clare, and Herald were at the basketball game over in the Soo. We struggled to get the deer up on the platform with the ravens gathering in the trees at the edge of the clearing and the old man calling them in with calls uncannily like their own. Afterward I made him coffee and a sandwich and he fell asleep sitting at our kitchen table. I was out in the laundry room and was startled when I heard convincing mooing. I returned to the kitchen and he said he had dreamt about a cow who was his best friend as a child. This man had spent thirty years of his life as a mechanic in the Air Force but when he returned home he slid back into the old ways. He no longer owned a car, didn't eat much or drink alcohol, spent much of his time fixing bicycles for the local kids and courting old ladies, who Donald said complained about his ardor.

My thought as I fell asleep was if ravens aren't just ravens what are they? I had a momentary dream about a small bear Clare once chased when we were blueberry picking and then awoke in despair at three a.m. I walked through all the rooms of our haunted house turning lights on and off as I passed through. I tried to pray in the den where Donald had lain so long but prayer is not my habit and I couldn't remember all of the Lord's Prayer so settled for "Now I lay me down to sleep, I pray the Lord my soul to keep," which my mother said with David and me in the evening before bedtime, her voice often slurred with booze and downers.

After a jumble of brief dreams I turned my night table light on at four a.m. and looked at a photo of Laurie in a tennis dress who had died at twenty-five of breast cancer. She was so instinctive and nonmental while I was always reading and trying to figure out my parents. Her own were as plain as day wanting so badly for her to become a famous tennis player. We had such fun behaving badly and though we were so unlike we were true pals. The parents kept her on a minimal five dollars a week so she would learn the value of money, or so they said. She envied the clothes my mother ordered me from Chicago but I was rangier in build so she couldn't wear them and that's why I hit my father with a garden stake. He offered her a hundred dollars to see her nude pussy and butt in the den while I was in the backyard and she did it. When she told me I broke into tears and she said, "What's the big deal. That's five months of my allowance. I'm buying something nifty." Next morning, I think it was Sunday, he said something rude so I hit him thinking I was defending the honor of my friend. Only recently when I checked out the war in the Philippines did I momentarily wonder if my father's obsession with girls was a result of the thousands of dead bodies he saw in the Philippines. It was too unpleasant in my memory to look further just as when I tried to read Nabokov's *Lolita.* I stopped on page 3 while I had enjoyed the rest of his books. At one point girls are gawky and ignored by everyone and then they begin to burgeon and certain men take notice while boys want them to have tits. Uncle Fred used to slouch down while reading on the sofa the better to look up our school skirts or loose shorts. I actually talked Laurie into being nice to David thinking it might help him but then she loved him and couldn't figure out why because he was such a dork. Sexuality is so varied, strange, and overwhelming compared to the way the culture presents it. Teenagers wander up and down the halls of school shrieking, punching, giggling, so puzzled at what's happening to them. I was a very precocious fourteen and seduced Donald into going *all the way* as we called it on the third date. After that it was just something we did like drinking a glass of cold water on a hot day. We'd do it and then I'd help Donald with his geometry assignment. That sort of thing. Sometimes we'd make love again after we finished our homework. My brother David caught on and was appalled but then he was using religion to control himself. One night after he was judgmental I got Laurie to open his bedroom door and moon him knowing that he would be miserable with desire.

It was about five a.m. when I fell into a deep sleep but then Polly called at six with a voice tight with hysteria. Her daughter Rachel had been busted selling drugs of some sort to an undercover cop in N.Y.C. and she was flying out of town on the eight o'clock plane via Detroit. I immediately dressed and drove down the hill to her place. She poured me coffee and wondered if she should suggest me as a substitute for the principal that day and I said no that I was exhausted by my Clare problems and I would have to back away from substitute teaching until I figured it out. Polly looked at me and we laughed a mournful laugh, two women whose lives had been taken over by wayward daughters, and then she said that K through a friend in Ann Arbor he had called when the news came had found a lawyer in New York City who specialized in dope cases. This required a hefty down-payment fee of ten thousand dollars and Polly pushed a signed withdrawal slip and the lawyer's address across the table. She had to fly off before the banks opened and could I wire the money ahead? I tore up the withdrawal slip and pocketed the lawyer's address and bank account number. I said to Polly that we were part of the same family and I was only doing what my mother would have done, adding that I had the feeling that Clare meant to hibernate in the woods this winter so my daughter's problems were cheap compared to hers.

On the way to the airport in the first light I was initially irked that I couldn't live in the little house I had bought because I had to look after Clare. K had told me that Clare had said she intended to move a cot into the den where her father had spent his last days. This was before what I thought of as her hibernation plan.

Polly was still uncomfortable about the money while we waited in the concourse for the plane. I explained that our parents had inadvertently taught us to despise money. David merely spent his on his cranky charity and in my case the money left to me made Donald uncomfortable. He'd only say "Save it for the kids." I kept the books and he did very well in the cement and construction business plus I had my teacher's salary. He even paid Clarence's debts when there was no real obligation. He would say, "I like to think I can put three squares on the table and a roof over our heads." The kids got straight A's and scholarships but Donald never knew that they couldn't accept financial aid because of the money left me by my mother and the occasional sale of Father's land. I even had to promise him I'd sell the big fancy SUV we drove him to Canada in. "What I'm saying is that I can't bear to see your savings going to a lawyer for your daughter's crimes when the amount isn't important to me." And that was that. I didn't feel a shred of virtue.

I was jangled and boneless when I left the airport and instead of doing something sensible like going back to bed I

drove toward Au Train thinking I might lay down the law
to Clare but then what is the law? I was confused and hungry enough to stop in Harvey for breakfast at the restaurant my father used to take David and me to for the turkey
sandwiches we liked. There were a number of tables of deer
hunters in the orange suits they wear to avoid shooting one
another. They were pointing at and discussing a big buck
deer draped over a pickup fender out the window and I had
the sudden image of Donald frying venison at the kitchen
stove. I could even smell it. At another table there was a
group of men I recognized as cement finishers and block
layers by the dried cement stains on their insulated Carharts
and hooded heavy sweatshirts. The oldest man, probably the
foreman, was eating a plate of fried potatoes and catsup as
if his life depended on it. He stared at me, then looked away,
then got up and approached my table.

"I was sorry to hear about Donald. There was a man
who could put in a day's work." I shook his hand as he offered this ultimate compliment of the north. His hand felt
like a semipetrified baseball mitt. "You might not remember me. Donny and me played football way back when, then
worked together. The name's Teddy." He bowed, his face
reddening, and walked away.

"You were the left tackle," I called out and he turned
and grinned.

When I made the turn near Au Train I wasn't a hundred
yards down the small road toward Flower's when I saw a
man lying on his back in an orange suit with a rifle across

his chest. I got out of the car and I called out to him but he didn't answer. I walked over and could see his footprints deep in the snow coming out of a swamp to where he lay. I said, "Hello" loudly thinking he was ill. I remembered Donald saying that about the same number of hunters die by heart attack as do of errant gunshots. He opened his eyes as if I were a dream. "I had a hangover and this fucking snow is too deep so I took a nap." The whiskey fumes rose toward my nose and I hurried away.

There was no one at Flower's but I could see a trail out the back door through the snow and from perhaps a few hundred yards in the woods I could hear a chain saw, which would be Clare and Flower working on the shelter. The house was overwarm and water dripped from the eaves. The temperature outside was rising above freezing and the midmorning sun glinted off the snow. I lay down on a small corner bed in the room where I had lain with Donald so long ago when I was fourteen and he sixteen. How we loved each other. There were five bearskins tacked to the wall from the time of Flower's dad, whom she said was so hard he broke like a stick. Flower had become angry when she discovered Donald had put a bearskin on the floor for our lovemaking. It evidently broke a taboo of some sort. Then as now I was decidedly a white woman and didn't want to know. This thought made me wonder how much Clare had absorbed from her father but then it's impossible to be quantitative about such matters. In my essentially white Episcopalian mind-set I could somewhat understand Uncle Fred's Zen Buddhism but when I tried to read a piece in *Harper's* about Tibetan Buddhism it seemed an alien country. I recalled in high school when the local Finns were angry because an anthropologist at the college had said that Finns were essentially northern European Indians. Clarence and Donald thought the whole fuss quite funny with Donald being half and half. Clarence would say, "I'm just an American whatever the hell that is." When Clare was a junior in college she brought her Sicilian roommate home on Easter vacation and this girl had thick, black kinky hair that was beautiful. At dinner Donald asked if he could touch her hair and when he did so we all laughed. She said that over a period of thousands of years Sicily was vulnerable and everyone invaded it, Muslim countries, Africans, and Greeks. Donald said, "I agree with the results" and blushed.

Now there were ravens surrounding Flower's house and I swear a large, bearded male looked in the window which cast a yellow square of light across my chest. I sniffled a bit over daughters missing their fathers. I never missed mine.

I slept until late afternoon when the cold November light began to fail. I don't think I ever slept more deeply and there was the pleasant illusion that I had become part of the bed. I turned to see Clare and Flower folding up the five bearskins and wrapping them in a large canvas tarpaulin.

"Mom, are you okay?" Clare said with a windburned smile. In the few days I had been in Chicago she had become ruddy, her skin coarsened by weather.

"I'm not the one in question," I whispered, which she ignored.

Clare and Flower dragged their heavy bundle out the door and left the door open. I got up and watched from the window as they skidded off their freight on a toboggan down toward a low area in the darkening woods where I once found a wild orchard. What a pair of women, I thought. The only thing my mother had in common with Flower was a fascination with wildflowers. Once when Flower drove her old Plymouth into the alley behind the garage to talk to Clarence my mother and I were in the yard and she acted frightened of Flower.

I went to the wood-burning kitchen stove and lifted the top of a Dutch oven smelling a venison soup made with dried corn and dried wild leeks. Herald was always leery of Flower but sent her packages of food from the Southwest that included chiles and a variety of dried corn and beans. When Herald was still a little boy Flower had sent him a hunting knife she had made with a deer-horn handle. He never used the knife but it was a prized possession.

I sat down at the table and tasted a chile sauce that burned my tongue pleasantly. Suddenly it was dark and I heard their feet crunching through the snow on the path back to the house. I tried to think of something to say to Clare, which made me want a drink. There was a jealous notion that Flower had become Clare's mother during this dark time. What did I have to offer? Should I say to Clare that your father is forever dead to you and you should resume your life? In my mind's eye I could see Donald and Clare packing for one of their countless fishing trips with Clare at age seven in pigtails sitting at the kitchen table going over her list of needed supplies saying, "Dad eats so much bacon I can't believe it."

While Flower dished up the soup Clare sat down beside me and gave me a hug as if I were the one with problems. "Don't worry about me, Mother, I have to do this."
What could I say? Nothing whatsoever, not even "Dress
warmly." We ate our delicious meal and ended up laughing
at a naughty joke about an old woman with one leg who
made love to a bear. Despite my laughter it was slightly
unnerving that Flower told the joke as if the story were
absolutely true. When I got up to leave I had decided not to
tell Clare about the problem with Polly's daughter in New
York. Though Rachel was younger Clare had patiently
taught her dance steps and how to swim. The thought of
this girl in prison made me think of Dickens's phrase "bleak
consternation."

When I got home I found my asshole father's martini
shaker in the pantry and made myself an overlarge drink.
At this stage, why not? There were two phone messages and
I chose David in Jalapa to come first over K in New York.
"How are you?"
"I don't know. How are you?"
"I don't know."
An exact transcription. We started over with me de-
laying the bad news about his ex-wife Polly and him telling
me about his first interesting day driving around to villages
taking samples from wells and water systems. The threat of
cholera made me think of the novel I was rereading. Bears
and cholera. I was a long way from Chicago. I took a big
gulp of my drink and told him why Polly was in New York
and he questioned whether he should fly up and help. I
asked, "How?" and he was offended. I said that I'd call

tomorrow when I knew more. I left a message at the hotel where Polly and K were staying and K called back in an hour when I was half bombed and dwelling on a passage in the García Márquez novel: "Only God knows how much I loved you." I nearly didn't answer the phone. K said he had given Polly a sedative and she was asleep. The arraignment had been perfunctory. The only things working in their favor were the fact that there were hundreds of similar cases on the docket and that the amount of heroin sold to the under-cover agent wasn't in the major category. The lawyer had covered the bail with my wired money and they would need more to pay him. I said I'd wire more in the morning and then heard a noise from his end. K said his sister was sob-bing in the bathroom because he wouldn't let her see her boyfriend or call him. After he hung up he was taking her to a detox center even though she claimed to be only an occasional user. He asked about Clare and I was noncom-mittal, then a little frightened because the night had been still up until fifteen minutes ago and now a strong wind from the north had begun.

"I think she means to hibernate to get close to the spirit of her father," I said, my voice quavering.

"Jesus Christ I knew it was something like that. I just have no idea what we can do."

"Me neither," I said, hanging up the phone because I could no longer talk.

I went into the kitchen and made another drink and then went out onto the open back porch and sipped it in the blowing cold. I looked up and watched the clouds of the oncoming front cover up the stars. Just like that, they're gone.

At some point in the night the furnace went off so that when I awoke at first light just before seven the house was frightfully cold. I put on a full-length sheepskin coat Donald had given me for Christmas, made coffee, and waited for the furnace man I had called to arrive. He turned out to be from the class behind me in high school though I didn't remember him. After he had replaced what he called the *igniter* I poured him a cup of coffee and he showed me what was wrong with the defective part with his oily hands. Heat was flooding the kitchen and I parted my coat. For an instant my left breast peeked out of my nightgown and we both blushed as I covered it. He left moments later and it occurred to me as I watched him walk out to his van that if he had made a move I doubt if I would have resisted. What could be erotic about oily hands and the scent of fuel oil? I had felt so naked beneath my robe and nightgown.

I dressed as warmly as possible then went out to Clarence's workshed and got my cross-country skis and poles. I still tasted last night's vodka in my mouth and my mind was unclear. I wanted to go to a wild area near Champion but remembered it was deer season and didn't want to be mistaken for a doe. Presque Isle would be too windy so I chose Trowbridge Park and skied for nearly two hours until I was soaked with sweat but hadn't quite dispelled the image of the repairman's large oily hands. My heart

jumped at the idea that I had forgotten the wire transfer
to K and Polly so I stopped at the bank, and then picked
up a steak at the IGA remembering how easily Donald
could eat a two-pound porterhouse or a whole chicken, for
that matter.

When I got home there was a call from Coughlin on
the answering machine saying that he had got some interesting information from both the anthropology professor
and a researcher at the Newberry. He was assembling it and
would FedEx it north. He sensed the inquietude in my voice
and we ended up talking for an hour. I covered the steak
with salt and pepper with my spare hand and at the same
time kept glancing at the stack of high school textbooks at
the end of the counter with extreme distaste. He said that
on all levels the main reason to live is because you're already alive. I tried to make a joke about my early morning
nonexperience with oily hands and he laughed and said,
"Real desire often takes us by surprise." He reminded me
that my own husband had told me to find a boyfriend and
that though some people are able to transcend their biology
I probably wasn't one of them. I admitted that I had thought
over the matter of whether I needed another man but hadn't
come to any conclusions. He was quick to remind me of the
limits of thought. I asked if he wanted to come up for the
weekend and go cross-country skiing and he was startled
saying that it was already noon on Friday but that he could
come up the following week for Thanksgiving weekend if I
wished. The hardest part of the conversation was about
Clare. He told me that it would be helpful to everyone directly
involved if I stopped saying "my child" and "my daughter."

Clare was twenty-three and past ownership, and I couldn't help her by pursuing her.

Despite this I panicked when I ate the steak and listened to the noon news. The weather said the front out of Alberta (a *clipper,* they called it) was passing quickly but that it would become still and very cold, perhaps drop well below zero. I was drowsy but immediately put on a coat and drove out to Au Train. My daughter simply couldn't be allowed to sleep in a fucking hut when it was that cold.

Flower wasn't impressed. She was making three venison mincemeat pies and said that Clare had driven over to the Canadian Soo (Sault Ste. Marie) to see her father's spiritual teacher for a few days. This was so totally unexpected that I sat there like a lump but close to tears of relief. I told Flower that I wanted to see Clare's shelter but she said absolutely not. She sat down and poured us each a glass of her homemade wine, for which she used wild strawberries and rhubarb. She looked at me overlong and I was reminded again how native people don't fill up all available space with chatter. They don't believe that talking is thinking. This unnerved me and I absurdly remembered a college term paper I wrote on the Welsh poet Dylan Thomas. I had read a book by his widow, Caitlin, called *Leftover Life to Kill,* which shocked me. How could these people have a good marriage when they appeared to be drunk every day? The professor told me that I was more than a trifle too bourgeois. Sitting there with Flower staring into my eyes made me feel like a hysterical PTA mother, the kind who used to crowd me as a teacher for ignoring her son whose sole activity was picking his nose and staring out the window as if it were a television screen.

"How could you help her get over her grief?" Flower finally asked.

"I don't know," I said, a perennial answer.

"What are you doing to get over your own?"

"Getting up in the morning, reading, eating, going to bed at night. That's about all except going out in the snow on skis."

"The snow is a good thing. I'm not sure there are any books for this. Just don't take up with a wet man."

"I don't know what you mean?" I had waited for a full minute for her to explain "wet man."

"A wet man is like a frog way back in the swamp that thinks he is the whole world, that the world starts and ends with him. I notice that most men are like that now. Donald wasn't like that."

"I just worry that Clare will freeze to death," I said lamely.

"Smart people have always known how to keep as warm as their bodies want to be." Now she began laughing so hard tears formed in the corners of her eyes. "I didn't know that was what you were worried about," she choked out. "I thought you were worried that your daughter would become a bear and be lost to you." She came around the table. "In the old days a few men became bears while they were living but it was real rare for women unless they made love to a bear."

Flower sent me home with a venison mincemeat pie and I ate it for lunch with a salad. It was better than any I had made for my family because she used lard for the crust and her own deeply flavored dried fruit including wild crab apples. A flash of sunlight came through the kitchen window and I felt happy with the only sour note being the stack of textbooks on the counter over by the toaster. I gathered the textbooks in my arms, opened the door to the basement, and threw the books down into the darkness. There was still a faint scent of fuel oil and I had a memory that was dimmed by the wine we drank when it happened. It was June and my parents had moved up to the Club. Mrs. Plunkett, our housekeeper, had the day off and David was off fishing with Glenn, who always smelled like beer. I was fourteen and Donald sixteen and we were dancing in the living room to the Rolling Stones. Laurie was over with her boyfriend and after we searched my father's den for a while we found the key to the wine cellar. We sat at the table in the wine cellar, smoked a joint, and drank two bottles of French wine. Laurie went off in the corner behind a rack with her boyfriend but we could hear her giving him a blow job. I had never done that before but Laurie said that you avoid getting pregnant by keeping boys soft. Donald was laughing and we left the wine cellar and went into a room full of stacked furniture and luggage and necked against the wall and I got grease marks on my pale blue blouse leaning against the wall on a greasy copper fuel line that led from the furnace to the buried outside tank. Donald would rub his prick through my underpants against my pussy until I wilted and his stuff came all over my thighs.

I was amazed that I had thrown the books down the basement stairs but it made the rest of my piece of pie and salad taste that much better. I opened *Love in the Time of Cholera* to my bookmark on page 47. "It had not been easy for her to regain her self-control after she heard Digna Pardo's shriek in the patio and found the old man of her life dying in the mud." It happens everywhere all of the time, I thought, but it never quite registers until it happens close to us.

It had become quite evident that I didn't want to teach in Marquette. All I had to do to rediscover this was to flick on the basement light and look down the stairs at the text-books sprawled there like book corpses that had lost their lives in my private war. Literature textbooks resemble anthologies where all the finest material is left out to arrive at a harmless product. I no longer wanted to be part of a system whose actual intent was to produce reliable employees. You could add on babysitting and the expectation of parents for you to instill a sense of discipline totally absent in the home. The smallest possible light bulb went off in my head when I remembered that in late September a young man who taught human geography at the college had suggested I might tutor some native students who tended to get lost out of shyness. This seemed like a better idea than wandering hither and yon in the Marquette school system. The professor had said that half the native students were new politicized Indians and in your face while the other half were withdrawn. He had introduced me to a brother and sister from Baraga who were bright enough but barely spoke above whispers and suffered from terminal homesickness in addition to being too poor to eat decently. A few were quite traditional and there was fatalism in their early return home from the alien cities of Sault Ste. Marie and Marquette to areas where unemployment was fifty percent and the rate of alcoholism very high.

It had begun snowing hard outside and I slouched forward on the kitchen table in a semidoze watching the snow gather in the barberry bushes outside the window. I hadn't noticed the green of summer enough and now the colors were gray and white and black. David and Vera were in green Veracruz abutting the blue Caribbean but I had to tend Clare. Coughlin said on the phone that I can't guide her unless I accept her. If I stridently oppose what she's doing she'll oppose me. How can the daughter be more like the father and the son more like me seemingly in full control of all of life's vagaries? I finished my master's degree tending the house with two little kids. Mother said on the phone, "You should have some help." No thank you. I'd rather be exhausted. Nearly prone I set García Márquez up on the table, skipping ahead. "For the next two weeks he did not sleep a single night." I've read so much fiction that I used to think my perceptions of life were merely a fiction I was writing, especially after the kids left for college and there was so little noise in the evening. Once Donald was watching *Monday Night Football* when a call came from the state police for help in finding two hunters from downstate in Flint who were lost. Donald was part of the search-and-rescue group for Luce and Chippewa counties and the lost people were usually hunters but sometimes summer campers with cheap compasses or no compasses at all, or children who had wandered away from campsites with mothers weeping that the lost child would be eaten by wolves and bears though this only happened once, near Brimley, when a bear killed a young girl or so I'm told.

The Flint hunters were lost nearby in the Hiawatha National Forest (silly poem). The swamp where the Flint hunters were lost was too thick for snowmobiles so Donald and a friend who was a commercial fisherman and large took off on snowshoes. I worried all night and the state police were parked in our yard at dawn when Donald and his friend returned with the two men over their shoulders. The two lost men weren't very big but they still must have been a burden. I cooked the biggest breakfast possible with the men smelling like pine smoke and snow. Donald had built a huge fire of tamarack and pine in the swamp so that they were fairly cozy. One of the men was of Italian descent and shipped us fifty pounds of Italian sausage, cheese, and salami by FedEx, which we loved. I fell asleep at the table, my eyes opening now and then to see the snow on the barberry bushes forming thick, fluffy white hats. I had seen in a sporting catalog of K's a sleeping bag used by mountaineers in the Himalayas that was good for weather down to fifty below zero. I would order one for Clare. One winter she and Donald camped by a remote lake for ice fishing and said they were never cold one bit.

I stumbled into the living room and collapsed on the sofa wishing I hadn't read Cleland's *Rites of Conquest* but Donald had asked me to because he needed help in understanding how the people he loved were utterly subjugated. What are any of us beneath the unbearable sweep of history including my father the elegant young Chicago gentleman heading off to the Philippines in his tailored officer's uniform only to see ninety percent of his men drop down into war's meat grinder. In my dreams everyone became blind and deaf in heaven and then I was back to earth dreams where everyone still couldn't see very well, and then I was back as a little girl in this doghouse down the block where I could hide out with this big black dog that seemed to like me a lot. When I awoke and had a cup of coffee and another piece of the mincemeat pie I thought maybe Clare's hut in the woods behind Flower's with its five bearskins was like my doghouse with only David knowing about it. I could sit up in the back and the world was reduced to lawn and forsythia bushes out the opening. If a robin landed or a squirrel trotted by the dog would growl.

Thanksgiving was a full house. Coughlin came north by noon on Wednesday and since deer hunters were still lurking in the woods we skied on the beach all the way to Presque Isle and then around it brushing the deep snow from a park bench and sitting there in the sunlight staring out at Lake Superior, which was only modestly rumpled in a northeast breeze. When he arrived Coughlin had given me the envelope of bear material but I had put it away for the time being. When he asked why I said Clare is coming tomorrow with Flower and I don't want to dwell on her today. While we were out on the park bench a small bank of clouds came across the sun turning our mood somber. He said, "After all, the fact of death is the most brutal thing we humans are forced to accept," but then the sun came out again and I told him that the day after the burial Herald had said, "Mother, it can't be awful if it happens to every living thing."

While Coughlin was roasting two nice chickens he had brought up from Chicago following a recipe he got from

David, who got it from Vernice, where you baste the chicken
with lemon, garlic, butter, and tarragon, I drove out to the
airport to pick up Herald, who was bringing home his Mexican girlfriend, Sylvia. I should have called ahead because the
plane was nearly an hour late, a frequent problem for those
coming up from Detroit and Chicago. Polly and K and the
wayward daughter Rachel were coming in from New York
City but the flight from Detroit was booked so they were
going to drive the mere five hundred miles from Detroit hope-
fully arriving by morning. Rachel was refusing to live with
her mother so she was going to stay in my little bungalow
down the street from Polly's with K to look after her until
things *settled down,* as Polly said. I was indeed relieved when
David said that he and Vera had decided not to come up from
Jalapa but maybe they would come for Christmas.

Sitting there in the terminal wishing I had brought
along my García Márquez I pretended to be intently studying the local newspaper, the *Mining Journal,* so no one I
might know would approach. I was anxious about meeting Herald's girlfriend. I was so pissed on the phone the
other day when Herald said that knowing his family were
odd ducks he hoped we all behaved well so that his fiancée
wouldn't cut and run. I was on the verge of demanding just
how we were odd ducks when I suddenly thought Clare hibernating like a bear might fit that category. In any event
they were only staying until Friday afternoon because Sylvia
wanted to visit a cousin in Ypsilanti, near Detroit. After
Herald's disastrous high school girlfriend jilted him Herald
has limited himself to foreign nationalities and lately until
Sylvia they have been either Japanese or Chinese young

women studying in the sciences. When I questioned him about the idea of a girl working in a fancy strip club and what was he doing there he said several of the girls at the strip club went to USC and that mathematicians occasionally go to strip clubs just like other men.

When they finally came off the plane I was impressed by how attractive they looked both separately and together. She was about five-ten when I'd expected her to be smaller like Vera. In the car she actually gave a little speech about her background so that I wouldn't have to be curious. Sylvia was twenty-two and her father was the manager of a car dealership in Hermosillo and not a very happy man because he would always be a decently paid manager but never an owner. She was the oldest of four children and had *escaped* to Los Angeles when she was nineteen because her mother was a bully and insisted that she marry the son of her best friend. She danced at a strip club four nights a week and during the days she took business courses at a community college in Pasadena because ever since she was a little girl she had wanted to be the manager of a hotel near the Pacific Ocean. She had been out of touch with her family for two years and her parents wouldn't answer her letters. She desperately missed her sister and two brothers so last year she and Herald flew to Hermosillo. Herald put on his best suit and went into the auto dealership just before lunchtime and introduced himself to Sylvia's father and asked for her hand in marriage when he finished his Ph.D. in mathematics this coming June. Sylvia's father called Sylvia's mother and they all met for lunch. It was wonderful because she got to see her brothers and sister again.

Herald had told me a very small amount of this on the phone but I was boggled by the whole story. She was obviously what they used to call a *tough cookie* but certainly no more so than I had been. We were nearly to the house when Herald upset me.

"Mother, you're not looking so good. You're too skinny. You have to take care of yourself."

"I've been worried about Clare," I said weakly.

"Clare has always been half goofy, whether it's Dad's Indian side or something else in addition. She either wanted to be in the woods or wanted to move to San Francisco or New York City. Don't you think that's a little schizophrenic? Clare will survive as Clare. You have to spend time paying attention to yourself."

This was certainly the longest speech Herald had ever made and I had no response except that unworded tremulous feeling you have when somebody tells you that you don't look well.

We had a nice dinner except that Herald kept an eye on me to make sure I was eating enough. I mean I am frequently hungry but it goes away after a few bites and I become lost in thought. Everyone was a little tired, which is what airplane flights do to people, except me since I'd slept at the table half the afternoon. Sylvia's laughter kept our spirits up when we talked about religion. Coughlin noticed when I glanced at his envelope of bear material over on the sideboard against the wall. He said that it was hard to imagine what any of a number of tribes of Indians felt when the first

Jesuit or Franciscan missionaries instructed them in the sacrament of communion and they were told to drink the blood of Christ and eat his body in the forms of wine and wafers. Sylvia said her mother had a cousin who was a *penitente* and at a parade before Easter every year he flailed his own body with thorn branches until he bled profusely. No one else seemed to mind but I was unable to eat the wild raspberry cobbler I had made for dessert.

Sylvia and Herald went up to bed at ten and Coughlin went to his hotel soon after. I felt abandoned and drank the nearly full remains of our second bottle of dinner wine, which didn't help when I tried to read García Márquez or the bear material. "No, not rich," he said. "I am a poor man with money, which is not the same thing." This reminded me overmuch of my nitwit brother David who might have been a bum if he hadn't had an inheritance. In the structure of his hardworking idleness his insanity required an outside means of support though he once seemed quite happy raking lawns with his landscaping crew. The bear material was simply frightening and I didn't get very far into it. In old Ojibway tradition a girl at the beginning of her first menstruation was called a *wemukowe* which meant she was *going to be a bear.* She covered herself with soot until her period was over but until that time everyone called her *mukowe,* which meant she had become a bear. Afterward she resumed normal life or so the material said. But what did that have to do with my twenty-three-year-old daughter? That was enough for one evening and I turned on a television program about the nature of dogs. The nasty little dog Clare had brought home from California had disappeared but K had told me later that a neighbor had given him its collar without comment. Maybe I needed a dog. We always had dogs until our last one died, at the beginning of Donald's illness. I fell asleep on the sofa but Herald woke me up at three a.m. and led me up to my bedroom, my parents' bedroom in fact, but that no longer seemed relevant. I looked at the phone on the night table and wanted to call Coughlin to see if I should come to the hotel but then thought better of it.

Thanksgiving went pretty well but not as I expected. I cooked a ham to go with the turkey because Herald had refused to eat turkey since he was a boy and we had tried to raise a few turkeys but a coyote had gotten in the pen and stolen them. There was only a single turkey foot left, which Herald buried in a funeral service with Clare, who continued to eat turkey. The surprise was Clare, whom I had hardly seen since before going to Chicago. She was thin and distracted but quite warm and ordinary toward me. She was proud of the three dried-fruit pies she and Flower had made that morning and was helpful during the dinner preparation making a roux so that the turkey gravy would look an attractive brown. She had also taken Rachel upstairs when she arrived with K and Polly, who looked bleak and exhausted from their New York City trip and all-night drive from Detroit.

After dinner Polly fell asleep upright in an easy chair. The young people, Herald, Clare, Sylvia, K, and Rachel, went for a walk though Rachel was sullen and slow to respond. Suddenly the house was quiet except for the faint snoring of Polly on the sofa. Flower stared at Coughlin and properly assumed he was to be trusted.

"Clare went on over to the Canuck Soo to see Donald's teacher. I knew him a long time ago when he wasn't too solid but he was real gifted at seeing things no one else sees. He once told me he was real surprised when he was born and probably would be surprised when he died. His mind flies around a lot so he became a land surveyor so he would always know where he was. I knew his teacher over in Manitoulin Island and he scared the shit out of everyone. I'm just an old lady and I stay away from most of this stuff. I live in the woods so I know a few things. Anyway this man spent time for three days with Clare. He took her back to a blowhole near her father's grave. A blowhole is where the sleeping bear's breath goes in and out of a frozen hole from the moisture in the bear's breath. I'm not sure of all that Clare had in mind but this man told her that the fair thing to do was to let go of his spirit. Donald's spirit might hang around a year, which would mean June, but she shouldn't be clutching at him. She could spend a night a week at most in her hut and talk to him a little but she shouldn't be holding on. It would be wrong to do so. He also said to her that it might drive her truly crazy to fool around with such matters. After all it took Donald fifteen years to sit his three days and three nights. He said she didn't know where she already was in the world, which makes it dangerous. That's about all of what she said the man told her." Flower paused for a while as if searching for a conclusion then looked at me with a trace of hardness. "You and Donald should have let her come home a few months earlier. It would have been better."

I began weeping because I knew what she said was true. Donald didn't want to be a burden to his children and that might have been right for Herald but not Clare.

In the morning I walked way out to Presque Isle with Clare and Herald. Sylvia turned us down because she couldn't get used to the cold on such short notice. We didn't talk about much, which was blessedly pleasant. The night before when we said our good-byes I asked Coughlin if he wished me to visit him and he teased, "Of course not, you've become a patient." I said, "No I haven't" but he was probably right.

When we were nearly to Presque Isle having walked quickly on the shore ice Clare said that despite K's best efforts as a guardian she was sure Rachel would escape as soon as possible. Herald agreed. This made me feel bad for Polly and I questioned them. Clare said Rachel was in love with her musician boyfriend even though he was an addicted asshole. Herald rambled on about the nature of love, then came back to earth by saying that Rachel knows Polly's world and doesn't like it. Polly doesn't know Rachel's world but still doesn't like it. Rachel's language is music and the tens of thousands of hours of simpleminded music she has absorbed has become the way she thinks however primitive. The drugs that will probably kill her are an appropriate adjunct to the music. Clare and I stopped in our tracks while Herald crawled up a snowbank and waved to the world. Herald was normally as unlikely to judge people as his father. Donald would say about people's behavior, "They likely have a reason. We just don't know what it is."

That afternoon when I returned from taking Herald and Sylvia to the airport for their Detroit flight Rachel was sitting in an easy chair with her eyes closed listening through earphones to music that was so loud I could hear it clearly. I went into the kitchen and from Clare's bedroom above me I could hear that she and K were making love. This made my stomach feel icy so I left the house and drove down to the hotel to see Coughlin, who said he would be involved in a long phone session with a patient until two o'clock. On the way up in an elevator a room service waiter smiled at me widely, which made me feel acceptably attractive, almost tingly. It turned out he was headed to Coughlin's room with a sandwich and a bottle of ale. Coughlin looked frazzled having been on the phone for three hours with a suicidal ex–pro athlete, a football player, who had lost his wife and two children in a divorce. The motive of suicide would be an unsuccessful attempt to hurt the ex-wife. Coughlin had talked to her and at this point she couldn't care less except for their two children, little boys, who would be emotionally destroyed if their father killed himself. This gave me an instant headache, which Coughlin obviously shared. He wolfed his sandwich and beer then drew a videotape from his suitcase. It was a Brazilian film called *Black Orpheus*, which he said he watched once or twice a year when a patient pushed him into dire straits. We sat on the sofa and watched the whole wonderful movie holding hands but that was all.

On Monday afternoon with everyone gone I began tutoring. There was a slight thaw so Clare had gone to

Flower's thinking it would be a judicious night to spend in her hut.

My first student, Vincent, was a hard case. Though in his mid-twenties he was only a freshman hoping to major in forestry. I knew his family name because he was born on Sugar Island from a Chippewa father and a mostly deaf French-Canadian mother. The father had disappeared into the armed services and the mother had moved down to Pickford, where she lived with a man who was foreman on a hay farm. Vincent had worked as a pulp cutter starting when he was fourteen but had moved up to being a timber cruiser (the man who marks the trees suitable for harvesting) for a big timber company. He was very bright except in freshman English, which he was flat-out flunking. I had talked to his English teacher, who thought we could get him through on some minimal level. Part of the problem was that Vincent had a small room in a house with seven younger students who caroused all night.

Our first hour was so basic in terms of grammar I felt as if I had been sitting in a dentist's chair. On another level he was very attractive in a rawboned way and I admit that I felt my bottom become warmer than the rest of my body. I immediately decided to offer him the use of Jesse's old apartment over the garage but I was too shy to say anything. He had taken off a sweater because the house was warm and he had the well-defined muscles of a workingman, so unlike those of bodybuilders. He smelled like Ivory soap and tobacco. He was highly nervous about his ignorance and I told him to go ahead and smoke. It made me want a cigarette though I had quit years before. When I came back into the den after fetching him an ashtray the way he hunched over the table studying the grammar book reminded me of Donald. When we finished our first two-hour session he bowed at the door and didn't look at me directly. As he opened the door of his old black pickup I could have called out something intelligent like "Vincent, come back here and make love to me."

Midway through Tuesday morning K called to say Rachel had disappeared when she was supposedly shoveling snow off the front walk. He had heard a car stop out front but thought nothing of it. There was a note in her bedroom under the pillow that said, "Dear Mom and K, Sorry. Love, Rachel." Polly came over during her lunch hour at school and sobbed her heart out. She had called the state police, who weren't interested in the problem. A twenty-two-year-old girl had freedom of movement since the heroin charge in New York City had been dropped. Vincent arrived for his tutorial and after meeting the distraught Polly said that he would leave, which was the last thing I wanted. I actually grabbed him by the elbow and said, "No." I had been laying a trap for him since he'd left the day before. The cleaning lady had been out in Jesse's old apartment all morning and I was wearing a modest low-cut sleeveless summer blouse and a fairly short blue skirt, not exactly a winter outfit. I pushed grief-stricken Polly out after inviting her for dinner. I had been upset in the morning when I'd studied myself in the mirror and realized that I had inadvertently lost too much weight since Donald's passing. This worried me because Upper Peninsula men in general favor a riper figure perhaps due to the colder climate. Donald had once picked up Clare's *Vogue* magazine and asked, "How come these women are all so skinny?"

Before dipping into the hell of grammar study I led Vincent out to Jesse's apartment. I was wearing flats and picked my way on the icy path and when I reached a pool of slush from the recent thaw at the bottom of the steps Vincent put his hands on my waist and lifted me over the slush to the bottom step. I felt a little wobbly on the way up the stairs and wondered if my butt was worth looking at. In the apartment we were standing next to each other and he looked around and said, "I can't believe my luck" and gave me an impulsive hug. I didn't let go and he looked at me oddly as if making sure of himself. The first one didn't last long but we lolled around on the bed for a while doing everything and the second time around I properly lost my mind. On the way back to the house I said I had been lonely for a while and he said, "Me too." We laughed quite a bit during our lessons.

Clare came home while I was fixing dinner for Polly. She was in a good mood but then was concerned when she studied my face at the kitchen counter. "You have more color in your face today," she said. Vincent's pickup pulled into the alley and Clare watched him begin to unload his stuff. I explained why I was loaning out Jesse's old apartment. Vincent waved at our faces in the kitchen window and she looked at me and laughed. "Everyone needs affection," she said.

Dinner with Polly and K wasn't as grim as I might have expected. She and our stalwart K had evidently talked for a while and he had convinced her that she had done what

she could. Clare piped up with the information that Rachel
and her boyfriend had been wanting to go to L.A. to break
into the music scene there. I said that maybe Herald could
look for her but Polly said, "What would be the point?" Both
Polly and K felt humiliated about the money I had spent and
I said, "Don't be silly. Jail would have made everything
worse for her. I didn't earn that money. Thank my dead
parents. Of course they didn't earn it either."

In the morning Clare went off to Ann Arbor with K, which
pleased me because at least I didn't have to worry about her
freezing to death in a hut. I made love with Vincent every
day for a week and admitted to myself I felt relieved when
the university went on Christmas break and he went home
to his deaf mother's in Pickford. He said that her greatest
insecurity was whether she had enough wood to burn for
winter and he intended to cut and split an extra dozen cords.
In addition to all of the pleasure he gave me he had begun
using *was* and *were* in the right places.

A few days after Vincent left I collapsed on the front walk
while shoveling a foot of new-fallen snow. It was a still day
and I could hear strains of Christmas music wafting up the
hill from downtown. I had been coughing a lot but attrib-
uted it to the occasional cigarette I had smoked with Vincent.
I also felt feverish and dizzy several times a day but ignored
it. I had put away my García Márquez for a while because
it had become unbearably poignant and then, absurdly

enough, had begun rereading Louise Erdrich's *Love Medicine*, but at breakfast the print had blurred and I thought my eyes might need a checkup. I had also been a bit dreamy and delusional not realizing it was because of the fluid building up in my lungs. It's amazing how dumb we can be. So anyway I collapsed facedown in a snowbank and luckily a neighbor down the street was walking past and called an ambulance.

I didn't remember much for a couple of days but when I came semiawake in the hospital I was told I had severe double pneumonia! Clare was standing at the end of the bed and K and Polly were peeking in from the hall.

In my two weeks in the hospital right through Christmas there was a nearly overwhelming feeling of embarrassment. I had expected Clare to end up in the hospital not me. In fact at age forty-four I had never been in one except to give birth and visit sick friends. Since childhood I'd rarely had a cold and growing up, when Mother and Father and David had the flu I didn't get it. In the second grade I had this poor girlfriend whose family was religious and when Father was hungover and puking in the bathroom we stood outside and sang, "Jesus loves me this I know for the Bible tells me so." My friend cried when my father hollered, "Cut out that goddamned racket."

I never had any interest in my dreams except when they were amusing though I'd had sense enough to be upset when my friend Laurie had said that she never dreamt. I had the half-learned assumption that they helped resolve mental

problems but when Coughlin and David talked about the
theory and practice of dreaming I yawned. However, early
in my hospital stay I was in a semicoma for three days from
either a drug allergy or contraindicatory drugs and in this
semicomatose state it was not so much dreaming as seeing
the inside of my brain in lurid Technicolor as if it were a
disjointed movie. I was too sick to be frightened but my mental movie was more vividly *real* then any waking reality I had
ever known. It seemed that at the depths of my illness the
idea of death wasn't frightening. Like movies there was often accompanying music. Once on a family camping trip up
near Crisp Point Donald and Clare were fishing the Big
Two-Hearted River and Herald and I went off to some clearing we had seen near a logging trail to look for wildflowers.
When you have your nose in a wildflower guidebook you
can lose track of where you are. After a couple of hours it
became warm and we were thirsty and the deerflies were
driving us crazy and it occurred to us that were lost. Herald climbed a tree but could only see miles of trees. Every
direction we walked was the wrong direction. We decided
we'd best stay in one place so we sat in the middle of a clearing and Herald started a smudge fire to drive away the flies.
Late in the afternoon we heard Donald calling and then
suddenly Clare appeared in her fishing boots and practi-
cally screamed, "You assholes shouldn't leave the campsite." Luckily she had a canteen of water. Anyway in this
fevered state I saw us all as a movie camera that hasn't been
invented yet. Bugs, beetles, spiders, a pink-eyed garter snake,
the birds called cedar waxwings, the shadows of ferns, rot-
ting logs, deer turds, Herald following me, or me following

Herald. Grass tickling my butt when I peed, the smell of perspiration, a cloud that looked like an elephant, everything was seen more clearly than I had ever seen before. You could even see the emotion of being lost.

This kind of thing seemed to go on forever though mostly in shorter segments: Laurie in the kitchen seeing my father's swollen penis through his parted robe and giggling, the speed at which I fell down the bank of the Deadstream River, the fear of the book *Wuthering Heights* when I was twelve because some aspects of Heathcliff reminded me of my father, the nutty fat woman jumping up and down near the Coast Guard station, me frying up an egg sandwich for the paperboy who one winter afternoon wore only one sock. I asked him, Why? His pants were too short and frayed. He said, I couldn't find my other sock. He wouldn't come in the house. He ate the egg sandwich on the front porch and when he dropped a piece in the snow he picked up the hard egg yolk and ate it. My brain couldn't make Donald look right. Often he was too hairy near a campfire near Muskallonge Lake when we heard a baby bear crying. Once he was in our hotel room when I took the kids to New York City but he'd never gone to New York City. Several times he was a painted warrior like he was with his friends at a Halloween party near Eckerman and when they rushed into the party howling they scared the shit out of everyone and kids cried.

When I came fully awake I was relieved that these visions never returned with close to the same strength. Clare was beside my bed and said, "You sure made some strange noises." When I would wake from a sweaty sleep she would be reading a botany textbook and then help me change my nightie. Sometimes in the night K would be sitting in the corner under a dull lamp reading this Frenchman Foucault and I'd wake up and ask, "What's that book about?" and he would say, "I'll tell you when you feel better." I said that I must look ugly and he said "Not to me." Vincent came several times bringing profoundly stupid flower arrangements that I liked anyway. My two main doctors were only faces but Donald's neurologist stopped by several times to say hello. He said that there had been questions by his colleagues about what happened to Donald but he had only said that Donald had moved to Canada.

The last big vision was the best and happiest and centered on our trip west when the kids were in their teens. We had stopped on the way out to see my mother in Evanston and Donald had loathed Chicago traffic. He had no experience with heavy traffic so I'd usually drive with him slumped low in the seat muttering. It was even a problem for him in Yellowstone Park, where we'd stop and he'd walk off in the forest for a while. We went home by a northern route and he wanted to see the Custer Battlefield because we'd listened to a tape of Evan Connell's *Son of the Morning Star* when we were driving west.

The dream started when we left the Best Western in Buffalo, Wyoming, at dawn and drove north toward Crow Agency, in Montana. It was a peculiar clear cool dawn that came after a heat wave and there were puddles of water in the parking lot only in the dream the puddles weren't dirty brown water but clear and pale blue. It had been the most enchanted day of the whole trip and the dream followed this course of enchantment. It was cool and windy and we wore

jackets at the Custer Battlefield and we were so early few
people were about. Donald was distressed to find an old
drunk man sleeping in a ditch and covered him with a spare
blanket from our car trunk. Donald laughed at the battlefield because he could hear shouts and small horses and in
the dream I could too. Herald was our navigator with altogether too many maps so we continued on the side highway,
Route 212, toward Belle Fourche, in South Dakota. Reality started to disappear in my version when we reached
Lame Deer on the Northern Cheyenne Reservation. Donald
was waiting outside the school with his green work clothes
smeared with pungent pine pitch as if he were a logger and
the kids were very young sitting out in a pickup reading
comic books. I came out of the school with an armload of
books and we went home to a gray weathered log cabin
overlooking a gulley and cooked dinner. In reality Donald
loved Lame Deer and had talked to a round woman in front
of the post office who said, "You're a big sonofabitch!" We
went farther southeast and turned in Alzada so that Herald
could see Devil's Tower, which was used in his favorite
movie, *Close Encounters of the Third Kind*. Clare and I hadn't
liked the movie and we drove back north to 212 and farther
through Belle Fourche to Bear Butte, north of Sturgis, where
we saw the largest buffalo in creation in a pen.

I awoke from this dream in an odd state of mind thinking of Donald's story and how his great-grandfather had
dreamed of this draft-horse farm where he eventually ended
up happily working. Did this mean I should write to Lame
Deer and see if they needed a teacher for the coming fall?
Maybe. Why not? I lay there with Clare snoring softly in

an easy chair next to the hospital bed wishing I had come to know that part of Donald that involved his religion but he was naturally reticent. I mean he wasn't secretive but the inquiries were up to me. He seemed quite open with Clare but I was always too busy as a schoolteacher and Herald was strictly interested in the sciences.

I was home by the day of New Year's Eve feeling not bad but horribly spindly in the bathroom mirror. I was five-ten but had dropped from nearly one-forty to one-fifteen. At my request Clare made me a cheeseburger and I ate most of it. That evening from my bedroom I could hear Clare and K quarreling downstairs through the hot-air register. He intended to return to Ann Arbor when possible but she planned to enroll in botany and horticulture at Michigan State in East Lansing, seventy miles from Ann Arbor. They would visit weekends. They nagged at each other like pissed-off cousins. I fell back to sleep and woke at midnight and heard from the television downstairs the sound of New York City on New Year's Eve and also the sound of Clare and K making love. She's noisy.

A few days later I made a decision and got in touch with Mrs. Plunkett, our old housekeeper and cook when our parents were up at the Club. She was now in her late eighties but managed to find a grandniece, a more recent emigrant from Italy, down in Kenosha, Wisconsin, who was willing to come north and take care of me. I was pleased to tell Clare and K that they were free to resume their lives. They argued with me but I could see that their concealed hearts were in departure. They left the next day after picking up Benedetta at the airport. She was round but light-footed and graceful, quite merry really, and by dinner, when she served me a lasagna in a béchamel sauce, she asked me about the men in Marquette. I said she would have pretty good luck if she wasn't too choosy. She said she wasn't, then brought me a veal chop and spinach. She meant for me to eat my way back to health.

Of course it was the strangest winter of my life. I was so impatient with my convalescent existence and the painfully slow increments of recovery. It reminded me of when Herald was a boy and would chart the progress of the Detroit Tigers on a bulletin board. We would all have to listen attentively when he explained how slowly the players improved their batting averages after midseason. A prolonged hot streak might only raise your batting average from .271 to .276.

David came up from Jalapa stopping in Chicago to see Coughlin, who decided to come along after they concocted a plan to snowshoe the five miles from the plowed road into his cabin near Grand Marais. At dinner with both of them glancing surreptitiously at Benedetta's butt at the kitchen stove they boyishly refined their adventure until I said that they were scarcely going to the North Pole, which they ignored. Their glances at Benedetta made me think of the silly filigree that surrounds our sexuality. The night before I had felt a slight pang of jealousy when I heard a noise and peeked out the bedroom window to see Vincent leading a woman up the garage-apartment stairs. Now David and Coughlin were huffing and puffing for Benedetta about the Great North and the five miles in to the cabin. I was tempted to mention how Donald and a game biologist had tracked wolves crossing from Canada to west of Paradise Point for twenty-five miles one cold February day. When he finally dropped his faux manliness during dessert (zabaglione) David admitted that Vera wanted to have a baby. I was stunned and Coughlin actually dropped his fork. At forty-one it was certainly possible for Vera and I tried to stop my mind from racing over certain aspects of what I had presumed was only their love affair. When they returned in two days they had to spend most of their time with Polly, who had become so depressed over her daughter she could barely speak. I invited her to come over anytime she wished but then I was still ill enough that I couldn't stay awake all that long. Sometimes we sat on the sofa holding hands and watching a movie. For unclear reasons Polly liked westerns but when I said I was thinking of moving out west to Lame Deer in Montana she was appalled. "You can't just go out there alone," she said, and I said, "Yes, I can."

It had occurred to me as my illness began to subside and my strength gradually regathered that at age forty-four I wasn't dead yet. It was hard to stop being a schoolteacher after twenty years so I would have to continue being a school-teacher until my mind led me elsewhere. To me life without work would become meaningless despite the fact that I didn't have to work, but now I felt the vertigo of freedom, remembering painfully a beginner's course in philosophy in college where the professor was obsessed with the French writer Albert Camus's idea of *terrible freedom.* My vertigo came from examining a half-full cup of coffee and realizing I was free to come and go as I wished. I had been taking care of a husband then two children since I ran off and married Donald when I was sixteen. Now this life had nearly disappeared and it occurred to me that part of my obsession with Clare's grief was that I didn't want to let her go. Even the house no longer had abiding ghosts. I couldn't imagine leaving Marquette forever but then I didn't need to. I had enjoyed my sexual extravaganza with Vincent but at the moment I couldn't imagine ever being tied closely to a man again.

Clare came north only once before March but we talked several times a week on the phone. Flower came twice a week, driven to Marquette by an old boyfriend, Joe, who had been a commercial fisherman down in Naubinway. Joe would sit sleeping in his battered pickup and when I asked Flower why he wouldn't come in the house she only said, "Joe's favorite thing in life is sleeping." She never came without bringing a dried-fruit pie. Benedetta was curious about the grand taste of these pies and Flower told her that you have to render the lard for the crust from young pork.

I was attentive to the increase in the winter light. I clocked dawn and twilight in a journal in the manner of Herald tracking baseball averages. The low point had been on the day of the winter solstice, December 21, in the hospital right after I emerged from the coma. I had awakened at dawn and Clare had said, "Mom, from now on the light is going to be with us an extra minute every day." But then

I fell asleep and didn't wake up until darkness fell, shortly after four. It was more than I could bear, this missing an entire day in my life.

I had started out walking five minutes a day in mid-January and by the first of March I was up to two hours of walking or cross-country skiing. I had also gained back twelve pounds. Benedetta even put good olive oil on steak after she broiled it. The only startling news I received from out of town was that Herald and Sylvia had caused a problem for everyone but themselves by running off to San Francisco and getting married. This was one of the few distinct times Herald reminded me of his father, who would have loathed the idea of a huge June wedding in Hermosillo. Sylvia told me on the phone that she was on her mother's *shit list* again but I said she'd get over it.

I found my father's Bronze Star from his service in the Philippines behind some books on the upper shelves of the den. I carried it around the house in its small leather case wondering what to do with it then put it back behind the same books. I also found a photo of him and Jesse wearing leis in Hawaii between the pages of a copy of James Jones's *From Here to Eternity*. They looked thin and drunk. In a small cookbook called *Canapé* I found a photo of Mother in her moonbeam costume for a Club party that had so terrified David. Our nanny Gretel tried to cover her whiskey breath by chewing entire packs of Dentyne gum.

In early March Polly and I drove out to Flower's bringing her a fifth of her favorite peppermint schnapps (Dr.

McGillicuddy's). Polly said that Rachel had written from
Burbank to say that her boyfriend had left her and returned
to New York but she was staying in L.A. and looking after
an unsuccessful rock band. We stopped on the beach and
listened to drift ice pushed by an east wind pile up against a
granite island with huge crunching sounds. Polly said that
it was curious but that despite the obvious horrors her husband thought that his two years in Vietnam had been the
best of his life. "Where did that leave me?" Polly had wondered at the time. I told her that once when David and I were
little my father had taken us for a walk in the woods at the
Club because Mother had a hangover. We had seen a big
black snake sunning on a log and my father said that during the war in the Philippines he and his men would eat
snakes. David and I caught a snake and took it into the
kitchen to cook but then David suggested that we eat tuna
fish and pretend it was snake. I had discovered that my
father had been with General Jonathan Wainwright on
Corregidor. My father, Jesse, and several hundred other
men had headed for the hills rather than surrender, which
was lucky for them because the mortality rate for those who
surrendered was very high. It takes a long time for a father
to drive the love out of a child.

We went for a walk at Flower's on the hard-crusted
snow but Polly turned around because she didn't want to
see Clare's hut, which Flower had finally decided to show
me. The hut was mostly buried in snow but I cleared the
entrance and peered in. The day was bright and the hut's
interior, really a cave, was black so I could see nothing.
I reached my hand in and Flower, who was behind me,

growled. I jumped up screeching and Flower laughed. We continued walking into the swamp for half an hour or so to where under the roots of a huge deadfall tree Flower showed me a blowhole, the breathing hole of a hibernating bear. I lay down and smelled the rank odor of breath and putting my ear to the hole heard what seemed like a single breath a minute. "It's not Donald, it's an old female bear," Flower said, and then did an eerie little dance and chant while I walked away. Back at the house Flower cooked us a beaver tail, which Polly didn't eat but I thought was rather good.

That evening I hastily looked through the bear material Coughlin had brought up at Thanksgiving. It made me feel uncomfortable, not in a spooky sense but with the feeling, semireligious, that it was not my business. There was a footnote that said in the ninth century the men who guarded the Swedish Viking king were thought to be half bear. In many native tribes the bear was thought to be redemptive because it rose from near death in the spring. One May Donald said that bears were lucky and fat after a severe winter had killed so many deer for them to eat.

I had an insomniac night over the matter marveling how certain beliefs managed to hold on. I finally got up at three a.m. and tried unsuccessfully to read *Harper's* magazine, poured a drink, and watched a movie about World War II set in France around the time of the Normandy invasion. Young men jumped out of landing craft at the beachhead and were mowed down by machine-gun fire. They floated facedown in the surf. The world seemed unacceptably temporary including love. I turned off the television and listened

to Beethoven's *Missa Solemnis,* which though I loved this
music failed to purge bears and war.

In mid-April when Lake Superior's ice had begun to break
up I flew out to Billings, in Montana, and then drove down
to Lame Deer for my job interview. The landscape was bleak
and horribly windy but I was happy. The reservation school
had a familiar feel and the superintendent was pleased with
my résumé, saying that "ordinary do-gooders" often didn't
make it through the first year. While we talked we were both
looking out in the school yard where under a set of swings
two little girls were punching a little boy. We laughed. When
I left I was confident that I needed this new landscape, which
was so unclaustrophobic compared to the Upper Peninsula's
dense forests. I would have to live in a mobile home the first
year but if I liked the place well enough I'd build a cabin
similar to the one I'd seen in my dream.

      I had thought about stopping in Chicago for a few days
on my way home but then suddenly I didn't want to see
Coughlin and talk about myself. I made a few phone calls
from my Billings motel, ate a wretched dinner, and then flew
the next morning to New York City via Denver. I stayed in
the same fancy hotel on the Upper East Side that my parents had favored. On one trip David and I had stayed in the
same bedroom and I had thrown his shoes out the window
but Mother had had a bellhop retrieve them. I visited museums and bookstores and went to the Bronx Zoo, where I
did not pause overlong at the bear cages. I went to an Italian delicatessen and had a big carton of food shipped home

to Benedetta, who still lived with me but had enrolled at the college. I had called her to remind her to feed a little female terrier that arrived on our back porch every morning for a snack. She didn't have a collar and wouldn't come in the house, eyeing me as if I were trying to trap her. She liked cheddar cheese and I had seen her crawling under the garage. I hoped she would stay. She was as footloose as me. On a cool morning walk I stopped at a construction site where the workers were dressed like Donald. A Mexican-looking worker yelled at me, "Hey, foxy lady" and I felt pleasant.

In June around the summer solstice and the anniversary of Donald's departure I went with Clare over to David's cabin. K had been there for a month and the place was more ship-shape than I had ever seen it. K had been surveying the roots of creeks and wanted to take us to a big hill where the watersheds of three rivers began but the insects were too thick so I preferred the idea of a hike in the dunes, where the sand supports less insect life. David wouldn't be able to come up from Veracruz until early July when he finished the first part of his water project. Vera had had second thoughts about having a child with him and they had begun the paperwork for adopting a baby girl. David had said something vaguely inappropriate about how it was better to adopt a homeless puppy from a dog pound.

Clare and I walked up the first tall edge of the dunes and watched K rowing on Au Sable Lake far below us. She then guided me a mile or so to a grove of poplar and birch, which K had showed her as a place he had taken Donald. We were sitting there on a huge low-slung branch of a birch tree moving in the breeze when Clare saw a large flock of ravens near another ridge of dunes out toward Lake Superior. Clare said that the ravens were probably following a bear and slid off the branch and started walking in that direction. I wasn't excited about seeing the bear but decided to trust Clare's judgment. When we got close to the ridge and could hear the ravens on the other side Clare saw the bear tracks, which had emerged from a neck of forest to the west of us. She said she had been out there with K a few days before tracking bears that came to the dunes to eat the vines of beach pea and wild strawberries. In the shade of the dune we found a patch of wild strawberries and ate some despite the sand granules that clung to them. We crept up the steep dune with difficulty in the sliding sand and peeked over the edge. About a hundred yards away and below us a large bear swagged his head between a patch of beach pea and strawberries nibbling quickly as if frantic to eat. And then the ravens above him must have warned him because he stood up and made a woofing sound. I know that Clare and I were thinking the same thing. *Is that him? Is that him? Is that Donald who is greeting us, saying a final good-bye?* The bear stared at us and Clare clenched at my hand. And then he trotted over a hill as we all must.

ACKNOWLEDGMENTS

I wish to thank Professor Richard Eathorne of Northern
Michigan University and Professor Kurt S. Pregitzer of
Michigan Tech for their help, also Ray Nurmi of Snow-
bound Books in Marquette, Michigan. I also wish to ac-
knowledge Professor Charles Cleland, whose seminal book
Rites of Conquest gave me bitter encouragement.

—JH